THE MERCILESS DUO RETURNS

A Gritty Psychological Thriller of Terror

(Most Wanted – Book 1)

Thriller

Merciless Ink Publishing

MERCILESS
INK PUBLISHING
Stories without apology, ink that leaves scars.

Ricarda-Huch-Straße 35
14480 Potsdam, Germany
www.merciless-ink.com
info@merciless-ink.com

Edited by Dr K. Ette
Proofreading: Stefanie Brandt
Cover design by Merciless Ink Publishing

ISBN: 978-3-911873-03-1

**To survive is not to be free.
It's a life sentence.**

CONTENTS

CHAPTER 1

Thursday, 1 March, 23:10

The air in the unfamiliar room was musty and oppressive, weighing down on him like a suffocating shroud. In total darkness, with no sound from the outside world, every chirp and hiss of the room's unseen nocturnal inhabitants sounded amplified.

Tiny, prickly legs crawled along his neck, sending a tingling sensation down his spine. He slapped his ear to shake off the unwelcome intruder and jumped up from the musty mattress on the floor.

A sudden spark leapt into the darkness for a split second, startling him.

Where am I? he wondered.

A match flared, lighting a candle, the glow of which revealed a girl in a school uniform chewing gum with youthful nonchalance. Her gaze was calm, but with a certain indifference and a hint of cold malice. Her right leg bent, she leaned casually against the wall, which was cracked in several places, flakes of paint curling away from the surface. Geckos and cockroaches scurried away, and cobwebs clung to the corners.

"Surprise, pastor's son!" A voice echoed through the room.

The so-called pastor's son snapped his head towards the sound. His mind vehemently denied what his senses of sight, hearing and smell had perceived.

"You look like you've seen a ghost," said the hostage-taker, his soft voice a stark contrast to his terrifying face.

An icy dread crept over the pastor's son as he struggled to make sense of the chilling scene before him. Instinctively, he closed his eyes and began his anti-panic ritual: "One, two, three—"

A thud jolted him back to reality. He stopped counting and opened his eyes – just in time for the next sound: the pop of a chewing gum bubble, almost comical amid the eerie situation.

The girl blew another bubble, stretching and shimmering in the flickering light.

"Has it dawned on you who we are?" asked the hostage-taker.

If it looks like a duck, swims like a duck and quacks like a duck ... The pastor's son's thoughts whirled. But it can't be true. Not in a million years.

"I will introduce us," the hostage-taker interrupted his mental carousel. "I was christened Scarface because of the scars on my face." Pointing to the girl, he said, "My assistant, always by my side. The press gave us an inappropriate nickname last year: The Merciless Duo. Basically, we are compassionate."

Jesus, Mary and Joseph! His eyes went wide with terror, and he stiffened like a man confronted by a hissing black mamba, coiled and ready to strike.

"Th-the Merciless Duo were k-k-killed in a car chase last year," he stammered. "They were b-burnt beyond recognition."

"Were they? Well, here we are again."

"How ..." His heart sputtered, paused for a fleeting moment, then erupted into a frenetic rhythm akin to the gallop of a racehorse. "How di-di-di..."

The pastor's son seemed to have his tongue glued to the roof of his mouth. His body sagged under an invisible weight, and his goosebumps almost turned into cystic acne.

The rumours about Scarface and his assistant echoed in his mind: The Merciless Duo are heartless, incapable of any compassion. They never grant their victims the mercy of death. Instead, they inflict wounds – both flesh and soul – that fester for a lifetime. Each survivor becomes a prisoner of his own shattered mind, tormented by agonies that no prayer can silence, no therapist can unravel, and no drug can dull.

Like a malignant cancer cell, fear began to spread through the pastor's son, eating away at his nervous system. A thick fog descended over his consciousness, engulfing him in all its intensity. His world went blurry, and his knees gave way, buckling under him like overcooked spaghetti.

Scarface swooped in just in time and held him upright. Gripping the pastor's son's right arm tightly, he applied pressure to the biceps until a prominent forearm vein bulged. The assistant disappeared, only to return with a glass vial and a hypodermic needle. She turned the ampoule upside down and filled the syringe by pulling on the plunger. After gently tapping it to remove any remaining air bubbles, she plunged the needle into the pastor's son's protruding vein and squeezed the mixture into his bloodstream.

"This will now strengthen you and sharpen your senses," Scarface said. "You must endure what is to come, with a vivid mind."

CHAPTER 2

Friday, 9 March, 19:00

Detective Chief Inspector Dennis Mugo of the Special Crime Prevention Unit sat in the living room of his modest suburban home. His wife Virginia, a quiet woman with a kind smile and warm eyes, joined him on the sofa with a steaming cup of chai and a glass of frothy beer. The flat-screen TV on the mahogany wall unit was on, the countdown to the evening news ticking down.

At 7:00 p.m., a sketch of a couple appeared on the screen: a man with a scarred face in a dark hoodie and an attractive girl in her late teens with box braids. The news ticker read: *The notorious Duo are back!*

> "Good evening, I'm Musamali Demba, and we have a critical update on the notorious criminal pair known as 'The Merciless Duo'. After a year in the shadows, they appear to have risen from the dead. Their reign of terror last March left a trail of unprecedented torture in its wake, sparking outrage and fear across the nation. It all came to a fiery climax on the night of 31 March, when the high-speed chase ended in disaster. The car in which the two criminals were believed to be travelling plunged off a cliff and exploded in a ball of fire."

The television showed a wide shot from the top of the cliff to the charred, twisted car, its frame barely visible under a layer of ash.

> "The bodies found inside were burnt beyond recognition. And yet, against all odds, whispers of their return have resurfaced. At today's press conference, the lead investigating officer, Detective

Chief Inspector Dennis Mugo, made the following statement to the media ..."

DCI Mugo appeared on the screen, his voice sounding frustrated as he spoke:

"We have reason to believe that the criminal duo are back. We are doing everything we can to bring them to justice. However, our biggest obstacle is the unwillingness of the victims to cooperate. Most victims are reluctant to seek legal redress. This makes our work even more difficult ..."

The shrill ringing of Mugo's mobile phone on the coffee table distracted him from the news.

"DCI Mugo," he answered, muting the television.

He listened to the voice on the other end. Sighing heavily, he ran his fingers through his hair.

"I'm on my way," he said and hung up.

The veteran, fifty-one years old, clean-shaven, with a military-style haircut, took a big gulp of beer and looked at his wife over the rim of his glass.

"A man managed to alert his security guards just in time as the Merciless Duo forced their way into his bedroom," he said, his voice tinged with urgency. "There's a chance the Duo are trapped in the house. I have to go."

Virginia nodded. "Then go. Take them down."

Mugo rose from the sofa, ready for another gruelling night in the service of public safety. He led a task force charged with investigating all cases across the country related to the Merciless Duo. Despite the tireless efforts of local police, every lead had evaporated, leaving only dead ends, unanswered questions and simmering frustration. And a nation on the brink of panic as more cases came to light.

◆◆◆

Almost as tall as a standard door, with broad shoulders and bulging muscles, the village chief could hardly believe that someone of average stature and height had knocked him down – years of undefeated wrestling had honed his body into a bastion of strength.

"What kind of ox gene has this skunk got?" he muttered, wrinkling his nose at the stench that filled his bedroom.

His eyes narrowed in indignation and disgust at the sight before him: a girl in a school uniform, a screwdriver in one hand and a burning candle in the other. She blew on a bubble of chewing gum until it popped with a soft snap.

"Who shit in your skull, you silly goat?" growled the village chief in a deep voice reminiscent of a buffalo's mating call. He was known for his vulgar language and obnoxious swearing.

Undeterred, the girl blew another bubble.

The village chief stood up, feeling his simmering anger boil. Proud as he was, he felt no need to cover his nakedness. He turned to face the intruder, a figure with a dark hood pulled over his head. Scars marked his face, and his right eye protruded grotesquely from its socket.

"You numbskull, how dare you break into my home and lay your filthy paws on me?" the village chief croaked belligerently. His name inspired admiration, respect, and awe in his village and beyond. His fame frightened the bravest. "Do you know who I am?"

The left corner of the intruder's mouth showed the hint of a wry smile. It disappeared just as quickly as he said, "What we already know about you is disgusting. Let's leave it at that."

A slight tremor betrayed the village chief's struggle to comprehend the audacity and insolence. He took a step towards the intruder.

"Do you know who you're messing with, you brain-dead nitwit—"

"Shh!"

The village chief's blood boiled; never before had he been silenced with a mere "shh", like an unruly child. He bent his knees in a stance reminiscent of his golden days as a wrestler. His fierce gaze concealed his plans: dismember the stinking idiot, wrap the body parts in a blanket, and deliver them to a hyena's lair, where nature would take care of the rest.

The frenzy of blood in his guts made him toss all his elaborate fighting strategies overboard. Like a raging bull, he lunged forward, ramming his fist into the intruder's right upper abdomen, just below the ribcage.

The girl blew out the candle.

Disoriented by the darkness, the hulking village chief swung wildly, his punches missing their mark and bouncing off the wall with a resounding thud.

A fist that must have been cast in cement slammed into his diaphragm. He took the blows with his stereotypical masculine stoicism, refusing to vocalise his pain. With the ferocity of a hippopotamus defending its territory, he lunged forward, delivering his blows with reckless abandon.

The intruder stopped his left fist in mid-swing and twisted his arm violently. Blows then rained down on his body like a rented mule.

The intruder's reflexes in the pitch-black darkness left him completely baffled, and he wondered: *does this stinking lump of puke have the genes of a house cat*?

In this extended traditional family in western Kenya, the homestead consisted of several structures and huts, each built in a specific location according to Luo culture and tradition. The ambush on the village chief took place in his first wife's house, which stood directly opposite the main entrance. To the right was his second wife's house, and to the left was his third wife's house. His first wife was absent.

Overwhelmed by a sense of powerlessness, panic gripped the village chief. The chokehold, tight as a vice and undoubtedly designed to suck out his soul, crushed any semblance of hope that he would survive this confrontation with dignity.

The girl lit her candle and blew a bubble with her chewing gum. The intruder let go of the village chief and watched as the nostrils of his boxer's nose flared and contracted as he gasped greedily for air.

"It should be clear by now that throwing tantrums will get you nowhere," the intruder sneered, his soft voice lacking the weight to be taken seriously.

The village chief clucked his tongue. He wrinkled his nose in contempt and retorted, "What have you been feasting on, you stinking one-eyed scarecrow?"

"You would do well to mind your manners," the intruder warned, his foul-smelling spittle landing on the village chief's face. "I must introduce ourselves and explain why we have chosen you. Then I will ask you a question and expect honest answers."

"What a sick mongrel?" hissed the village chief with renewed confidence.

"Final warning: watch your language," the intruder said without showing the slightest sign of annoyance. "From now on, call me Scarface." He gestured to his accomplice. "My assistant. You must have heard of us."

"Heard of what? Your slimy face and rat eyes?"

Scarface pulled a flip-book business card from the kangaroo pocket of his hoodie, held it up to the village chief and ordered, "Read the title out loud."

This wasn't a coherent speech, but a senseless jumble of words that had no place in his household. He looked down at Scarface with disdain, then at the business card. For seconds, he stared at the letters on the card, which seemed to him to be a string of more or less abstract, meaningless symbols.

"I said, read the title out loud."

"Kiss my hairy arse, you greasy slime face!" the village chief boomed, clenching his fists.

The assistant blew out the candle.

CHAPTER 3

Friday, 9 March, 19:35

DCI Mugo veered off Kiambu Road and pulled up behind a line of police vehicles parked at the edge of a newly built gated community.

As he turned off the engine of his Mercedes Benz 280 SE, a police officer approached him.

"It was a false alarm," said the officer. "We searched the house and the area but found no sign of the Duo. Then, the man's wife came home from work and suggested it must have been his nightmare. He keeps waking up from his dreams in a panic, claiming the Duo are in the house."

Mugo slammed his fist down on the steering wheel.

◆◆◆

Scarface grabbed the village chief by the neck, pressed his head against a metre-high sideboard and held him there.

The village chief watched as the assistant approached, her gaze predatory, like a lioness on the hunt, her candle in her right hand, a stained screwdriver in her left.

The village chief felt the tip of the screwdriver plunge into his back, the metal biting deep into his flesh. With agonising slowness, it began to carve a shape. Blood trickled down his back, and he bore it stoically. As an iron-willed alpha male, he couldn't afford to show any signs of pain, fear or terror – especially in the presence of a woman.

In his warped notion of male camaraderie, he whispered conspiratorially to Scarface: "This klutz is not a girl, is she?" To the male chauvinist, it was inconceivable that a woman – let alone a girl – would have the temerity to make aggressive advances towards him.

"She's a girl," Scarface confirmed. "Now zip it, boy."

"You didn't call me a boy, did you?"

"Yes, I did. Now keep your mouth shut; we have work to do."

The village chief felt Scarface's fingers tighten around his neck and feared the stinking man was trying to cut off the blood flow from his heart to his brain. Every fibre of his body screamed for him to flee, to fight, but his limbs seemed to be encased in solid steel.

He watched as the assistant drew a bottle of yellowish powder from her skirt pocket. She sprinkled it on his back, and the burn hit him like a habanero pepper on an open wound.

As the stranglehold loosened, the village chief seized the opportunity. Standing at full height, he wrapped his powerful hands around Scarface's throat. Every fibre of his being was devoted to sucking the last bit of life out of Scarface. With the ferocious tenacity of a rhino defending its calves from predators, he rammed his knee into Scarface's stomach and slammed his head into the sideboard.

Scarface's hoodie fell off, exposing his scarred and blistered scalp.

"You disgusting, bulbous-nosed fiend!" roared the village chief with fervour. Out of the corner of his eye, he caught a glimpse of the assistant unflinchingly blowing a bubble with her chewing gum. "You're next, you stupid sewer rat."

The assistant blew out the candle.

The village chief's eyes darted around the dark room, unable to comprehend the impossibility that had unfolded – Scarface had broken free from his iron grip.

The village chief's breath caught in his throat as a violent twist snapped the wrist bone, sending a jolt of pain through his arm. As a heavy kick shattered his knee with an unpleasant crack, he couldn't help but groan in pain. He fell down.

Two hands jerked him to his feet. Before another sound could escape his throat, a chokehold snuffed out his breath.

The assistant rekindled the candle. She tilted it so that a small puddle of wax formed on a shelf beside her, then pressed the base of the candle into the melted wax.

Dexterously, she unzipped the rucksack on her back and reached for a thick roll of duct tape. She unrolled it, tore off a length with her teeth and handed it to Scarface, who was now pinning the helpless man to the wall.

"Only a fool would prefer to flaunt his male ferocity rather than ask why we singled him out," Scarface remarked. He wrapped the tape around the village chief's mouth and shoved him away.

The once-undefeated village wrestler fell to the ground. He felt both his hands being pulled behind his back. A cable tie was tightened around his wrists, cutting deep into his skin.

The assistant set down her rucksack and took out a small plastic bottle. She poured a yellowish-white powder into it, added a clear liquid, and swirled the mixture several times.

Scarface opened his blue, rusty metal toolbox, the hinges creaking as he lifted the lid. He took out parts of a watering can, modified to suit his grim needs, and ran his fingertips reverently over them. With a glimmer of satisfaction, he began to assemble his makeshift instruments of torture, piece by piece. He attached a sturdy plastic shaft to one end, which would typically hold a simple garden sprayer. At the other end, he screwed on a trigger guard and attached a black tube to its valve.

The assistant took the assembled device from Scarface and dipped the tube into the plastic bottle with the prepared mixture. Then, using her teeth, she tore off a piece of tape and wrapped it around the tube to hold it in place.

Scarface approached the village chief, grabbed his arm and squeezed his bicep. In a well-coordinated team effort, the assistant put down the torture device and took an ampoule and a needle from her skirt pocket. She filled the syringe and injected the mixture into the village chief's bloodstream.

The village chief's erratic breathing subsided.

The assistant moved to the sideboard. With one last look at the huge man lying helplessly on the floor, she snuffed out the candle, plunging the room into darkness.

A relentless torrent of violence tore through the village chief's nerve endings, each more vicious than the last, ripping his insides apart with unprecedented savagery.

The burly man writhed and convulsed. His jaw clenched against the tape, and the struggle to make any sound added a raw, almost feral edge to his muffled moans. Reduced to a pitiful shell, his muscles seized and clenched as though high-voltage currents coursed through him, his mind buckling beneath the crushing weight of humiliation.

After what seemed an eternity, the vicious torture stopped. He felt a finger pressed against the jugular vein in his neck, apparently to check his pulse.

The surreal horror began all over again.

Oh, god of thunder and lightning, god of the brave, I abandon myself to you. Take me now, the village chief prayed. He felt that death would have been a far better choice.

The suddenly flickering candlelight on the sideboard cast a glow over the scene. Scarface dropped to one knee and tore off the tape with ruthless force, stripping away the village chief's moustache along with a layer of skin.

The village chief threw up. Like waves breaking and receding on a beach, his consciousness faded and reappeared. Through the haze, he faintly noticed the assistant approaching with a glass ampoule and a syringe. Before he could react, he felt the sharp sting of a needle piercing his neck.

"We don't want you to lose consciousness," said Scarface. "It would be unforgivable to leave you without feeling."

"What have I done to deserve this?" the village chief demanded, but his usually strong bear voice was too weak to be heard.

◆◆◆

Oliver Morgan's event management office in Abingdon-on-Thames, Oxfordshire, was a mess: files, documents, and a greasy box containing the half-eaten remains of a salami pizza lay scattered across the cluttered veneered desk, obscuring the Kenyan SIM card he was still searching for.

Although cleanliness was not his strong suit, the five-foot-eight, red-haired, blue-eyed Oliver was a talented all-rounder. Six years earlier, he had set up a company in Mombasa, Kenya's oldest city on the Indian Ocean, exporting goods from Britain. The business flourished, employing twelve people in marketing, accounts and human resources. From his base in Oxfordshire, he monitored stock levels and managed order books. Every few months, he travelled to Kenya to oversee the growth and development of his company.

Oliver Morgan breathed a sigh of relief when he discovered the SIM card under a lens-cleaning tissue. His attention shifted to the vibrating phone on the table, his wife's name flashing on the touchscreen.

"Hello honey," he replied, shutting down the computer.

"Hey, where are ya?" Charlotte Morgan asked. "Your flight's in less than four hours. You should have been home ages ago."

"Work went bonkers. I lost track of time."

"Oli, we had plans. I was hoping for a proper send-off before the little one wakes up."

"I feel awful, honey." Oliver got out of the chair and grabbed his jacket. Through the glass door, he saw the cleaner waiting for him to leave so she could start tidying his office. "I'll make it up to you, swear down."

"Where are you at right now?"

"I should be there in a jiffy."

The piercing cry of the nine-month-old baby droned on in his ear. The adorable bundle of joy had a mind of her own, capable of squirming and screaming incessantly when things didn't go her way. When she was awake, she expected undivided attention. In fact, she demanded it.

He heard Charlotte sigh.

"Uh-oh, the little troublemaker's up," she said and hung up.

Oliver's three-year-old daughter, wearing a pretty little dress and her hair pulled back in a cute ponytail, ran up to him as soon as he entered the compound.

Oliver scooped her up, tickled her and blew on her neck, eliciting laughter as she clung to him. With a sense of urgency, he carried her into the house. The tantalising aroma of his favourite dish filled the air: fried prawns in a homemade garlic and lemon sauce.

"I had dressed up lookin' fly for the occasion," said Charlotte. She was sitting on the edge of a white sofa by a large window, cradling her little 'troublemaker'. The sheer white shirt hugged her curves and exuded a certain seductiveness. "Gotta heat the food. Hope them prawns stay glassy!"

"I'm hella behind schedule. Just gonna grab me a sandwich at the airport."

"Daddy, where are you going?" the daughter asked.

"I'm jetting off to Kenya, sweetheart." He bent down to her level and stroked her hair.

"You're going on the big plane?" A pout played around her lips. "I want to go on the aeroplane with you!"

Sighing, Charlotte moved the baby into a more comfortable position and called, "Come to me, darling, or else, pops' gonna miss his plane!"

Oliver glanced at his wife for a moment. Her face was an unreadable mask, but the rapid rise and fall of her chest gave her away. Every breath seemed a struggle to keep the turmoil bubbling inside her from spilling out. Oliver could feel it all and understood the reason only too well. He was leaving for three weeks, and their farewell would be anything but dignified – reduced to a goodbye kiss. Oliver knew that the last few weeks had added to her frustration. He had been constantly on the road organising events for an international musician and had come home late and exhausted every night – if he had made it at all.

A pang of guilt rippled through him, but it was quickly eclipsed by the prospect of the exciting adventures that awaited him in Kenya, the pride of Africa.

CHAPTER 4

Saturday, 10 March, 05:45

For some villagers, the rooster's crow was an original, organic alarm clock, heralding the dawn of a new day. The second wife of the village chief began her duties by preparing her husband's breakfast of sweet potatoes, yams, and a large pot of chai. The third wife had long since risen to milk the cows. Her daughters were busy in the kitchen – the youngest dipping slices of white bread in beaten eggs and her older sister, Beatrice, frying them to perfection.

"Why don't you say anything today, Beatrice?" complained the younger sister.

"Everything is fine," Beatrice replied with a sad look in the corner of her eye. The abuse she suffered at home affected her deeply. Once before, she had dropped her schoolbag and run to Lake Victoria, but a fisherman had thwarted her attempt to disappear into the water.

Balancing her husband's breakfast in a basket on her head, the second wife called out to the village chief in the customary way: "Wuon Oseko." – A term that affectionately referred to him as Oseko's father.

There was an unusual silence.

She turned the knob and was surprised when the door gave way. As she entered the house, an acrid, sickening smell hit her like a physical blow. Her eyes fell on her husband. He lay grotesquely sprawled on the floor, stripped of all dignity, drenched in blood and vomit. His face, swollen and bruised, was almost unrecognisable.

A primal scream escaped her lips, the breakfast basket slipping from her head as her eyes darted around the room, scrutinising every corner and shadow.

Alarmed by the scream, the family members rushed over. Only the third wife dared to enter the house without permission. *Wuon* Oseko greeted her with a fart.

What has that filthy wanker pumped into my body? wondered the village chief in embarrassment. The attack had caused him to lose control of his bowels, and he could no longer hold back the annoying bursts of flatulence. In silence, he cursed Scarface like a farmer whose herd has been ravaged by hyenas.

"*Nyieka, konya tingo Wuon Oseko e kitanda*," said the second wife – she had asked the third wife to help her lift their husband onto the bed.

"Aaaargh!" The pain that rippled through every nerve ending was more than Wuon Oseko's hardened body could withstand, shattering his stoic demeanour and ingrained toxic masculinity.

"Uuii!" the third wife screamed, then clamped a hand over her mouth.

◆◆◆

Oliver Morgan retrieved two suitcases from the baggage claim at Jomo Kenyatta International Airport. Working his way through the crowd of travellers, he spotted Omari Sekibo, whose infectious grin revealed a missing canine tooth. Omari was more of a friend and confidant than a mere employee, valued for his loyalty and companionship.

"*Jambo sana rafiki yangu,*" was Oliver's greeting.

"*Karibu sana*, boss." Omari's smile radiated warmth. "How was your flight?"

"Same ol' same ol', *rafiki*. Either glued to the screen for mad hours, or catching zeds, or munching on that pre-packaged grub."

"Boss, use simple language or switch to Swahili," Omari said, pushing the luggage trolley towards the car park.

Jumping into the car, Oliver's eyes drifted to the back seat. The hairs on the back of his neck stood up with joy and excitement.

"How old?" he asked dryly.

"Nine. Your belated birthday present."

With the excitement of a child on Christmas Eve, Oliver took another look at the back seat, examining Omari's acquisition with an expert's eye.

"Wow!" he marvelled with a lopsided grin. Without another word, he pulled a wad of twenty-pound notes from his wallet and slipped it into Omari's breast pocket.

An ambiguous smile played on Omari's lips as he patted the bundle.

The two met and struck up a friendship a decade ago when Oliver Morgan and his then-fiancée, Vitória García, stayed at a hotel where Omari worked as a manager. A few months later, when Oliver sent Omari a consignment of products bearing the prestigious 'Made in Great Britain' and 'Made in Germany' labels, he had no idea that the goods would attract so much attention from Omari's neighbours and friends.

The export business was born. Feeling unappreciated, underpaid and undervalued, Omari quit his job at the hotel to concentrate on selling the goods arriving at the port of Mombasa. Over time, his responsibilities expanded to include running discreet errands for his boss. Now, after seven successful years in the export business, Oliver was looking forward to the grand opening of his production facility in two weeks.

Oliver switched on the radio and watched the fluffy, cauliflower-shaped clouds drift lazily across the sky. It was a heartwarming sight, but a short-lived one. News of the Merciless Duo filled the car.

"How does the Duo keep wreaking havoc and evading the cops?" he asked, turning down the volume.

"Don't fret about those crooks; I have booked you a place that will guarantee you total privacy and security."

"How do you watch your back?"

Omari shifted into a lower gear and slowed behind a minibus in the busy streets of downtown Nairobi. Stroking his hair, he replied, "I have baseball bats and axes under my bed and in my living room."

"I've read that Scarface is pretty much untouchable, innit? That his stench alone will knock you out cold."

"Shit! You just reminded me. I need to buy torches. They say Scarface only acts after his assistant has blown out the candle she carries. Absolute darkness will confuse your senses; you will lose your bearings. Even if you could defend yourself, you will be helpless."

"Cor blimey!"

"We are all freaked out," said Omari, honking at a handcart driver to clear the way. "The Duo's torture is next level. It's like nothing you've ever heard of from the other weirdos, dead or alive."

CHAPTER 5

Monday, 12 March, 17:15

The 12-member task force of the Special Crime Prevention Unit, a semi-autonomous directorate of the National Police Service, convened its first official crisis meeting. It was held in the Criminal Investigation Department's boardroom, which had been converted into the unit's exclusive incident room.

Team leader Detective Chief Inspector Dennis Mugo stood at the front of the room, behind him a wall-mounted screen displaying miniature photographs of the wounded backs of the Merciless Duo's victims.

"We are all aware of the brutality of the so-called Merciless Duo," DCI Mugo began in a bureaucratic tone. The charismatic, always impeccably dressed superior had a knack for brevity. His deep, reserved voice matched his dismissive expression, and his six-foot-two, broad-shouldered frame gave him a commanding presence. "More and more cases are coming to light this year that bear the unmistakable signature of the Duo. Presumably, it's the same Duo as last year, consisting of the man calling himself Scarface and the young female accomplice he introduces as his assistant."

He sipped his coffee – his unapologetic addiction to the dark brew set him apart from his colleagues in a department where chai reigned supreme.

"Scarface appears to be well-trained in martial arts and uses darkness to outwit his opponents," he continued, his dark-brown, bloodshot eyes scanning the room and his subordinates. "The Duo consistently follow a pattern of torture. Sadism and a lack of empathy characterise the attacks, which are designed to torture the victim to the brink of death. In most cases, adrenaline injections are used to stabilise the victim's circulation and vital signs."

Mugo pressed a key on the keyboard, and a colour composite sketch of the Duo materialised on the screen.

"The Duo always appear with their faces uncovered, carrying their instruments of torture in a rucksack and metal toolbox. However, some victims believe that Scarface wears a mask."

He picked up a remote control and stepped aside to give his team a clear view of the screen. A subtle eye roll betrayed his nostalgia for the old bulletin board on which he used to pin photos of murder victims, crime scenes and suspects, weaving a web of connections with lines and arrows.

"As these are not murders, the police are not called immediately. As a result, the crime scenes are tampered with or contaminated. So far, no fingerprints or biological evidence have been found to link the Duo to the crime scenes. The only evidence found at some of the crime scenes is a business card belonging to Dalilah Beale, the chair of the DS Savekids Foundation."

He clicked on a thumbnail, which started a slideshow of the victims in ascending order of attack. Each victim had an inscription on their back, either a number, a letter, or a hashtag.

"The physical injuries suffered by all the victims are as follows: The left eye socket is broken, the teeth are knocked out, and the back is abraded. Some victims also suffered broken fingers, toes, or dislocated joints. As a result of the attack, they have irritable bowel syndrome and faecal incontinence. Some have had to undergo rectal surgery. They suffer from erectile dysfunction and chronic insomnia. Many are in psychotherapy. Some have seen no way out of their situation and have taken their own lives."

Mugo paused the slideshow, then scrolled to the first image, which showed the inscription on a victim's back.

"In this picture, we have the lowercase letter 'm'," he said. "Depending on your point of view, it could also be a lowercase 'w', the number 3, or the uppercase letter 'E'. Any other ideas?"

The question hung in the air like smoke.

Mugo clicked on the next picture and announced, "This could be the number 6 or 9, or the small letter 'g'."

"Flip the photo horizontally," suggested Detective Sergeant Rahab Atieno-Masinde, a woman of average stature who always sported a short, curly pixie hairstyle. Her feminism had led her to choose a hyphenated surname after tying the knot. She had argued that dropping her maiden name in favour of the groom's surname perpetuated the patriarchal idea of marriage, in which a woman is seen as "belonging" to her husband and his family.

Mugo turned the photograph.

DS Atieno-Masinde grinned and said, "It could also be a 'q' or a 'b'."

"Flip the picture vertically," thundered Detective Sergeant Killian Bakari, Mugo's brother-in-law, married to his twin sister. His voice was deep and husky from decades of cigarette smoking. "It could be a capital 'Q' or a zero. I usually write 'O' clockwise, starting at the top, and rarely connect the ends properly. The victims must have wriggled and squirmed as the assistant carved their backs, and the screwdriver may have slipped in the process."

Mugo cleared his throat. "To decipher the message, or to see if this is a psychopathic ritual, we need to get all the inscriptions on the victims' backs and know the position they were held when their backs were inscribed.

There are certainly more victims who have not yet reported their attacks."

"Whether the Merciless Duo from last year, who were thought to be dead, are back, we can't say for sure, can we?" asked a colleague sitting next to DS Bakari. "The current duo could be copycats."

"The Merciless Duo are back," said Atieno-Masinde. "Our graphologist has confirmed that this is the handwriting of the accomplice. Their description and modus operandi match last year's Duo."

"Digital Sleuth," Mugo called, nodding to the burly Detective Sergeant Bernard Osendi, whose squinty eyes and thick glasses gave him a distinctive look.

Detective Sergeant Bernard Osendi, who wore the nickname "Digital Sleuth" like a badge of honour, nodded. Beneath his unathletic exterior was a sharp mind that had never worked in the field, only in the digital world of crime fighting and intelligence gathering. His unrivalled skills behind the computer screen had earned him the nickname among his colleagues. He was happy to be called that.

"We have five new potential cases," the Digital Sleuth reported. "Potential because the victims have physical injuries consistent with the Duo's M.O., but their statements tell a different story."

He took off his glasses, blew on them, and wiped the lenses on the hem of his shirt. Then he put them back on and glanced down at his laptop.

"Potential victims in Nairobi include property mogul Francis Moshari and German model scout Moritz Rosenthal, who was attacked earlier this month," he continued. "In Machakos, there are two victims: a youth volleyball coach named Amos Mutisya and a local musician. A village chief is hospitalised in Kisumu. He says he was attacked by two huge men."

"Fine ... or maybe not," Mugo mused aloud. "I'll fly to Kisumu." He turned to DS Bakari and said, "Killian, you head to Machakos."

"I'll pay the property mogul a visit," DS Atieno-Masinde offered.

Mugo nodded, then turned to the Digital Sleuth. "Send us any relevant details you can gather on these victims."

"Right away," affirmed the man, diving into his digital domain to gather pertinent information for the team.

"The rest of the team will check all private hospitals and morgues," Mugo instructed. "Our goal is simple: we need to find every victim. We have to figure out what the messages on their backs mean. And find out why they're so reluctant to come forward. That's the key. It'll lead us to the motive." He paused, letting the weight of his words settle over the team.

None of the team members had anything to add.

Mugo concluded the meeting: "Ladies and gentlemen, let's get to work. We must put an end to this reign of terror."

CHAPTER 6

Tuesday, 13 March, 10:40

DS Bakari stood by the bed of youth volleyball coach Amos Mutisya in a hospital room in Machakos. His brusque, demanding tone revealed his growing frustration and impatience with the uncooperative patient. How else could he convey the importance of cooperation in the interest of justice? What else could he say to make this man understand that it was his civic responsibility and patriotic duty to help fight the terror plaguing the country?

Bakari noticed a hesitant shift in the man's posture, suggesting that his lower body, most likely his buttocks, had been viciously mutilated. His gaze fell briefly on the doctor's report, which stated that the patient had expressly refused to have his injuries photographed.

"Look, I respect your privacy." Bakari changed his abrasive tone, which was getting him nowhere. "These criminals need to be brought to justice for attacking you. So let me check your back. It'll help us crack the code they're sending."

The man rolled his eyes, a typical passive-aggressive reaction seen in many of the victims the Duo had attacked.

"We can't let these criminals continue their rampage," Bakari patronised. "We must ensure that others don't have to endure the same terrible ordeal."

"God sent his angel of punishment, Kushiel, to chastise me for my transgressions."

"Excuse me!"

"You can't serve God and give in to the devil's temptations without suffering the consequences. The matter is between me and my Creator. I have nothing to discuss with a mortal being. Now leave me alone."

Bakari sighed theatrically and shuffled out of the room in frustration, just in time to answer an incoming call.

"Hello."

"Any progress?" asked the Digital Sleuth.

"Negative. The man appears to have been blackmailed, coerced or intimidated into silence."

"I'll send you some ammunition I've just found. Let's see if that knocks him off his guard."

◆◆◆

Four days after the attack, and after countless traditional remedies and painkillers, the lion-hearted village chief showed signs of a swift recovery. His body was an abstract masterpiece of bruises, swelling and plaster casts, coagulated blood completing the work. A bandage covered half of his left face, hiding the shattered socket and injured eye. Blood smeared his swollen lips, dripping from the raw gaps where his teeth had been knocked loose. But he was unflappable, showing no sign of discomfort that could undermine his alpha-masculinity.

With his right hand dislocated and his left fingers broken, he had to be fed. So he had insisted on an opaque partition between his bed and his neighbour's to avoid the embarrassment of being spoon-fed like an infant. His henchman held out a cup from which he drank a traditional brew through a straw. On the other side of the bed sat his first wife, her fingers fidgeting with each other.

After a single knock on the door, DCI Mugo, accompanied by a deputy chief constable, entered the room, approached the bed and introduced himself and his partner.

He turned to the man – the henchman. "Would you mind stepping outside for a moment?"

"He stays," the village chief growled, exposing the torn tissue of his gums as he spoke.

"As you wish," Mugo said, picking up the medical report. Every now and then, he licked the tip of his middle finger as he turned the pages.

He lingered on one page, reading the doctor's barely legible handwriting.

Right distal radius fracture.
Left orbital floor fracture.
Right knee dislocation.

He skimmed the long list of injuries and turned to a page with a Polaroid picture of the village chief's back. The inscription, which undoubtedly bore the Duo's signature, was either an 'O' or a zero.

"The report says that you were attacked by two huge men," Mugo began, putting the report back on the bedside table and taking a notepad and pen from his breast pocket. "Is that true?"

"It's in the records, isn't it?" the village chief spat, punctuating the words with sharp, ragged breaths. Out of false pride, he had lied about the gender and size of the attackers. "Those cowardly cocksuckers were lucky they came at me armed to the teeth." The bruised gums and swollen lips made him slur his words.

Mugo's interest was piqued. "Could you please explain what you mean by them being armed to the teeth?"

"That filthy toolbox was packed with all kinds of weapons: knives, chisels, hammers, pliers, and so on."

"Those are tools, not weapons," Mugo corrected.

"They're lethal weapons if you misuse them." A hint of condescending resolve punctuated his words. With a piercing, unyielding stare, he added, "Hand me a chisel, and I'll drill a hole in your skull."

Mugo picked up the medical report again and leafed through it.

"Allow me to quote your statement: 'A stinking, butt-ugly googly eye. He stank from each and every pore.' I will refrain from making assumptions without sufficient information, but your description fits the notorious criminal duo – a man of average height and a girl in a school uniform." He narrowed his gaze, sharp and intent on uncovering buried truths.

"Don't look at me like that," the village chief shot back with a disdainful expression. "I wasn't so wasted that I couldn't tell a guy from a girl."

Were the Duo afraid of this mountain of a man? Mugo wondered. Had they decided to replace the girl with a man?

"Can you describe the second perpetrator? What did he look like? What was he wearing? Any distinguishing features?"

"The jerk had a nose like a melon and a bug eye that looked like someone had tried to yank it out. When this scumbag pulls down his filthy hood, his scalp looks like a festival of blisters. His ears are like lumps of rotten, melted flesh. The jerk looks like a plucked chicken. He hasn't got a single hair on his slimy face and skull."

The deputy chief constable's shoulders bounced with silent laughter.

"Those sneaky scoundrels pulled off a bunch of tricks to outwit me. I couldn't breathe. That skunk ... the bacteria in his mouth had mutated out of control, like he'd been licking on a raw zorilla all day long."

"Can you describe the second man who inflicted the injury on your back?" Mugo asked a trick question.

"She ... aaargh!"

With the swiftness of a housefly fleeing a threatening slap, the village chief's wife got up and came to his bedside to attend to his agony.

◆◆◆

Flashing his service card, Bakari introduced himself to the musician from Machakos.

"Can you take off your shirt?" Bakari continued, sitting on a chair by the bed in the private hospital room. "I need to see the wound on your back."

"It's reassuring to know that the CID is personally involved in my case," said the musician, sitting bolt upright in bed. Bandages covered his body, but his eyes and teeth were intact. "I swear I've learnt my lesson and won't make any more stops in the middle of the night because of a supposed car breakdown. In fact, I only stopped out of pity for the young woman."

"Take off your shirt and turn around."

"They stole my new Nikes and my leather jacket," the musician lamented as he unbuttoned his pyjamas. "I spent thirty-two thousand on them for a music video. You need to know the price, don't you?"

"No, I don't."

Bare-chested, the man rose from the bed and turned around. There was no typical inscription on his back, just jagged knife wounds.

"Got a sore bottom?" There was an indifferent, almost mechanical quality to Bakari's tone. He got up from the chair.

"What do you mean?" asked the musician.

"Did the goons mess with your bum?"

The man frowned. His lip curled as he shook his head.

"Something important is that I have a photographic memory," the musician said. "When the man picked up my shoes, the mask fell off his face. He has bushy eyebrows and—"

Bakari held up his hand to silence the man. "Report this to the local police."

He turned to leave but stopped abruptly as a voice from outside, tinged with alarm, called out: "Scarface! Scarface!"

The musician clutched the sheet, fear in his voice as he asked, "Did you hear that?"

Bakari didn't answer. His hand on the holster, he hurried to the door.

CHAPTER 7

Tuesday, 13 March, 13:30

"Can you describe the person who inflicted the wounds on your back?" Mugo broached the subject again. "You used the word 'she' at the beginning of your sentence."

He sensed the man's unease – the subtle shifts in his posture, the flicker of hesitation that said more than words ever could.

"I will deal with these empty-headed morons myself," the village chief blurted out. "I don't need you for that."

The deputy chief constable took a step closer to the bed.

"I'm afraid I'm going to have to disappoint you," he sneered. "Such retaliation is against the law. So, answer the question."

The village chief's face hardened like granite. "*Excusez-moi?*"

Mugo adjusted his blue-striped tie, his gaze steadfast.

"Did the perpetrators introduce themselves or explain the reason for the attack?" he asked. "Did they say why they had to inflict these wounds on you?"

"You never learnt that such brainless morons just get a kick out of their diabolical deeds. They don't need any rhyme or reason for their perverted mind games." The village chief snorted like a warthog. "Go. Do your homework properly."

"Let me be clear," Mugo said, fixing the village chief with a penetrating stare, "obstructing justice by providing false information to law enforcement can have serious consequences."

"Ridiculous," the village chief croaked.

Mugo leaned forward slightly and lowered his voice. "Were you attacked by a man calling himself Scarface and a girl in a school uniform?"

The village chief's face betrayed his shock, but there was something else beneath it – something Mugo couldn't quite place.

"You can bounce back to your offices," the village chief growled. "I need my rest."

"You won't cooperate with us because you're being threatened?" the deputy chief constable asked.

"Or do you have something to hide?" Mugo added. "Are you proud to admit that a schoolgirl is responsible for your hospitalisation?"

The rise and fall of his chest betrayed the village chief's painstaking attempts to appear calm. He turned to his henchman and hissed, "Show these cowboys the bloody door."

"Are you aware I could arrest you for insulting a police officer by calling me a cowboy?" Mugo shot back. "The charges? Damaging my reputation by implying incompetence and unprofessional conduct."

"Then arrest me."

"Would you rather go to jail than talk about Scarface and the schoolgirl who attacked you?" Mugo asked. "What do they have against you?"

◆◆◆

"There should be a law against men wearing dark hoodies," muttered Bakari, slouched in the corner booth of a crowded Internet café, a half-empty beer bottle on the table before him.

"Why's that?" asked the Digital Sleuth on the other end.

"People are jumpy these days. Someone sees a guy in a dark hoodie, and they freak out. Happened at the hospital today. Male nurses and patients panicked because some guy thought he'd seen Scarface. Started shouting, "Scarface! Scarface!"

"Dark hoodies are getting a bad rap," the Digital Sleuth said, half-joking. "But if the name Scarface is enough to shake up a hospital ... damn! Have you got it?"

"Got it," Bakari said, clicking on the email attachment the Digital Sleuth had sent. It was a photograph of youth volleyball coach Amos Mutisya standing behind a kneeling girls' volleyball team. "Are the Duo playing vice squad?"

"We'll see. Use it as ammunition. See where it takes us."

"Later." Bakari ended the call, his gaze lingering on the photo for a moment.

He clicked on the print icon, drained the last of his beer, logged off and walked over to reception.

"How much?" he asked, "I also have two prints."

"That's one hundred and seventy-five," said the clerk, handing over the A4 prints.

Bakari slid into his car, put it in reverse and backed out of the car park.

The radio came to life.

> "... Pastor Jacob Lamai is appealing for anyone with information about his son's disappearance to contact him or the local police. His son, Noah Lamai, a husband and father of three, has been missing since the beginning of the month. He was last seen leaving his office in Westlands at around ten p.m. Noah Lamai ..."

The sound crackled and sputtered. Bakari turned off the radio.

The volleyball coach watched as the eager officer entered his private hospital room and pulled up a chair beside his bed.

"Here I am again, Mr Mutisya," Bakari said.

"I have nothing to say to a mere mortal." Mr Mutisya's voice barely rose above a whisper.

He was in for a surprise: the officer held a printout of his photo with the volleyball team right in front of his face. It was uncomfortably reminiscent of his encounter with Scarface when he brandished a business card and announced, "*This is the smoking gun. Irrefutable proof.*"

"Either you cooperate, or ..." Bakari paused. The allusion was clear.

The unspoken alternative jolted the man out of bed. He unbuttoned his hospital gown, pulled it off and turned around.

Bakari used his smartphone to take pictures of the wound.

"You can put your shirt back on now," Bakari said as he sat down. "I've got a few questions I'd like you to answer."

"Please leave me alone now. You got what you wanted, didn't you?"

"Let's get something straight; I'm not here to weigh in on your moral compass. I'm a crime fighter." Bakari demonstratively placed the printout on the bed. "Just because something may be morally questionable doesn't necessarily make it a crime."

"What else do you want to know? Was I attacked by the Merciless Duo? *Yes*. Was it Scarface and the assistant? *Yes*. Are we done now?"

"We have only just begun, Mr Mutisya."

The volleyball coach swallowed hard. There was an undeniable authority to the officer's voice, quite unlike

Scarface's, yet both had the same unflappable assertiveness.

"Scarface held you in a bent position while the assistant inscribed your back. Is that right?"

Mr Mutisya nodded. "Yes."

"Which side was the assistant standing? Right, left or—"

"She was standing to my right."

"I suppose Scarface told you why they were after you. What was their motive?"

Plagued by feelings of guilt, which he wore like a second skin, he avoided direct eye contact.

"I bet you are married, sergeant," he managed feebly, his eyes fixed on the bed. "We are only human; we fall into temptation."

"I agree with you." Bakari gestured with his head at the A4 photograph. "Have you ever laid a hand on your lover or wife?"

He looked up. "No. I was never violent."

"I'm leaning towards thinking you're not the violent type. Then enlighten me: Why did Scarface attack you in such a vengeful way?"

"It was hypocritical of me to preach high morals in Sunday school and not practise them."

"Can you explain that?"

He shook his head. "What I have done is a sin in the eyes of our Creator. It's not a crime for you to concern yourself with."

"Scarface is suffering from a God complex. He had no right to make you pay for your sins. Who do you suspect has been in contact with the Duo to expose you?"

"Why does it matter? Whoever it was, I can't blame them. I should have seen it coming."

"Scarface usually leaves a business card, which belongs to Dalilah Beale, chair of the DS Savekids Foundation.

I'm sure Scarface mentioned what the card meant and why he had to leave it behind after the attack?"

"I'd rather not talk about it."

"I totally understand that it's difficult for you to talk about the ordeal. But here's the thing: your cooperation could be key to catching these criminals. I promise that your extramarital affair—"

"It wasn't about the affair," he muttered, voice taut.

"Then what was it about?"

"It was something terrible," he breathed, his voice distant, laced with deep regret. "Something I should never have done."

"What did you do?"

He covered his face and shook his head repeatedly.

CHAPTER 8

Friday, 16 March, 21:00

Dalilah Beale arrived at the chic restaurant on Kimathi Street almost half an hour late. She spotted Musamali Demba, the popular KNN TV presenter with whom she had a rendezvous.

The financially and professionally accomplished bachelor with the warm, friendly features that made him irresistible to women rose from his chair and planted a tender kiss on the back of Dalilah's hand.

"African time!" he greeted with a broad smile, his gaze gliding over her like a silent 3D scan. Dalilah felt his scrutiny but kept her composure, lifting her chin slightly. She was aware of the effect of her high cheekbones and large brown eyes. Her ebony-black Brazilian extensions cascaded over her shoulders, each strand deliberately perfect.

Musamali Demba, dressed in a light blue pinstriped suit, pulled out a chair for her and whispered, "You look so stunning. I'm almost intimidated."

"You don't look bad yourself," Dalilah remarked as she sat down.

His face lit up, revealing his bleached teeth. He settled into his seat and turned to the waitress, who had just placed the menu on the table.

"Another glass of the same wine for the lady, please," he ordered. "Or, you know what? Just bring the whole bottle."

"And a bottle of sparkling water," Dalilah added.

"Your beauty," he gushed after the waitress had left, "could cause a lot of women to develop an inferiority complex."

"That was almost music to my ears, but the inferiority complex bit ... that's in bad taste," retorted Dalilah, a prominent women's rights activist dedicated to ending gender-based violence in Kenya. She co-founded the DS Savekids Foundation, which provided support and counselling to victims of domestic and sexual abuse, particularly children and women.

The self-confident, assertive man seemed to take it in good humour, his wry smile confirming it – or so Dalilah thought.

A pretty-faced sommelier in a tight white-and-blue uniform accentuating her belly ring weaved between tables with a bottle of red wine.

"*Château Les Rambauds Bordeaux*," Musamali boasted to Dalilah. "Nothing but the finest for someone as enchanting as you."

The sommelier poured the wine into Dalilah's glass and refilled his. A waitress brought two plates of avocado bruschetta with salmon.

Musamali raised his glass and asked, "What shall we drink to on this glorious evening?"

Dalilah smiled indulgently, holding his gaze as she struggled to maintain her composure despite the nagging thoughts tugging at her mind.

"Is something wrong?" he enquired, putting down his glass.

"The Internet is currently abuzz with fake stories claiming a link between me and the Merciless Duo. A special unit of the CID has summoned me for questioning."

"Don't get worked up," he said, his hand hovering awkwardly before hesitantly touching Dalilah's arm. "These internet trolls think you have something to do with the Duo simply because they always leave your business cards after the attack. The Duo probably had duplicates printed."

"No, they didn't. Analysis confirmed that the business cards are from the same print run."

"We all give out our business cards at random. It's also possible that you may have misplaced some cards."

Dalilah took a bite of bruschetta and washed it down with a sip of wine. She glanced over the rim of her glass and said, "I've never lost or given out any of my business cards at random."

"Really?"

"You know that the DS Savekids Foundation supports victims of domestic and sexual violence. I focus on children up to eighteen, whom I call my protégés. Before I give my business cards to my protégés or their parents, I always write their case numbers on the cards. I keep a list of who I give them to."

"Why give a business card to someone under eighteen?"

"Well, these aren't your typical business cards – they're more like four-page mini booklets with a comic strip inside. On the front are my telephone numbers and a toll-free number."

"You don't hand out your business cards indiscriminately, and you've never lost one. You also keep a record of who you give them to. Did the Duo politely ask your protégés for the business cards? Or did they use their burglary skills to get them?"

"I have a strong hunch. But the picture isn't complete enough to draw a conclusion. First, I have to confirm that all the business cards found at the crime scenes bear my handwritten case number. You have connections; can you find out for me?"

A faint pout tugged at his lips, the subtle smirk of a man basking in a compliment but feigning nonchalance.

"Yes, I have many connections. But why can't you just ask the task force in charge of the investigation?"

"Working too closely with the police could inadvertently expose my protégés' identities before they're ready. Many find it difficult to talk about what happened, especially with authority figures. Some would then only share fragments, while others would distance themselves from their experiences altogether, claiming it happened to a friend and not to them."

Musamali took a bite of bruschetta and dabbed the corners of his mouth with a cloth napkin.

"This is an aspect I never seem to understand. Why do they twist their stories or lie?" he asked.

"They are often insecure. Emotionally fragile. Confused by the betrayal of trust by those who are supposed to care for and protect them. Some deny the abuse because they fear the consequences. Some may have been led to believe that the abuse was a form of deserved punishment."

"Let's not forget that some children are imaginative and inventive storytellers."

The words shattered her self-control. Leaning forward slightly, her eyes fixed on him like a laser sight, she purred, "Where ignorance is bliss, it's folly to be wise. Count yourself lucky you've never had to walk in the shoes of a sexually abused child. That you've never had to grow up feeling useless or worthless. That you never had to live a lonely life filled with mental and physical anguish ..."

The waitress returned to the table.

"We haven't decided yet," Musamali said. He turned to Dalilah. "Pay no further attention to my remark. I'm going to call in a favour and gather information about the business cards. But tell me, why does it matter to you that those business cards found at the scene have your case number on them?"

"It proves that the man who was attacked isn't a victim – he got what he deserved."

For a man who thrived on words, the TV presenter was rendered mute, his expression of disbelief louder than any words he could have spoken.

CHAPTER 9

Friday, 16 March, 23:40

As stubborn as Milka, his parents' donkey, there was no stopping Member of Parliament Jared Kosgey from driving while drunk. The MP had taken his family to a golf club on the outskirts of Nairobi to meet a sponsor of his political ambitions. When the man failed to turn up, his mood plummeted.

Lucy, his wife of many years, opened the back door for their sleepy 13-year-old twins, Rebecca and Robert. Then she climbed into the passenger seat of the green Range Rover her husband had bought her years ago.

With squealing tyres, the car lurched out of the parking space.

"What have you done with the headlights?" snapped the MP, his characteristic reaction whenever things did not go his way. His patience at such times dangled on an unusually short fuse, ready to explode at the slightest provocation.

"The headlights do not switch on automatically," Lucy explained. Her husband hadn't driven the old Range Rover for years. He only drove his new SUV – or had someone else drive it for him.

"What?"

"The headlights are switched on manually." Tilting her head towards him, she added, "*Mheshimiwa.*" Her tone suppressed any hint of sarcasm. She didn't want to come home with bruises on her face.

The dignified title of *Mheshimiwa*, a mark of prestige for certain government officials, restrained his usual condescension. (*Mheshimiwa* means Excellency, Your Honour or Nobleman, and most holders of the title felt honoured to be addressed as such.)

Mheshimiwa's typical response when he felt disrespected was an exaggerated display of emotion, often accompanied by vehement cursing and swearing. When he ran out of curses, he would resort to a 'bitch slap' – a backhand slap. Or he would rap his forehead against his wife's, as if to avoid getting his hands dirty.

Lucy and the MP had known each other for nearly two decades, the last thirteen in the bonds of marriage. But the joviality that had characterised their relationship had faded over the past six years, giving way to a quiet, unquenchable resentment. The thought of ending the life of the man who had become an abusive partner came to the fore. Throughout this tumultuous time, Lucy had been as patient as a vulture watching its prey from a perch. Despite the turmoil, she maintained her role as the ever-supportive wife, hiding her inner struggle for self-redemption behind a carefully crafted façade of happiness and contentment. Tonight would mark the beginning of a new chapter in her life – she had set her plan in motion.

Her phone vibrated in her hand. She discreetly checked the message.

ALL SET.

The message was from her uncle, the mastermind behind the murder plot. It confirmed that the escort vehicle was no longer roadworthy. The car was supposed to carry five men, two of whom were the MP's unofficial bodyguards.

Lucy replied with a thumbs-up emoji.

The journey unfolded in tense silence. With each passing minute, Lucy felt like a turtle slowly emerging from its shell. The drive wasn't going fast enough for her, and the deserted streets at this ungodly hour added to the cold sweat running down her back. Her heart raced, pounding louder with every bend they took, fearing her husband would spot her uncle's hired car behind them.

The car crashed into a high kerb, jolting the MP from his microsleep. Nothing earth-shattering for the man with the sleep-drugged eyelids. He steered the vehicle back onto the carriageway.

Will we make it in one piece? The thought pounded in Lucy's head, as sharp as the knot tightening in her chest, fuelled by the tension of the murder plan ahead. She gripped the edge of the seat and noticed that her husband was rocking his legs, a telltale sign that his weak bladder was about to burst.

"There's a public toilet up ahead at the junction, *Mheshimiwa.*"

The MP mumbled something incomprehensible that could have meant anything, or nothing. He stepped on the accelerator.

The car came to a halt at the junction, a few metres from a rectangular public toilet. A toilet attendant sat in his small cubicle with burglar-proof bars reminiscent of a prison. To his right was the men's toilet, and on the other side, the women's.

The MP walked briskly to the toilet. He left a tip on a plate on the counter and was given a key. Then he slipped around the corner, out of sight.

Rebecca woke up to see a strange-looking man standing outside the toilet.

"Mummy, Mummy," she whispered, "look, look."

"What is it?"

Rebecca pointed to the toilet, but no one was there.

"Oh, nothing." She looked around and asked, "Where are we, Mummy?"

"Go back to sleep, sweetheart; we're not home yet," Lucy said, looking worriedly down the main road.

"Shit!" the MP cursed as he struggled to undo the jammed zip.

The light went out, and an unbearable stench assailed him. A candle flickered behind him, and out of the corner of his eye, he spotted someone.

"Damn! I forgot to close the door," he muttered, struggling with the jammed zip, on the verge of wetting his trousers. "Sorry, mate, you need to get out."

"You called me mate?" the intruder hissed, rudely shoving him aside. "You sure have a strange sense of humour."

Useless TV programmes, the MP thought. He occasionally watched the hidden camera shenanigans of a reality show, some of which he found distasteful. But to have his privacy invaded in a toilet was pathetic, demeaning and not at all funny.

"I'm going to be a party pooper," he hinted with a broad grin as he looked around, not even dignifying the man with a cursory glance. "Where are the hidden cameras?"

The intruder's fist struck him across the mouth, loosening the teeth that had recently cost him a fortune in Turkey.

Seized by a furious primal instinct, he acted on impulse, lashing out with a burst of violence. He locked the intruder in a tight headlock, heedless of the millions of spectators who might be watching the spectacle live.

The candle went out, plunging the toilet into darkness. The blackness triggered his nyctophobia, a pathological fear of the dark that he would never admit even to himself. His body went into flight mode, he let go of the intruder.

Letting go of the intruder proved to be his undoing. The burly MP, who could take a beating, realised this was an enemy action. He strung together all the platitudes uttered in desperation and fear.

"*C'est la vie, Mheshimiwa*," the soft voice hissed, and the candle was rekindled.

This can't be happening! But there they were, the unmistakable criminal couple, in the flesh, right before him.

"Hey, I am MP Jared Kosgey." His pulse pounded against his ribs. "I've got at least fifty thousand in the inside pocket of my jacket. Take it and get out of here before my boys come in."

"Neither wealth, nor fame, nor power will save you, *Mheshimiwa*," Scarface said, his voice an icy shroud of doom, each word tolling like a death knell. He slammed the toilet lid shut, placed his toolbox on top and opened it.

The MP's eyes fell on the neatly arranged, blood-stained tools. His mouth opened, but the words lodged deep in his throat, refusing to come out.

◆◆◆

"First time in my house, hope to see many more," Musamali began, pouring wine into Dalilah's glass. They had mutually decided to continue their sensitive conversation in a more private setting – much to the delight of Musamali, who needed no further persuasion to end up with Dalilah in his opulent home in the upmarket suburb of Kilimani. His mind was filled with the sizzle of a warm, intimate weekend of snuggling and cuddling with the woman of his dreams.

Dimmed red LED lights, five scented candles, and a flat-screen TV transformed into a crackling fireplace created a romantic atmosphere. A subtle mix of blues' songs played softly from his surround-sound system.

"We've been so close for so long, and we get on so well together," he stated with a smile. "I think we could be even happier if we stopped pretending we're just friends."

Caught between his demands and his partner's expectations, the 39-year-old struggled to start a family. A seemingly perfect partner had turned out to be the most jealous he had ever met. Four potential partners had offered simplicity, modesty and the prospect of lifelong commitment, but they were saddled with pre-existing burdens such as financial debt or parental responsibilities. Dalilah stood out as the epitome of his ideal partner, possessing all the qualities he wanted in a spouse. Her only flaw, he felt, was her fierce feminist stance and her passionate advocacy of girl power.

"Would it be wrong if I thought about proposing to you soon?" he asked. "I promise to treat you like a queen, spoil you with the best life has to offer. I'll make sure—"

The phone in Dalilah's handbag vibrated.

She fished it out and answered, "Hello."

Musamali watched as Dalilah's radiant face grew darker and darker as she listened to the person on the other end of the line.

◆◆◆

Pinned against the wall in a chokehold, the MP flailed his limbs in panic.

"You mentioned that your boys might be here soon, so let's skip the formalities and get down to the nitty-gritty," Scarface said with a certain grim satisfaction.

He loosened his grip, and the MP gasped for air like a fish out of water. From the kangaroo pocket of his hooded sweatshirt, Scarface pulled out a flip-book business card and held it up.

The MP silently read the words on the card.

Dalilah Beale.
DS Savekids Foundation.

Scarface's hand lunged forward, seizing the MP's throat in an iron grip. With each squeeze, the acronym 'DS' on the business card seemed to move apart, and new letters filled the widening gap to form a new phrase: *Dahdi Stoppa Savekids*.

The MP vowed never to mix alcohol and drugs again – the line between reality and hallucination was dissolving before his eyes.

"This card embodies the crime for which you will pay today," Scarface hissed. Releasing the choke hold, he flipped the card open and commanded, "Read the title."

The title, 'Children are the future,' got stuck in the MP's throat.

"Are you disobeying me, *Mheshimiwa*?" Scarface asked, a yellowish fluid oozing from his intimidating right eye.

Before *Mheshimiwa* could react, a blow shattered his left eye socket. Another punch knocked out his already loose teeth. When he tried to scream, all that came out of his dust-dry throat was a hoarse rattle.

The assistant collected the teeth and placed them in a plastic bag. She pulled a roll of tape from her rucksack, unrolled it, tore off a piece with her teeth and held it out to Scarface.

While Scarface taped the MP's mouth shut and bound his wrists with cable ties, the assistant took out her box cutter. The blade left raw, bloody marks as it sliced through the MP's clothes.

Completely naked, the MP looked down at his torn suit strewn across the toilet floor.

Scarface waved the business card in the MP's face and whispered in a voice that was chillingly calm: "Whoever offends one of these little ones who believe in me, it would be better for him if a great millstone were hung around his neck and he were drowned in the depths of the sea."

The misquoted Bible verse struck a chord.

The MP's phone buzzed.

My men? he wondered. Check on me. Now ... before it's too late.

CHAPTER 10

Saturday, 17 March, 00:25

"Please, Teresia, think again – for your daughter's sake," Dalilah pleaded with the woman on the other end of the line. "You can't let Ruby down now." She shook her head at Musamali's attempt to refill her wine glass.

"Dalilah, please accept my wishes without contradiction. Everything I have told you about my husband has been a lie. He does not abuse Ruby in any way."

"How do you explain the traces of semen on Ruby's underwear, which you yourself brought to us?"

"Ruby has a boyfriend. I was jealous."

"Why don't we arrange a face-to-face meeting to discuss this matter?"

"I'm sorry, Dalilah, but I can't see you anymore. Every time I do, all my lies come flooding back. I don't know what devil got into me. My husband is innocent. I have had a mental disorder since my accident."

This sounds rehearsed and forced, Dalilah thought.

"Just so you know, Dalilah, we have cameras in every corner of the house. And guards. The Merciless Duo should know that. They shouldn't dare come here and attack my husband."

"I have nothing to do with the Duo, Teresia—"

Teresia's husband, sitting next to her wheelchair, snatched the phone from her hand and turned it off. His angular bulldog face contorted into a predatory snarl. He grabbed Teresia's braids and pulled her head towards him.

"Woman, I will make your death slow and agonising if you so much as think about contacting these devils again," he growled, his voice a deadly promise. "How can you be so ungrateful and cold-hearted after all I have done for you and Ruby?"

A single large tear rolled down the cheek of 36-year-old Teresia. A car accident four years ago had derailed her life in ways she could never have imagined. Confined to a wheelchair, she was largely dependent on her husband and a carer. Worse still, her paraplegia prevented her from adequately satisfying her husband's sexual needs. In a gesture of fairness, she had allowed him to have an extramarital affair. But the man's credo was that sweets should not be eaten with the wrapper on – a principle that explained his rejection of condoms. With AIDS raging and claiming countless lives, he saw his 15-year-old stepdaughter Ruby as the safest alternative and meticulously tracked her ovulation calendar to avoid the risk of pregnancy. That his semen would end up in the girl's underwear and that his wife would stumble upon it was something he hadn't thought possible.

The irony of fate: Teresia had done everything in her power to teach her daughter about the dangers of strangers.

"Never get into a stranger's car."

"Never accept gifts from strangers. This is called street smartness."

Never in her wildest dreams had Teresia imagined that danger would lurk within her own four walls. Teresia was helpless to protect her daughter. She was powerless to hold her husband accountable as he maintained complete control over her under the guise of conjugal duty and care.

A few months ago, while watching Dalilah Beale's interview on television, Teresia felt hope begin to blossom within her.

"... In accordance with our foundation's constitution, we provide support, advice and assistance to

> victims and their families affected by domestic and sexual violence. We prepare them for legal proceedings and accompany them if necessary. A key aspect of our work is investigating suspected incidents without direct police involvement. The involvement of police officers, some of whom are not adequately trained in this sensitive area, can be a stressful experience for victims. There is a significant need for improvement in this area, particularly among male police officers. Victims feel harassed and mistreated by them when they talk about their situation ..."

Teresia called the Foundation's helpline and was put through to Dalilah Beale. She poured her heart out.

Teresia and her daughter Ruby received comprehensive and discreet professional support, including medical and trauma counselling. A thorough medical examination of Ruby provided compelling evidence of sexual abuse. But legal action proved difficult. The main obstacle was Ruby's inability to identify the perpetrator. Her stepfather, a respected and well-connected neurologist, had habitually drugged her before molesting her.

Now, Teresia had no choice but to drop the case and sever all ties with Dalilah Beale and the DS Savekids Foundation.

As her husband dismantled her phone, a question flashed through her mind: If the Duo are planning to attack him as he fears, would they dare now that I have warned Dalilah Beale about the cameras and guards?

Dalilah gazed down at her phone, her fingers hovering mid-air above the screen. Teresia's sudden change of tone and abrupt disconnection made her head spin.

"Do you want to talk about the phone call?" Musamali asked.

"Another proven case of child abuse for us to shelve. Adding insult to injury is the woman's belief that we are in contact with the Duo."

"What makes her think that?"

"Free speech on the Internet is both a blessing and a curse. I guess she believes what the internet trolls are saying, that I'm behind the attacks."

He covered her hand with his and squeezed it gently.

"It's such a shame that so many women are financially dependent on their husbands," she said, a note of concern in her voice. "It only deepens their sense of powerlessness and undermines their self-esteem. Things that need to be brought out into the open are instead swept under the carpet. Some even end up denying or twisting the truth – despite clear evidence of abuse, both against them and their children."

"You know, our society's pretty patriarchal, and that's part of the reason why the idea that it's OK for husbands to 'discipline' their wives still exists. So a lot of women just put up with the abuse without speaking out. And then there's that old saying, 'Spare the rod, spoil the child,' right? It's led to corporal punishment being so normalised that when kids end up with bruises, people might mistake it for abuse. Hard to tell sometimes—"

"When I said abuse, I didn't mean punishment or physical child abuse. I meant sexual child abuse."

"This woman knows that her husband is sexually abusing the daughter? But she wants nothing more to do with you because she read that you hang out with these psychopaths?"

"I wouldn't exactly call the Duo psychopaths. I don't think they have any emotional deficits. Like I said, those men who were attacked got what they deserved. They got a taste of their own medicine."

"You can't be serious, Dalilah!" he gushed, his eyebrows knitted in confusion. "These men were attacked because they're paedophiles?"

"They are not necessarily paedophiles, but child molesters."

"Is there a difference?"

She nodded solemnly. "A child molester commits the heinous crime of sexually abusing a child. A paedophile, on the other hand, is sexually attracted to children. Not all paedophiles abuse children."

Dalilah's phone rang, showing an unknown number with a Kisumu area code.

She pressed the green button and said, "Hello."

"Is this Dalilah Beale?"

"Speaking. Who am I talking to?"

"My name is Dorcas. We don't know each other. Sorry to call so late. I just wanted to thank you for what you've done. He got what he deserved a long time ago. He was rightly punished. I know it was the Merciless Duo. Thank you, Dalilah, for—"

The connection broke. Dalilah's left hand instinctively cupped her breast.

"The woman thanked me because someone had been beaten to a pulp, apparently by the Duo. She called me from Kisumu and sounded like a mother who knew of her husband's misdeeds."

Dalilah called back the number, watching Musamali's astonished expression.

A woman answered with her name and the name of a hospital.

Dalilah said, "This is Dalilah Beale. Can I speak to Dorcas, please?"

"Ah, Dalilah Beale. It's nice to speak to you. Is Dorcas a patient or a staff member?"

"She just called me from this number."

"Oh, her. She's gone. I'm afraid I can't look for her; I'm alone at my desk."

"Do you know if her husband has been admitted to the hospital?"

"Yes, he's interned here. If you are planning to visit him, you should know that he has big problems with women. He won't even let a female doctor look at his wounds; it has to be a male doctor."

"Thanks for the warning. Have a good night." Dalilah ended the call.

"Thanks for the warning." Musamali's tone was somewhere between question and remark.

"The man who was attacked is apparently a misogynist."

"I suggest that we go to Kisumu tomorrow. I will talk to the man, and you will meet the woman."

"Good idea." Dalilah emptied her wine glass. "We better get some sleep."

Musamali drooled at the prospect like a dog waiting for a treat. He stood up and whispered, "Will tonight be the night of nights?" In the cheap soft porn he watched from time to time, women got horny after a gunfight or bad news.

Dalilah stood up.

"Fuck, fuck, fuck!" he whispered to himself. All he had at home was a three-pack of condoms. "Not enough!"

"Will you drive me home?"

He just stood there like a wet poodle, blinking as if he had to translate the words into a language he actually understood.

As Hi-Five's *She's Playing Hard to Get* drifted in the background, a wry smile tugged at the corner of his mouth. Dalilah saw it – something had changed in his eyes. The song had triggered something. Something she couldn't quite put her finger on, but she felt it.

Suddenly, she wasn't so sure she wanted the lift home, but she needed to get out of there fast.

◆◆◆

Ungodly hour or not, Mugo adhered to the official dress code. He selected a bespoke royal blue double-breasted coat from his wardrobe and pulled it over his long-sleeved shirt with contrasting elements on the collar and sleeves. His wife Virginia tied his tie – a tradition that had not changed in their 24 years of marriage.

"The Duo are growing more unscrupulous and brazen with each passing day," he remarked.

"You've dealt with worse criminals and nailed them. Don't let the Duo rattle you."

He opened the combination lock on his gun cabinet and pulled out his service pistol. As usual, he removed the magazine, checked that everything was in order and reloaded.

By the time Mugo arrived at the scene, MP Kosgey had been taken away, the area was cordoned off, and two police officers stood guard at the entrance to the public washroom. The forensic team was at work, and many onlookers, mostly night owls who had seen nothing, swarmed the scene.

Every millimetre in and around the toilet was examined. The numerous hairs, blood samples, clothing fibres and fingerprints found on virtually every solid surface were collected for microscopic examination. Fresh footprints on the soft ground were photographed, moulded and documented for immediate transport to the laboratory for analysis.

Detective Sergeant Rahab Atieno-Masinde had arrived at the scene early and was questioning an employee of a nearby fast-food restaurant.

When she saw Mugo's car pull up, she said to the employee, "Give me a minute."

She hurried to meet her superior.

"Hello, boss," she greeted Mugo as he stepped out of the car. Gesturing to a group of men gathered by a black SUV, she said, "Those are MP Kosgey's escorts. They arrived about ten minutes ago. I asked them to stay for questioning. Mrs Kosgey drove away. She claimed she was barely awake, and her children were fast asleep. They hadn't seen or heard anything."

"She was here with her children?"

"Yes, she was. She testified that she went to the toilet attendant and asked him to check on her husband because he had been in the toilet for a long time. The attendant went to check and immediately called for help. Mrs Kosgey found the attendant crouching beside her husband. The sight of his bloodied and bruised face shook her, and she rushed back to the car and dialled 999."

"Did the MP say anything?"

"He was in a pitiful state; he couldn't speak. I couldn't interview the toilet attendant either. He vomited and collapsed. He was taken to the hospital. Dalilah Beale's business card was found at the scene."

Mugo puffed out his chest in indignation and pulled a notebook and pen from his breast pocket.

"Proceed with the witness," he instructed. "I'll question the escorts."

"Please continue," Atieno-Masinde continued the conversation with the witnesses, "from the point where you took a cigarette break."

"I was just chilling and smoking when I saw a white Suzuki Swift over there," the man said, pointing to the spot where the car was parked. "The dude got out of the

Suzuki. He was talking on his cell and eyeballing the loo."

"What did the man look like?"

"I couldn't see his face. He was wearing a dark Kaunda suit and a black baseball cap."

"Did you see the number plate of his car?"

He nodded and gave Atieno-Masinde the number.

"Did you see the driver of the Range Rover go to the toilet?"

"No."

"Did you see anyone else go to the toilet?"

"No."

"Do you know what happened in the toilet tonight?"

"I heard that MP Jared Kosgey got jumped." The witness was playing with his hair. "Me, I wouldn't dare use a public toilet after dark, no way."

"Can you think of anything else that seemed out of place at the time? Another person on the road or near the Range Rover?"

"The chick in the Range Rover was talking on her mobile and peeping around like she was on edge or something."

"Why do you think she was nervous?"

"She was acting exactly like my ex. My ex always glanced sideways and over her shoulder coz she was always scared she might get busted while chatting up her side piece."

"You have been very helpful, thank you. I will need your full name and contact details in case we have any further questions."

He unbuttoned his breast pocket and pulled out an ID card.

"Oh, one more thing," Atieno-Masinde added, almost as an afterthought. "The Merciless Duo. Have you seen anyone who looks like them around here, recently or in the past?"

The colour drained from his face, his eyes widening in disbelief.

"It all makes sense now," he gasped. "The reporters ... the cops." His hand shot up to his forehead. "Lord, have mercy! If the Duo can jump an MP in a public place, who's safe anymore?"

CHAPTER 11

Saturday, 17 March, 09:15

DCI Mugo stopped his Mercedes Benz 280 SE in front of a wrought-iron gate. One of the guards from the gated community approached the car with lethargic movements.

"We're here to see MP Kosgey's family," said DS Atieno-Masinde in the passenger seat, holding up her service card.

"Straight ahead and then left," the guard instructed her. "Third house on the right."

The guard opened the gate. Mugo drove through, his eyes drawn to the manicured central island with the blooming flower beds. The vibrant colours of the blossoms harmonised with a group of brightly dressed children singing with infectious joy at an outdoor birthday party.

He parked in front of a large blue gate, which was ajar. Lucy Kosgey stood at the door in an elegant sleeveless top tucked into a ruffled skirt with a bow at the side. Her left hand, held akimbo, was adorned with several silver bracelets.

"The amulets she is wearing are those worn by the superstitious for good luck and health," Mugo observed. "But don't you think her make-up is so bold and, in a way, conveys the image of a woman who is not shaken by her husband's precarious situation?"

"Well …" Atieno-Masinde had nothing more to say.

They got out and went inside.

"We met a few hours ago," Atieno-Masinde said as she shook Lucy's hand. "This is my partner and boss, Detective Chief Inspector Dennis Mugo."

"Come in," Lucy offered.

She led the officers into an open-plan living and dining room. Atieno-Masinde sat on a large corner sofa with a quilted seat. It was upholstered in white leather and partially covered in anthracite linen, matching the curtains behind it. Mugo sat in a wicker chair at right angles to the sofa.

"May I offer you something to drink?" Lucy asked. "Mango juice or tea?"

Mugo flashed a glance at Atieno-Masinde, then back at Lucy.

"Juice, please," he said, taking a notebook and pen from his breast pocket.

"Tabitha," Lucy called to her maid as she sat in an armchair opposite Mugo.

The maid appeared in the living room, and Lucy immediately ordered, "Bring us some mango juice."

"Mrs Kosgey," Mugo began, "please tell us again what you remember before, during and after the attack on your husband. Perhaps something has occurred to you since. Any detail, no matter how trivial it may seem, could be important."

"As I told your colleague yesterday, I didn't see or hear anything."

"Why did your husband use that particular toilet?"

"He had to pee. The toilet was on the way."

Mugo jotted down a note. "The severity of the injuries suggests he spent a long time in the toilet. Didn't that worry you? It took some time before you asked the toilet attendant to check on him."

He saw a disapproving look and caught a hint of mockery in Lucy's voice as she asked, "Is there a time limit that sets off an alarm if a man spends too long in the toilet?"

"Did you notice anything unusual on your journey? Perhaps a suspicious car following you?"

"There were no suspicious cars in front of or behind us. The roads were quite empty."

The maid came in with a tray containing a juice pitcher and three glasses. She placed it on the table, filled the glasses, and left the room.

"Mrs Kosgey," Mugo said, "how did you know there was no suspicious car behind you?"

"I looked back once or twice to check on the children. I didn't see any cars behind us."

"Didn't you wonder where your escort car was? They were supposed to follow you."

Lucy crossed her legs and placed her hand on her thigh, a gesture Mugo noted as an attempt to mask her discomfort at the question.

"I didn't imagine anything dramatic," she replied. "We have never had reason to worry."

"And it didn't occur to you to call the men to find out where they were? I'm sure you noticed they weren't there when you were sitting in the car next to the toilet."

"I was asleep. And like I said, there was no reason to be nervous."

"We have a witness who saw you talking on a phone in the car with your eyes open and looking around," Atieno-Masinde said.

Lucy shrugged. "It's his word against mine."

"Were you asleep or wide awake and talking on the phone?" Atieno-Masinde pressed.

"I heard nothing suspicious, saw nothing suspicious, felt nothing suspicious, smelt nothing suspicious."

Lucy's mobile phone rang.

"I have to take this call," she said. "Excuse me."

She got up and left the room.

◆◆◆

Dark storm clouds cast shadows over the A104 motorway, providing a sombre backdrop as Musamali demonstrated the enhanced engine efficiency of his sleek silver BMW. For more than a quarter of the 360-kilometre journey to Kisumu, he was less talkative, looking glum and reserved.

Dalilah thought she knew why, and reflected on perhaps the most widespread cliché: *men are always after one thing – sex. Did he think he was going to sleep with me last night?* At least he'd been gentlemanly enough to blame the alcohol for not driving her home. She'd called a taxi.

"Do you remember the polarising educational programme we ran on the ChiPo channel two years ago?" she asked, offering him a stick of chewing gum.

He took the gum. "Why was it cancelled?"

"We faced accusations that we were misleading our audience by presenting an inaccurate picture of child sexual abuse in the country. Some critics argued that it was a problem of Western societies."

"I have interviewed people who believe that psychological crimes such as serial murder, paedophilia and racial discrimination only occur in the Western world."

Dalilah rested her left elbow on the armrest and popped a chewing gum into her mouth.

"The World Health Organisation estimates that around nineteen million children under the age of eighteen in Europe have experienced sexual abuse," she said. "Almost thirty per cent of these cases are thought to go unreported."

"Eighteen million children?" He silenced the soft music playing in the background before asking, "What do the figures say about our continent?"

"The number of reported cases in our African countries is extremely low. Mostly because of shame, fear of reprisals, a general mistrust of the authorities and things like that." Squinting against the glare of the sun, she pulled down her visor. "I recently came across a meta-study by the University of Barcelona. It found that Africa has the highest rates of child sexual abuse."

"You believe that?" He flipped down his sun visor.

"The fact is that we are a proud community. Few are prepared to air their dirty laundry in public. I know many parents and guardians who use phrases like 'stranger danger' to try to protect their children from possible abuse by strangers. They often argue, 'We don't have that kind of immorality in our homes and communities'. Funnily enough—"

Musamali honked. Then he dazzled a car in front of him with his headlights.

"Apologies," he said, overtaking the cars ahead. "Please continue."

"A recent survey we conducted revealed a stark reality. Ninety per cent of respondents admitted that child abuse was widespread in families and close circles. Strangely, eighty-five per cent believed it would never happen in their own family."

"Finding out that your partner, relative or someone close to you is abusing your child must be incredibly devastating. Do you come across many of these cases?"

"Sadly, yes. The numbers are staggering, so many children are affected. Their mothers often struggle with denial. They feel guilty about the failed relationship, the problems at home, the betrayal of trust. It's difficult to convince them that their problems are not their fault."

"How do the abused children come into contact with your foundation, if I may ask?"

"The older and more confident children, usually girls, approach us directly. Abused boys tend to hide their suffering for fear of stigma or shame. Some children are referred to us by their mothers or neighbours, mostly women, through various communication channels."

"I don't understand why a mother would hold back from reporting the abuse to the local authorities."

"The biggest challenge is the manipulative behaviour of the perpetrators. Some hold respected or influential positions in their communities or are family heads. This creates an environment where few dare to speak out against their abuse. The end result is often an ambivalent dynamic: 'hate the sin, but love the sinner'."

"Isn't it sometimes tricky to figure out whether the information you're getting is accurate?"

"Why would anyone make up a story about sexual abuse in our society, where it's almost taboo to talk openly about sex?"

◆◆◆

Lucy Kosgey returned to the living room and sat down.

Mugo turned to a new page in his notebook. "Mrs Kosgey, I want you to think about the guests at the country club last night. Was there anyone who didn't quite fit the bill?"

"Sorry, but I don't judge people by their looks."

"Was your uncle ..." Mugo consulted his notes, "Jonathan Wasike part of the entourage?"

Lucy seemed taken aback by the question. Mugo noticed the tell-tale expression on her face as she absorbed his words.

"He wasn't part of the entourage. Why are you asking me about him?"

"We have a list of suspects and possible accomplices. We need to clear them," he explained. "How close are you to your uncle, Jonathan Wasike?"

Lucy wiggled her finger. "I have a good relationship with my family. That includes both my immediate and extended family."

"Did you see or speak to your uncle, Jonathan Wasike, that day?"

Mugo noticed a look of surprise on the woman's face.

"Now you're getting personal!" Lucy Kosgey, maiden name Wasike, protested.

"A man matching his description was spotted in a rented car," Mugo said, his gaze fixed on Lucy with laser-like precision. "The car was stopped on the main road. The man was on the phone at the same time you were. This overlap is rather strange, don't you think?"

"I find this question impertinent and annoying."

"This is not the first time I have heard such a complaint, Mrs Kosgey."

"Usually, the victim's relatives provide valuable information," Atieno-Masinde interjected. "It would be important for you to cooperate fully so that we can rule you out as an accomplice or co-conspirator."

The words may have been trite, but that didn't make them any less true. Lucy's composure was beginning to crumble.

"Can you imagine why someone would attack your husband in such an inhuman way and leave him naked?" Mugo inquired in a softer tone.

Lucy straightened in her seat, blinking rapidly.

"If he was inhumanely attacked and left naked ... then ... then it must have been the Merciless Duo, right?" she put the situation into perspective.

"We haven't confirmed that yet," Atieno-Masinde replied. "Why would the Merciless Duo be interested in him?"

Lucy's lips formed a subtle 'O' shape, which she covered with her left hand.

Mugo shot a telling glance in Atieno-Masinde's direction. They could have pressed further, but by tacit agreement, they left it at that – for now.

"Are your children at home?" Atieno-Masinde asked. "We would like to ask them some questions."

Without answering, Lucy got up, walked to a half-open door and called, "Rebecca, Robert, come down for a minute."

Rebecca entered the room and shyly shook hands with the officers. Lucy noticed the way her shoulders hunched, but she shrugged it off, telling herself that Rebecca was still reeling from her father's attack.

"What is it?" Robert demanded, standing in the doorway.

"These people are from the police," Lucy explained. "They want to ask you a few questions about last night."

"Jeez, Mamaaa," Robert whined. "I was asleep the whole time. You know that. I didn't see anything," and with that, Robert went back upstairs.

Lucy watched Rebecca chewing on her fingernails and wondered, *What's wrong with her? Had she seen Uncle Jonathan?*

"My children were asleep," Lucy said. "Rebecca, go back to your room."

"What has caused this sudden change of heart, Mrs Kosgey?" Mugo asked. "I was under the impression that you wanted to help us with this investigation. Was I wrong?"

"If you'd been paying attention, you'd know I can't help you," she snapped at him in an irritated voice. "For the last time, I saw nothing. My children saw nothing."

"Do you consider your marriage to be happy?"

"Are you a marriage counsellor now, DCI Mugo?" Lucy's response was sharp, her voice cutting. She got to her feet. "I'll see you out."

Mugo stood up. "You know why your uncle was parked in that area at the same time as you, Mrs Kosgey, don't you?" He held her gaze. "A lie never lives to be old."

Lucy's fingers tightened around her phone.

CHAPTER 12

Saturday, 17 March, 10:45

"Damn this wretched body," the village chief ground out through clenched teeth, his face contorting with each sharp sting radiating from within. But nothing cut deeper than the humiliation of being swaddled in nappies – a cruel blow to his once-proud alpha-masculinity.

His chest tightened as his henchman entered the room, a worried expression on his face. He thought grimly: *Misfortune seldom comes alone.* And added, *Woe betide you! I'm warning you!*

"Chief, um ..." The henchman looked away, took off his cap, and put it back on. What he held in his hand was a contemptuous attack on the dignity and reputation of the man he looked up to and respectfully called Chief.

"Spit it out!"

The henchman unfolded the paper that a journalist had handed him, leaned closer to the village chief and said, "A man from the press asked me to show you this drawing. He says this must be the couple who attacked you."

One look at the sketch was enough to send the village chief into a frenzy.

"Has your brain turned to mush?" His dislocated knee prevented him from kicking the henchman to teach him a lesson. "How dare you accept this inflammatory propaganda from retarded busybodies?"

"Chief, I suspect the source of this propaganda is this hospital. Someone here has drawn conclusions from your injuries."

"What fucking conclusions?"

"A couple known as the Merciless Duo appeared out of nowhere last year. The man who calls himself Scarface is said to smell terrible. A schoolgirl always accompanies him. Rumour has it they target men involved in domestic violence."

"What a load of bullshit!" the village chief croaked, swallowing a lump of pain in his throat. "Do those lunatics want to tell a man how to handle his old lady?"

"There's also a woman here who claims to be Beatrice's teacher. She has requested a private audience with you."

The village chief's stomach clenched, and bile rushed to his mouth. He feared the woman's motives. Suddenly, he heard the voice of his 15-year-old adopted daughter, Beatrice, echoing in his head, begging for mercy.

The memory of the first time Beatrice had screamed and begged for mercy two years earlier flashed through his mind: It had been a stiflingly warm, starless night when he had been on his way to the market for a nightcap. He had caught a glimpse of movement at the edge of the footpath – a lone figure holding a flickering torch, crouched low in the bushes. The splashing sound had been unmistakable and, in some inexplicable way, aphrodisiacal. He had approached her like a ravenous vulture circling its prey. The fact that she was his adopted daughter had done nothing to arouse his parental protective instincts; instead, it had stimulated his raw, unbridled desires.

Beatrice had begged and pleaded for mercy. She had convulsed with pain and wept bitterly. Coupled with disgust, she had felt soiled and defiled.

"If you ever speak of this to anyone, I will curse you and your little sister and throw you out of my homestead. This is your fault, Beatrice."

Beatrice had blamed herself and felt ashamed. She had even hated herself. Eight years earlier, her father had died, leaving a legacy of debt and despair. Her mother had become the third wife of the village chief, in line with the tradition of polygamy and female inheritance. Worse still, she had no say in the marriage – Beatrice had no one to turn to.

"Chief, what should I tell Beatrice's teacher?" the henchman asked, bringing him back to the here and now.

The village chief feared that his veneer was cracked and could crumble at any moment, revealing the ugly truth beneath. The thought of his legacy, reputation, and the virtues he had championed being irrevocably tarnished made his skin prickle with cold unease.

But his alpha-masculinity returned to its flaccid shell, inflating him like a hot-air balloon.

A true warrior does not sit down with an enemy; he takes revenge and teaches the enemy a lesson. This teacher is part of the 'coup d'état' to ruin me.

He forgot his henchman's question. His mind wandered back to the village Easter festival three years ago. He had been the guest of honour before a tense, disconcerted crowd. The emergency meeting had been called because a *kwer* – a grave taboo – had been violated by a close member of the clan. Without swift action, the community risked the wrath of *chira* – an insidious curse that knows no bounds, threatening not only the perpetrator but his family and perhaps the entire clan.

"*Incest is kwer*," the village chief had begun. "*Sexual abuse of a handicapped minor is kwer*," he had roared, his voice like a thunderclap, his carotid artery throbbing, his fist pounding on the table to underline the gravity of the taboo. "*If we do not take decisive action now, we will be putting our collective future at risk.*"

"*Jabilo must be executed,*" his henchman had shouted, eliciting a symphonic chorus from the crowd.

"Jabilo must be executed. Jabilo must be executed."

The memories gnawed at the village chief, dredging up a past he could no longer hide from. This life no longer felt like his own. He was now a *jabilo* – a man cursed by the ultimate disgrace he had brought upon himself. He had plunged into the deepest abyss of shame and dishonour in the eyes of the community.

His face, etched with pain, guilt and a crushing sense of hypocrisy, twisted as he looked at his henchman. In a strained voice, he murmured, "Get me two packs of fentanyl. The pain's getting worse."

His henchman hesitated. He saw the concern in his eyes – uncertainty, even fear.

◆◆◆

No sooner had Oliver Morgan woken up in his cosy apartment-hotel than he glanced into the adjoining bedroom. His gaze lingered, tracing the faint outline beneath the white sheets. It was the "belated birthday present" Omari Sekibo had given him on his arrival at the airport, and it was proving to be a test of character.

A tingling sensation crept under his skin, both invigorating and nerve-wracking, as he made his way to the bedroom.

He reached for the sheet, pulled it back and called to the nine-year-old, "Wake up, Bahati, it's time for your bath. And then a yummy breakfast."

◆◆◆

Some 500 kilometres away, in the coastal city of Mombasa, Bahati's mother, Zahara Balozi, was in a state of euphoria. Omari Sekibo had arranged for her son Bahati to be adopted by a wealthy family. Omari had assured her that their bond would remain intact, that this was Bahati's chance at a future she could only dream of. Zahara clung to the hope of a bright future for her son abroad, inspired by the daughter of a neighbouring family who had found her way to Europe under Omari's guidance. The neighbour had once proudly boasted, "*My daughter earns more in a month than a local teacher does in a year.*" Little did she know that her daughter's life abroad had taken a dark turn. She was unaware that most of her daughter's earnings were being siphoned off by a pimp and Omari.

The timing couldn't have been better for Zahara. She had been in desperate need of money, and Omari's initial financial support had enabled her to pay off some of her debts and outstanding rent.

Zahara took a long drag on a joint before handing it to her long-time friend, a university graduate with a serious drinking problem – Zahara wasn't any better.

"My boy's about to hop on a plane, you know? That *mzungu's* got a heart of gold, I'm telling you!"

The friend took a hearty puff from the joint.

"Where's the *mzungu* from?" she asked, smoke billowing from her nostrils.

"He's straight from the land of milk and honey." Zahara laughed.

"For sure, man. This party is already lit, and Bahati hasn't even crossed the border yet." She passed the joint back to Zahara and took a long swig from the vodka bottle.

"Bahati's aiming high. Wants to be a lawyer or a doctor."

"Cool, man! Best believe, in a few years, Bahati is going to roll up in a fancy ride and hook you up with a crib."

"Absolutely. Bahati is going to live up way better than we did with our fucked-up lives, man," Zahara philosophised, filling her lungs with the joint again.

"True that, sis. He deserves every bit of it. God bless that cool *mzungu*."

"Amen. Amen."

◆◆◆

Initially, Oliver Morgan had reservations about being called a *mzungu* – a white man – after stumbling across misleading information online. Over time, however, he grew to like the name and found a sense of superiority in it.

This *mzungu* swallowed hard: the sight of the petite Bahati playing naked in the bathtub with a lather of shampoo had so aroused him that he secretly used his five against one with a little lubricant.

He vowed to himself: "Just this once, I will use my hand."

CHAPTER 13

Saturday, 17 March, 13:10

Clutching a steaming cup of coffee, Mugo entered the incident room already occupied by the eleven members of the task force.

He had barely sat down when the Digital Sleuth opened the meeting.

"After checking with hospitals and morgues, we have eleven new cases. Nine are from last year. Three victims are dead, two live abroad. This brings the total number of victims to thirty-nine."

"The first time I visited Mutisya, the volleyball coach, he refused to cooperate," began Bakari. "The second time, I showed up with a group photo of him and his girls' volleyball team. His involuntary reaction hinted at a possible intimate relationship with one or more of the girls. I leveraged this reaction to get him to cooperate, and he indirectly admitted that the Duo had taken revenge on him for extramarital transgressions. But he refused to divulge details. He did, however, claim that he had never physically abused his wife or mistress, and I believed him."

Kebaso chuckled. "I took a similar approach with Rosenthal, the German model scout. He is single. I hinted that I would call all the models he had worked with to the police station to investigate the motive for the attack. He reluctantly agreed to cooperate, but there was no one he suspected of orchestrating his entrapment by the Duo."

"If these victims knew who was behind it, would they reveal it?" Atieno-Masinde observed, tracing a finger across the table. "It's clear they have something to hide."

"I managed to find two girls from the volleyball team and interviewed them separately," Bakari reported. "They both spoke highly of the coach and couldn't imagine him being involved in adultery. Mutisya was described by his wife and neighbours as a loving and caring man."

"In Kisumu, I had one-on-one interviews with the village chief, his three wives and a number of his relatives," Mugo said, rubbing his temples in deep thought. "The man claimed to have been attacked by two assailants. His account of events resembled a Swiss cheese, but with more holes than the finest Emmentaler. At one point, though, I wondered if the Duo had replaced the girl with a man, given the village chief's towering stature and undefeated wrestling prowess in his prime."

A buzz of voices filled the room. Mugo waited for the hubbub to die down.

"This village chief has a penchant for foul language," Mugo continued, looking down at his notebook. "However, he made a statement that is not in our records. I quote: 'When this scumbag pulls down his filthy hood, his scalp looks like a festival of blisters. His ears are like lumps of rotten, melted flesh. The jerk looks like a plucked chicken. He hasn't got a single hair on his slimy face and skull'."

The Digital Sleuth typed this statement into his laptop and said, "The interviews with this year's victims didn't reveal anything new, but they did confirm what we already knew. The perpetrator calls himself Scarface. His face is scarred, and his injured right eye protrudes from its socket, occasionally oozing a yellowish fluid."

He pressed a key on the keyboard. The monitor on the wall came to life, showing the composite sketch of Scarface.

"Scarface is of average height, standing between five feet nine inches and five feet eleven inches," he continued. "The scars on his face make it hard to tell his age, but he could be between twenty-five and forty. His clothing typically consists of a dark grey hooded sweatshirt, black tracksuit bottoms with two faded yellow stripes down the sides, and sturdy black boots. His voice is soft and soothing, like a lullaby that could soothe even the most unruly child."

"This could be part of the way he manipulates his victims," interjected a colleague. "A soft voice is often considered one of the most effective tools for inducing a hypnotic state. Could explain why victims are always helpless in his presence."

"Hypnosis requires cooperation," Atieno-Masinde explained. "If someone doesn't want to be hypnotised or actively resists, it won't work."

"Scarface speaks mostly in English," the Digital Sleuth continued. "His Swahili accent is melodious, with the softer intonations typical of a coastal accent. He always carries a blue, weathered metal case containing a variety of tools."

The Digital Sleuth punched a button, and a blue metal toolbox appeared on the wall monitor. Each press of the arrow button toggled the image, first showing the closed exterior, then the lower storage area and four smaller compartments.

"Similar toolkits, often sold under different brand names, can be found in many hardware stores nationwide."

A faint murmur filled the room. The sketch of Scarface's accomplice filled the screen.

"Scarface introduces the accomplice as his assistant," he continued. "She is a strikingly beautiful young woman, no more than twenty years old and about five feet five inches tall. She wears her hair in box braids and is always dressed in what most victims describe as a school uniform: a light greyish-blue blouse, a blue skirt, white socks with red and blue stripes at the top, and black strap shoes. Her rucksack contains various tools, including duct tape, a carpet knife, a screwdriver and a syringe. She remains silent throughout, occasionally breaking her silence with the loud popping of her chewing gum bubbles."

"Most of the victims agree that Scarface is terrifying. But it was the callous and ice-cold attitude of the assistant that sent shivers down their spines," Atieno-Masinde added. "Their testimonies suggest that the Duo have perfected their torture methods to the point where they no longer need to communicate with each other. They are very well prepared."

◆◆◆

Dalilah stepped out of the car in the Kisumu Hospital car park and was immediately engulfed in the scorching afternoon heat that characterised the region in March. She wore a wide-brimmed straw hat and dark sunglasses, less to shield herself from the intense sun than to avoid being recognised. Musamali donned sunglasses and a stylish red baseball cap.

Not wanting to touch the hot bodywork, she pushed the door shut with her feet and noticed Musamali watching her with a horrified expression on his face.

Men and their cars! she thought. I bet he'll check the paintwork for damage later.

They walked towards the hospital building, past a small group of mourners.

"Welcome to the district of professional mourners, who grieve louder than the bereaved," Musamali joked, nudging Dalilah with his elbow.

"That's in bad taste," she said stiffly, heading for the hospital reception.

A petite woman with chestnut brown hair, who was talking to the receptionist, made room for her.

Dalilah approached the reception desk and said, "My name is Dalilah Beale. I—"

"Dalilah Beale?" the petite woman broke in, her expression changing to one of surprise.

"Yes, that's me. Dalilah Beale."

The woman looked around, her expression now wavering between grief and fear, perhaps embodying both emotions at once.

"I am Dorcas. I phoned you last night about my husband." Her voice was taut. "He is dead now."

"Dead?"

"Yes." Dorcas hesitated, then lowered her voice. "I need to speak to you urgently, Dalilah. Meet me at Timo's Masala Restaurant in about an hour. Please. Don't talk to anyone until then."

CHAPTER 14

Saturday, 17 March, 13:45

The Digital Sleuth clicked on a thumbnail on his laptop. The image projected onto the wall screen showed MP Kosgey's back. It was a 6. With a few taps on the keyboard, he rotated the image 180 degrees. The wound could now be seen as the small letter 'g' or the number 9.

"The MP's case raises the question of whether it was premeditated or spontaneous," he said, drumming his fingers on the table.

"The attack seems to have been opportunistic rather than premeditated," Atieno-Masinde remarked. "According to his wife, he stopped there by chance because he had to go to the toilet."

"His wife gave the impression of having secrets," Mugo said. "When we asked her about Uncle, she skilfully dodged the question. But it was striking how visibly shocked she was when she realised that the Duo might have been involved in the attack. Another mystery was the escort car. A flat tyre before departure had held up the men. This could have been an accident or deliberate."

"Strange that the MP didn't wait for them," Bakari remarked.

"They said he was in a bad mood when he left the club and ignored their calls. One of them tried to call his wife, but her phone was off."

"The toilet attendant has been discharged from the hospital," reported Kebaso. "All he remembers is giving the MP the key to the toilet and then finding him brutally beaten. A toxicology report will determine if the toilet attendant was drugged. Foul play is suspected."

"Locking themselves in a public toilet and waiting for their victim, or following them there, does not fit the Duo's modus operandi," the Digital Sleuth mused aloud.

"Ritual offenders usually stick to their strict pattern," Kebaso said. "They tend not to be guided by their gut feelings. Counting on the MP to stop at a public toilet ... I mean, visiting a public toilet can hardly be part of the MP's routine."

"The safest bet is that the Duo are not ritualists," Atieno-Masinde argued. "This is torture with an undercurrent of revenge – or rather, vengeance. One thing is certain: the MP was on their radar."

"With the recent late-night raids on public toilets, a man would rather pee on a street corner than risk using a public toilet at night," said a colleague whose thick moustache above his grin gave him an almost theatrical air. "Maybe he was lured there. Or he stopped there for a clandestine transaction."

Mugo shook his head. "The premise that he was there to meet someone doesn't seem plausible to me for several reasons. First of all, I could imagine he has errand boys for shady deals, if he is involved in any."

"There's a strong possibility that the MP's wife and her Uncle Jonathan Wasike are somehow involved," Atieno-Masinde suggested. "Wasike could have acted as a lookout to warn the Duo in time. At the very least, he's a material witness – he must have seen the Duo leave or enter the toilet."

"Jonathan Wasike lives alone and runs a car repair shop specialising in spare parts," the Digital Sleuth said. "He's practically gone off the grid. It's worth noting his political history: four years ago, he ran for MCA but lost to MP Kosgey's brother-in-law. During the nomination process, Wasike raised concerns about vote-rigging and nepotism. This could be a motive against the MP."

"We will follow the trail of this Jonathan Wasike," Mugo said. "Back to the wounds on the backs of the victims."

"So far, the Duo have repeated last year's inscriptions unchanged," said the Digital Sleuth, "only the hashtag seems to have been engraved at random. I arranged them in chronological order and left out the hashtag. For the sake of simplicity, I suggest calling it a code."

He projected the codes he had compiled onto the wall screen.

35a-p31mom/96s&ed/-d13m12l56
msa_d3imo3/6g58ep1/di3m12l59
wsa1p3-3o3166s&epl1p-3w-2i5g
35a-p3/wq3-9g5&edl1p13m12sg
msa-d3imo3i6gs8ep11di3m12ls9

"I have assumed that the assistant was always to the right of the bent victims and that the inscriptions are in lowercase. There are about 30,000 possible combinations. The permutations increase to over a hundred thousand if both upper- and lower-case letters are used. Any deviation from this chronological order would result in millions of possible combinations."

"But we cannot crack the code until we have identified all the victims," Bakari pointed out with a smug smile. "Some are dead, buried without an autopsy and probably decomposed. I think it's too early to start scratching our heads."

"Is this a code we need to crack?" Kebaso asked. "It could be the Duo's signature, or their twisted calling card."

"I think we have to stick to the idea that this is a code that needs to be deciphered," said Atieno-Masinde. "The assumption that it could be a calling card suggests that the Duo are playing a game of cat and mouse. It's now clear that they are out for revenge. Or, to be more precise, retribution."

"We need to bend the law a little to get victims and their families to cooperate," Kebaso suggested. "Otherwise, we'll always end up in a dead end."

Mugo, the charismatic team leader, raised his hand dismissively. "We will not go down that road. We have the Digital Sleuth to dig up dirt on these victims that we can use as leverage and ammunition against them. There are skeletons in these men's closets. We need to find them and see if they are connected to the Duo's retaliation."

"Chances are these men's digital footprints are as squeaky clean as a new shilling," Bakari blurted out.

The room was suddenly filled with a muffled buzz of voices.

"Ladies and gentlemen," Mugo boomed, his eyes slicing through the room like blades, "I need answers – from each and every one of the victims. And while you're at it, I want to know everything about the Duo: where they come from, how they move, how they choose and stalk their targets, and how they always manage to disappear without a trace. Leave no stone unturned."

◆◆◆

Dalilah and Musamali entered Timo's Masala Restaurant and found Dorcas, the third wife of the late village chief, sitting next to an unknown woman.

"This is Musamali Demba from KNN. I invited him," Dalilah began, still standing. "I hope you don't mind."

She noticed Dorcas crossing her arms defensively and raising her ample breasts theatrically.

"We will only speak on the condition that we are never quoted," Dorcas said in a firm tone. "Otherwise, it could be our death sentence."

"I assure you of absolute discretion," Dalilah promised. She and Musamali Daudi sat opposite the two women.

"My husband's men want revenge. They are determined to find out who is behind this treachery." Her gaze became reproachful and bored into Dalilah's eyes. "My daughter only told her teacher. This is my daughter's teacher," she said with a quick gesture of her head towards the woman next to her. "The teacher only wrote to you. Neither she, nor my daughter, nor I told anyone what he had done. I never wished for his death."

"You had nothing to do with his attack, any more than I or my foundation had anything to do with—"

A waiter placed the menus on the table, silencing Dalilah.

"Today's special and a Coke for each of us," Dalilah ordered, not wanting to distract Dorcas unnecessarily.

The waiter collected the untouched menus and left.

Dalilah turned to the teacher. "Can you tell me how and when you contacted DS Savekids Foundation and what pseudonym you used? The name Dorcas is not on my list."

"I emailed you last year, and you replied," the teacher said. "After some correspondence, you sent me your business card by post, which I passed on to Dorcas. I no longer have access to that email address and cannot remember the pseudonym I used."

Dalilah's curiosity heightened. She turned to Dorcas. "Do you still have the business card?"

"I had given it to my daughter. She was supposed to call you from a phone box near her school, but she stayed home with a sprained ankle. A few weeks later, she told me she wanted to call you but couldn't find the card ..." Dorcas paused as a waitress approached their table.

"We've already ordered." Dalilah's voice was hollow and urgent.

The waitress nodded and walked away.

"I found it when I was cleaning up the room where my husband was attacked," said Dorcas, reaching into her skirt pocket and pulling out the business card.

Dalilah's heart raced as she saw her handwriting on the card: 1459. In a flurry of emotion, she grabbed her phone and unlocked it. She opened an Excel app, navigated to a spreadsheet, and scrolled down to row 1459.

"Beatrice." She read the name linked to case number 1459.

"Ah, now I remember," the teacher said. "That's the alias I used in the email."

Tears suddenly streamed down Dorcas's cheeks. She wiped them away with her bare hand and murmured, "Beatrice is my daughter. She has suffered terribly at his hands."

"I'm sorry the business card got lost before you could reach me," Dalilah comforted.

"I'm partly to blame for what he became," Dorcas breathed. "When the rainy season started, we were all very busy." She cast an appraising glance at Musamali Demba, then leaned across the table, closer to Dalilah, and whispered, "I couldn't give him the marital satisfaction he needed. I was always tired after working on the farm."

"He had no right to horribly abuse your daughter just because his wife couldn't meet his needs," Dalilah rationalised. She couldn't help but think, *What an insensitive mother*!

"It's just ... Now that he's gone, I feel infinitely sorry for him. He really had his heart in the right place. He saved me and my children from great grief when my first husband died." Her voice carried the weight of a lifetime of oppression and exploitation in a marriage.

Seeing no point in continuing the conversation, Dalilah said with a friendly smile, "I need to speak with Beatrice."

Dorcas's eyebrows shot up, her widened eyes reflecting fear. "You don't suspect my daughter of setting him up, do you?"

CHAPTER 15

Sunday, 18 March, 22:40

Oliver Morgan and Omari Sekibo, sipping drinks and munching on finger foods at the aparthotel, had reason to celebrate – the electrician and painters had put the finishing touches to Oliver's factory.

As the boss and employee toasted with whisky glasses, the electrician's fingers drummed a restless rhythm on the steering wheel of a stolen car parked inconspicuously on a street corner. His eyes were fixed on the gate of the aparthotel in front of him.

He swallowed his bitterness that the foreman, Omari Sekibo, had cheated him out of his wages. Omari had pressured him into signing the contract without reading the small print. Determined to get what was rightfully his, the electrician had hired two ruthless thugs and followed Omari unnoticed until he disappeared into the guarded grounds of the aparthotel.

Omari's car rolled out of the gate.

"There he comes," the thug in the passenger seat announced, his head covered by a dark hoodie.

"Here's the plan again: after the next roundabout, I will overtake the bum and block his path," the electrician explained as he followed Omari's car at a safe distance. "You grab him and stuff him in the boot. Then follow me in his car."

Omari exited the roundabout and stopped beside a gaunt woman and a man in sunglasses. The electrician overtook him, stopping about 30 metres in front of him.

Just as the two thugs threw open their respective doors, the electrician shouted, "Wait!" as he watched the unexpected development in his rear-view mirror.

"Wait for what?" growled the thug. He looked behind the car and commented, "No sweat, we'll take care of his friends."

"No. Innocent people will not be harmed," the electrician said emphatically. His gaze followed the sight of a small child emerging from the back seat – it was Bahati, destined to be reunited with his mother in Mombasa for a while.

The gaunt woman took Bahati by the hand and walked across the road to a waiting car while the man in the sunglasses – a pimp – climbed into the passenger seat.

The electrician shadowed Omari inconspicuously.

Omari stopped abruptly and let the pimp out. The headlights went out. Omari stayed in the car.

To avoid attracting Omari's attention, the electrician stopped 80 metres away. The thugs jumped out. Crouching, they ran across the road towards Omari's car. But the approaching sirens and flashing lights forced the two police-allergic thugs to take cover behind parked cars and wait for the patrol car to pass. While they waited for the patrol car to pass, the pimp hurried back to the car with a young street urchin. The boy jumped into the back seat. The pimp disappeared around a corner.

The thugs scrambled to their feet, but couldn't catch up with Omari, who had already backed the car out of the parking space. They hurried back to their vehicle and the discreet pursuit resumed.

The electrician kept a cautious distance as Omari's vehicle navigated the deserted streets – one bend, then another, until the gates of the apartment hotel yawned open, swallowing Omari's car whole.

The electrician rolled to a stop at a safe distance. He and his hired thugs had to wait in the car again.

◆◆◆

"Scarface is undoubtedly a psychopath. But what kind of twisted young woman would watch such monstrous torture while mindlessly chewing gum?" the Digital Sleuth asked Atieno-Masinde, who sat beside him in his office.

"Good question. Next question." Atieno-Masinde rubbed her tired, squinting eyes. Hours of watching the grainy video footage from the airport, recorded over the past two weeks, had taken their toll.

A unit within the task force coordinated police efforts, combing highways and country roads, moving from petrol stations to motorway restaurants, and questioning staff about the Duo. Wherever CCTV cameras were installed, the footage was reviewed.

Hundreds of witnesses had been interviewed, thousands of phone calls had been logged, some of which contained leads that required further investigation and verification. Several car thefts had been conclusively ruled out as linked to the Duo's activities. In addition, two make-up artists had been questioned and subsequently cleared of any involvement.

To intensify the hunt, roadblocks were set up on all the main routes into the capital, and officers at these checkpoints scrutinised motorists, focusing in particular on men accompanied by young women.

The Duo remained elusive and untraceable.

Bakari strode into the office holding two A4 printouts and asked rhetorically, "Any leads?"

The Digital Sleuth took off his glasses. "It's like chasing shadows in the dark."

Bakari placed the printouts on the table before his colleague and said, "This man suffers from the autoimmune disease psoriasis. The two snapshots were taken eleven months apart. The scars are virtually identical in both pictures."

"What are you getting at?" asked Atieno-Masinde, massaging her eyelids.

"Both this year's and last year's victims described Scarface as having large, fresh-looking scars. Could this be related to a chronic skin condition such as psoriasis?"

"Most autoimmune diseases would affect a person's agility and strength. Yet Scarface was active every day last March," the Digital Sleuth countered, typing a note into his digital diary. "I'm going to talk to Dr McKenzie tomorrow to find out more about this skin condition."

"There should be a pharmacy or drugstore where Scarface regularly buys his ointments or medicines," Atieno-Masinde remarked, stretching out her arms. "But he is in the news and on billboards all over the country. Someone has to do the shopping for him, and that person will likely use cash instead of M-Pesa."

"Still, it's a solid starting point," observed Bakari. "A few small mistakes have brought down the careers of some hardened criminals."

The Digital Sleuth yawned, stretching his arms.

"Damn, I feel like I've been through a meat grinder," he admitted. "It's bloody late, and I know exactly where I belong now."

"How can two perpetrators, always acting in concert, leave no trace?" Bakari wondered aloud. "It's beyond comprehension."

"The secret of success lies in the daily routine. Where did I read that?"

"The quote is from the American pastor and speaker John Calvin Maxwell," the Digital Sleuth jogged Atieno-Masinde's memory. "Funnily enough, Scarface's prowess reminds me of the traditional Luo folk tale of the unconquerable warrior, Luanda Magere. No arrow or spear aimed at his body could harm him, even if it pierced his shield."

"I was surprised that Luanda Magere has a Wikipedia entry," Atieno-Masinde said with a chuckle. "But that's folklore. The Duo are real."

Bakari shifted his weight from one foot to the other, tapping his fingers on his thigh.

"The Duo," he purred. "Aren't we dealing with an organised crime gang here?"

"What kind of criminal group would send a schoolgirl to carry out their mission?" asked the Digital Sleuth.

"Symbolic," Bakari replied with a blank expression. "Or a tactical move. What kind of gentleman would instinctively unleash his wrath on a young, beautiful girl without hesitation?"

"In any case, the Duo exude an air of criminal sophistication," the Digital Sleuth said, shutting down his computer. "They also seem to be equipped with the latest surveillance technology to keep track of all these men. But how can they stalk and strike across the country without making a mistake?"

CHAPTER 16

Sunday, 18 March, 23:50

The blaring alarm jolted Omari Sekibo from a deep sleep. He was sitting in his car in the underground car park of the aparthotel.

Yawning, he walked over to the lift. The double doors slid open. He stepped inside and rode to the seventh floor. Using the spare key, he unlocked the apartment door to find the street urchin he had delivered to his boss an hour earlier curled up on a sofa. Tears ran down the child's cheeks. The sound of Oliver Morgan's snoring could be heard from the bedroom.

Omari reached for a chocolate bar in a bowl on a coffee table and pressed it into the boy's hand.

"Stop crying and dry your tears," he breathed, grabbing the boy's arm and pulling him up from the sofa. "Let's go!"

Omari saw a car in his rear-view mirror. Something about it set his nerves on edge. To test his intuition, he deliberately missed the exit from a roundabout and drove around it again.

His hunch was confirmed, and Omari put the pedal to the metal as he exited the roundabout, increasing the distance between him and his pursuer.

Tyres squeaked as Omari brought his car to a halt in the same spot where he had picked up the street urchin.

"Get out!" he shouted. "Quickly."

The boy jumped out of the car and had barely closed the door when Omari sped off, disappearing around the next corner.

Realising the futility of continuing his pursuit, the electrician turned his attention to the little boy who had just emerged from Omari's car. The boy, slim as a broomstick, was in tears. From a corner, a glue-sniffing teenager approached the crying boy.

The electrician drove up, jumped out and walked over to the boys.

"Hey, I need to talk to you," he said.

"What do you want, dude?" the teenager growled.

"Why is the kid crying? What happened to him?"

"Fuck off, dude!"

The teenager put his hand on the boy's shoulder and encouraged him to leave. But the electrician came closer and grabbed his shoulder.

"Listen," he said, "I just want to help."

"Back off, dude," the teenager shouted, slapping the electrician's hand away. "Or I'll holler for my squad, and they'll fuck you up."

Huffing like a bullfrog, the thug in the front seat jumped out of the car. His bloodshot eyes, gruff demeanour, posture and clothing were those of a man you didn't want to mess with.

"Spit it out, homie!" he growled.

The tear-streaked boy swayed awkwardly from foot to foot, his hands twitching at his lower back before clawing at his sides.

Noticing his discomfort, the electrician enquired, "Are you unwell?

"Listen, dude," the thug thundered, "I'm from the hood. I know the score. Listen, this kid has ..."

From the periphery of his vision, the thug noticed the boy casting a sad look in his direction. Despite his blatant callousness, he seemed to have experienced a change of heart that prevented him from saying the words out loud. He leaned forward and whispered something to the electrician.

"Yuck, disgusting!" exclaimed the electrician, reacting both to the thug's lack of euphemisms and to what had allegedly happened to the boy.

His eyes lingered on the boy, his lips pressed together in a thin line as if to hold back a sigh of helplessness. He was a devoted father to a son of almost the same age, but now he found himself paralysed, unable to comfort a child who had been through such an ordeal.

He turned to the thug. "Get me their full names and ages. Let them know I'll be back with help."

The thug rolled his eyes grumpily. "Now you're tripping, man. You're not even allowed to set foot in that bougie joint, and now you want to fuck up the man in there."

"Just do it. Okay."

"The kid's going to have to face the cold reality, just like I did until I wasn't worth it to those creeps anymore. Nobody ever came to help us, bro."

"I need to know their names and ages. Can you do that?"

The thug smirked, one corner of his mouth curled up as he turned to the boys.

"Hey homies, I need your names and ages."

"Mickey. I'm seventeen," the teenager replied. "He's Sammy, he's eleven."

The thug turned to the electrician and blurted, "There you go. Let's split."

On the way back to the car, the electrician snapped his fingers to jog his memory, his lips moving to form the beginnings of various words. But the name he sought remained unreachable in the depths of his memory.

Hoping for an answer, he turned to the thug and asked, "What's the name of that foundation that fights child abuse?"

With an *Are you kidding me, bro?* look, the thug jumped into the front seat.

"What's the deal now, dude?" the backseat thug asked. "We still getting paid or what?"

Sensing the rising tension, the electrician decided to lighten the mood by asking a question that would stun the thugs.

"What's the name of that beautiful lady with the big behind who's married to Kanye—"

"Kim Kardashian," the two thugs shouted in unison.

Holy moley! Someone must have pulled the wool over his eyes. He remembered the name: *Dalilah Beale. DS Savekids Foundation.*

"The police may not be able to help this child, but Dalilah Beale can," he said, more or less in soliloquy.

"Clever, that," shouted the thug. "Dalilah Beale's got ties to the Merciless Duo, right? And if anyone can break into that posh place and finish off that guy in there, it's them."

◆◆◆

The Bluetooth device muted the radio and seamlessly switched to an incoming call.

"Musamali Demba," the TV presenter answered. He and Dalilah were on their way back to Nairobi.

"Musamali?" MP Kosgey's voice sounded questioning from the loudspeaker. "I must have dialled the wrong number." He slurred his words, his voice sounding sluggish. "Sorry to have disturbed your sleep."

"I'm wide awake. We can talk." He paused for a moment. "I am sorry for what happened to you."

"Sticks and stones may break my bones, but not my commitment to my constituents and constituency. Now that I have you on the phone, when will you have time for an exclusive interview?"

"Are you in hospital?" Musamali asked, slowing down as he approached a traffic jam on the Mathore-Soko Mjinga road.

"I have to stay in hospital for a while. I have tests in the early hours of the morning. Shall we say around eleven tomorrow?"

"Eleven o'clock is fine."

The MP ended the call, and the radio came to life again.

"Sticks and stones may break my bones," Dalilah said, clumsily trying to imitate the MP's voice. "What a weirdo! Are you friends?"

"He has been to the studio a few times and twice with his family. We became friends, exchanged phone numbers, and are on a first-name basis."

A gospel tune emanated from Dalilah's handbag. She reached for her phone and answered, "Dalilah Beale."

"I am a witness to an alarming incident in the city," said the deep voice on the other end of the line. "A man picked up a street boy and returned him an hour later. It's disgusting what's happened to him. His name is Sammy, and he is only eleven years old. He's in tears ..."

Musamali stopped in front of a police officer holding up a stop sign.

Dalilah looked at the two officers approaching the car and said into the phone, "Could you please tell me your name and the city you're calling from?"

"Put the phone down!" shouted an officer.

"I'll call you back," Dalilah said and hung up.

Leaning forward slightly, the officer scanned the interior of the car.

"Musamali Demba. Dalilah Beale," said the officer, "I recognise you both, but you still need to show me your ID cards."

They handed over their identity cards.

"Mr Demba, open the boot. Dalilah, get out of the car."

Dalilah's height of five feet eight inches alone was enough to rule her out as the assistant. But the instructions were clear: *leave no stone unturned, nothing to chance.*

"Forgive me if this sounds insulting, Mrs Beale, but you look like the assistant. Or let me put it this way, the assistant looks like you."

◆◆◆

A pungent smell woke Francesco Lombardo from his wettest dream yet. The Italian immigrant, in his early twenties, was in his Airbnb apartment in Tudor, a suburb of Mombasa.

Wrinkling his nose, he got off the four-poster bed, decorated with sex paraphernalia and numerous pillows in various shades of red, and flicked on the light.

His breath caught in his throat, as though the sight before him had punched him square in the chest. He rubbed his eyes and looked again. It was real. And she was wearing a school uniform – just like on the Most Wanted posters. Casually chewing gum.

"*Porca puttana*!" escaped from his constricted throat.

An avid follower of local gossip on the internet, Francesco knew what was at stake. Suddenly, he remembered a discussion on an Internet gossip forum about how the Duo's victims suffered from erectile dysfunction despite months of therapy.

Madonna Santa! Is life worth living if you can't get a hard-on? he wondered.

The bursting of the bubble of chewing gum blown by the assistant broke the silence.

Francesco glanced at the girl.

"*Mamma mia*!" The indifferent expression on the assistant's face suggested that a direct appeal to her would be akin to begging a hungry grizzly bear for mercy.

His heart raced, pounding against his ribs with a force that bordered on torture. Turning to his left, he watched as Scarface placed his toolbox on the floor and opened it, revealing stained, rusty, and modified tools.

Didn't the Duo only target men in abusive or violent relationships? Since moving to Kenya, he had lived carefree – no violence, no commitments, no messy entanglements. He had never even raised his voice when arguing with a date.

Determined to proclaim his innocence, Francesco cleared his throat.

Scarface turned towards him.

Francesco's courage wavered under the menacing gaze of the terrifying eye protruding from its socket.

"Cazzo! Cazzo!"

"Sounds Italian," Scarface remarked in English. "I only speak English, Swahili and passable German. It would be to your advantage if there were no linguistic misunderstandings between us."

The haze in Francesco's mind grew thicker by the second, enveloping him like the protective wings of a mother hen shielding her chicks. He had the unsettling feeling that he had forgotten the art of speaking.

"Do you understand me, Mr Italiano?"

With his vitality at its nadir, his legs like overcooked spaghetti, Francesco collapsed into the soft embrace of the bed, wishing it would swallow him up.

◆◆◆

The BMW's engine growled as it pulled away from the roadblock.

Fragments of the afternoon flickered behind Dalilah's closed eyelids: the winding, endless drive into the countryside to meet Beatrice; the uneasy silence as they collected the girl from the village market; Dorcas's abrupt protest – her voice trembling as she refused to stay in the car and listen to her daughter recount her harrowing ordeal.

"No, I … I can't stay here," Dorcas stammered as she got out of the car. Dalilah watched as she made her way to the shores of Lake Victoria. Musamali headed in the opposite direction to the market.

Dalilah and Beatrice remained in the back seat, the tinted windows slightly lowered.

"Do you like Fanta or Coke?" Dalilah asked, opening a shopping bag she had brought with her. She could sense that Beatrice, like many other victims of sexual abuse, was enveloped in a sense of loneliness, isolation, confusion and fear.

"Fanta," Beatrice said. The scars on her wrists and legs told of the emotional turmoil she had been through.

"I also brought you meat samosas. You're not a vegetarian, are you?" Dalilah began a warm-up conversation. She knew from her mother that Beatrice had a taste for meat.

Beatrice chuckled. "No, I'm not a vegetarian." She accepted the oil-smeared brown paper bag of snacks. "Thank you."

"Rather hot today. I'm sweating," Dalilah said, dabbing at her damp forehead with her handkerchief. She unscrewed her water bottle and took a sip, admiring the shore, draped in a lush carpet of greenery and shrubbery.

Beatrice took a samosa from the greasy paper bag, smelled the delicious aroma, and took a bite.

"I've got more samosas and Fanta for your little sister," Dalilah said, lightly tapping a second shopping bag between them.

"Thank you. She likes samosas. Mum doesn't know how to make them."

"Then I know what to bring next time I visit."

Beatrice giggled and took another bite of her samosa.

"I know who beat him," Beatrice said, her voice shaking. "It was the Merciless Duo."

"How do you know that?"

"I was there when they came into the house. At first, I was really scared of Scarface. But he spoke to me nicely. He even knew my name."

What a coincidence! Dalilah thought. She tactically changed her tone to that of a schoolgirl confiding in her best friend. "True. Scarface looks scary, but he speaks kindly. What did he tell you?"

"I should leave and not tell anyone that they are in Mikayi."

"Mikayi is the house built for the first wife, right?"

"Yes. He had asked me to clean Mikayi. He was out. Then ..."

Beatrice's jaw clenched, and her nostrils flared. A large tear fell on her hand, spilling all over the samosa.

Dalilah placed a reassuring hand on Beatrice's lap.

"Ah, now I remember, it wasn't the first time I'd smelled that foul odour," Beatrice said. "It smelled awful when they were in the room."

"When was the first time it smelled bad?"

"I used to hurt myself. Sometimes, I would dislocate a leg to avoid going to the market when it was dark. It was a way of keeping him from sneaking up on me."

Disgust clawed at the pit of Dalilah's stomach, then seized her in an iron grip. She had to pull herself together – stay objective, not let emotion take over.

"When I was well, and he got sick, I had to go to the market to buy medicine for him. It was dark. He was waiting for me on the way back. He grabbed my hand, and when I shouted for him to stop, he hit me, and my torch fell to the ground. Then I smelled this stench and heard something like a footstep. Then he went away."

"How ... er ... what exactly did you shout at him when he grabbed your hand?"

"Daddy, stop it!" After a moment, Beatrice added, "Please."

A voice echoed in Dalilah's head – that of her former primary school teacher: As girls, you should always say 'stop' loudly, clearly and confidently to stop annoying and unwanted catcalls, harassment and sexual advances. Don't say 'stop, please' in a nice way. Your timidity and shyness will not put these men off.

She heard Beatrice say, "My mother always insisted that we call him Daddy, not Chief."

A shadow flickered across Dalilah's mind, curling like smoke, dragging long-buried ghosts to the surface. In the depths of her mind, she heard her voice screaming: *Daddy, stop it, please*!

Her breath caught as the memory sharpened.

CHAPTER 17

Monday, 19 March, 09:45

MP Jared Kosgey's spacious private room on the third floor of the hospital overlooked a colourful garden. He lay in bed, deliberately half-covered, so that the ECG electrodes from the morning's examination were fully visible – this was essential for the press photographs and their impact on the public. His usually immaculately coiffed hair was dishevelled, with dried bloodstains here and there. A large white bandage covered his left eye, partially exposing the bruise underneath. His lips were swollen, his gums were bruised, and three front teeth were missing. Intermittent bouts of crippling stomach cramps, nausea, and faecal incontinence were brutal reminders of his internal injury. Insomnia, relentless nightmares, and the lingering stench of Scarface haunted him, a testament to his shattered psyche. Nevertheless, the MP was determined to exploit the situation, using demagogic tactics and smear campaigns against his political opponents to gain sympathy from the electorate. The first step was a press interview, even though the doctor had advised against it. Morphine and oxycodone, obtained from dubious sources, eased his excruciating pain a little.

Punctual as bricklayers, Musamali and his camera crew entered the hospital room.

"How are you holding up, *Mheshimiwa*?"

The MP squirmed and shifted, trying to find a position that would give him more relief.

Musamali, a man with a reputation for stepping over corpses to boost his TV ratings, pulled a chair closer to the bed and sat down, his expression that of a meerkat facing a traumatic scenario.

"I wouldn't wish what I'm going through on my worst enemy. It's hell, maybe even worse." The MP gingerly pressed a handkerchief to his swollen lips, wincing at the pain. "The CT scan showed some blunt trauma to my abdomen. Since there's blood in my stool, they're planning a gastroscopy with a biopsy to see how bad it is."

"Oh, I'm so sorry."

"They also found some weird semi-solid thing in my colon and took a sample."

"How the hell did that get in there?"

The MP squeezed his eyes shut and gritted his teeth. The painkillers had worn off, stripping away the layer of numbness and leaving his body defenceless against the onslaught of pain. His fingers trembled as he reached for the blister pack under the blanket. A "plop" sounded as he pressed it down, releasing an oxycodone from its compartment. He reached for a glass of water by the bed and swallowed the pill, the threat of an overdose looming dangerously close.

◆◆◆

After fortifying himself with chai and chapati, the electrician disappeared from the first-food restaurant, leaving Dalilah with the two homeless boys, Sammy and Mickey. Their breakfast consisted of samosas, sausages and vanilla milkshakes.

"Mickey, can you tell me who arranged for Sammy to be picked up?" Dalilah pressed. Mickey had constantly hesitated or avoided answering her questions, and Sammy had difficulty remembering important details of the incident. Dalilah suspected that Sammy was suffering from dissociative amnesia, a symptom of post-traumatic stress disorder.

"The *mzungu* did something bad to me," Sammy finally revealed. "He hurt me."

"I swear to God, man, that wasn't the deal," Mickey said in a tense and defensive tone, avoiding eye contact.

"What was the deal, Mickey?" Dalilah asked in a motherly tone. She took a sip of what she thought was a sublime coffee, generously sweetened with cream and sugar.

"Man, what's happened is happened," Mickey replied. In a mad rush, he grabbed the last sausage, stuffed it into his mouth and chewed noisily. He stood up with his paper cup, sucked noisily and announced, "I have to go now."

"I'll bring Sammy back when we're done, okay?" said Dalilah. "You don't mind if I take him to the doctor, do you?"

Mickey shrugged and left.

Her gaze shifted to Sammy's innocent eyes, which held a haunted look that spoke volumes about the horrors he had endured. The harrowing reality, Dalilah believed, was that the trafficker would be back for Sammy. She was convinced that Mickey was a beneficiary, acting neither willingly nor maliciously. One lesson Dalilah had learnt from her time on the streets was that poverty and hardship force people to choose degrading alternatives.

How can I protect this poor child? she wondered, knowing she'd have to fight her way through a maze of rules and bureaucracy. That would consume so much time. Involving the police would inevitably lead to a dead end, mainly because the electrician wouldn't answer the most critical questions, namely, how he had witnessed the nefarious activity. He was even less willing to name the two witnesses he had been with.

Dalilah weighed her options carefully, determined to protect Sammy at all costs. After much deliberation, she chose the only course of action left to her – the one that had once saved her from the clutches of her abuser.

◆◆◆

The MP pressed a remote control, raising the adjustable back of his bed. His personal assistant came over and fluffed the pillows before placing them behind his head.

"I am still emotionally and psychologically shaken to reconstruct the exact sequence of events that day," the MP said. "Please ensure that the interview is published in logical order. And edit out my temperamental expressions, which may not be relevant to the public."

Musamali grabbed the wireless microphone and stood in front of the camera.

"I am in the hospital room of *Mheshimiwa* Jared Kosgey. This is an exclusive interview. *Mheshimiwa* was attacked in a public toilet in the heart of Nairobi city on the sixteenth of this month."

He turned to *Mheshimiwa*, and the camera followed.

"Mr Kosgey, how do you feel now and how serious are your injuries?"

"I feel quite ..." He paused as a searing jolt of pain shot through his back and hips, then turned his gaze to the intravenous fluid dripping into his bloodstream.

After almost a minute of silence, he pulled himself together and looked into the camera.

"For those who know me, I always advocate peace. I therefore ask my supporters, friends and family to remain calm and entrust everything to God. The verdict will be delivered on election day ..." A throbbing spasm in his stomach made him grimace involuntarily.

He averted his eye from the camera lights and whispered, "I have to bite the bullet."

His face to the camera was now one of determination. "I would like to express my sincere gratitude to all those who have kept me in their thoughts and prayers. Evil will be defeated. My service to the community will prevail. I will not be shaken—"

A loud stomach rumble interrupted his monologue.

"Cut that out!" he ordered. "It's not necessary for the audience."

"All right. Start with the last sentence."

"I will not be shaken by the guerrilla warfare that has been waged against me, nor will I—"

There was a knock at the door. Two figures entered the room with conspicuous authority.

Detective Chief Inspector Dennis Mugo introduced himself and his partner, Detective Sergeant Rahab Atieno-Masinde.

"You'll have to wait until I'm done with the press," the MP declared.

"I would advise you to talk to us first," said Mugo.

"No. In case you haven't noticed, we're in the middle of a press interview."

"As you wish, Mr Kosgey." Mugo pulled a notebook from his breast pocket. "I hope you don't mind if we stay and take some notes."

"Go ahead." The MP turned to face the camera. "I will not be shaken by the guerrilla warfare against me. Nor will I myself resort to guerrilla tactics to ensure victory for the disputed post. I bear no animosity towards my opponents, adversaries or the architect of this senseless attack on me—"

"With all due respect, Mr Kosgey," Mugo interrupted, "the accusations you've made are false and irresponsible. Perhaps you would like to start again and explain why the Merciless Duo tortured you."

"Turn off the camera," the MP demanded.

Only when Musamali nodded did the cameraman react.

The red recording light went off, and the MP snarled, "Are you an inspector or a gossip reporter?"

"Detective chief inspector."

"Then act like one, or leave this room. The journalists have work to do."

Mugo clasped his hands behind his back, his steps measured as he approached the bed.

"I won't stand idly by while you lie to your viewers and supporters," he said. "Tell the truth about what happened that night."

Is he bluffing, or does he know what he is talking about? the MP wondered, especially as his personal assistant had told him that the police were at a loss in his case and had appealed to anyone with information to come forward.

It's all a bluff, he concluded. Then, with a theatrical sigh, he protested, "I have suffered a painful trauma. Don't interrupt me just because you think I'm not making sense. Take your notes and let me finish."

"While you're at it, stick to the facts and refrain from the infamous smear campaign," Mugo shot back.

"What my colleague is saying," Atieno-Masinde interjected, "is that making false statements to the police is a serious matter." She gave the MP a look that was enough to calm the waves.

"Are you playing bad cop, good cop?"

"I rarely slip into that role; it comes naturally when dealing with people who are trying to waste police resources." Mugo drawled, his words like a slow-turning screw. "Mocking our work is something I will not tolerate, Mr Kosgey."

A grey pigeon with white patches on its shoulders perched on the windowsill, distracting the MP. As it flew away, he couldn't help but think of his wife, who had a habit of "flying off" in the middle of a discussion.

Suddenly, a scream ripped through his skull: *LUCY*.

Believing he had the crucial piece of the puzzle, he whispered, more or less dogmatically, "You sneaky green snake in the grass."

"Have you thought of something, Mr Kosgey?" Atieno-Masinde inquired.

The MP was silent as a grave, his mind racing like an antelope cornered by predators. *Why did Lucy suggest that toilet, of all others?*

"It looks like something has occurred to you, Mr Kosgey," Mugo broke the silence. "I suggest that we talk to you first before you pass on any information to third parties that might alert the perpetrators or those involved."

In sheer disbelief, the MP shook his head repeatedly and whispered to himself: "She didn't even ask if I had to pee."

"Who are you talking about, Mr Kosgey?"

Mr Kosgey, who had momentarily forgotten that he wasn't alone, suddenly began to tremble. The room suddenly seemed cramped, stuffy and dark, and the air felt as if it were polluted with the stench of Scarface. Despite his best efforts to remain calm, his breathing became erratic, and his body convulsed. Panting, he opened his mouth wide, desperately sucking in the oxygen molecules from the seemingly thin air.

"Is he faking it?" Mugo asked Atieno-Masinde in a hushed tone.

"Doesn't look like it. He needs a doctor."

"Damn it." Killian's voice hardened. "If we can't get these men to talk, we're no longer investigators, just suits chasing shadows based on hearsay."

CHAPTER 18

Monday, 19 March, 10:50

In a taxi on the way to the doctor, Sammy enjoyed his milkshake while Dalilah stared out at the busy streets of the capital as it passed by. Ever since her conversation with Beatrice, the ghost from the past had been haunting her.

Dalilah's first desperate cry of "Daddy, stop!" had summoned her frail and ailing grandmother, who had rushed into the room just in time to thwart the abusive father's ominous intentions.

"Let Dalilah sleep for now and punish her during the day," was all the grandmother would say. Sexual abuse of children was an unheard-of taboo in the family – inconceivable.

Dalilah's last desperate cry was not long in coming. She had been awake in bed, fiddling with her talisman – a ballpoint pen adorned with a skull cap. When the door opened, she quickly curled up into a foetal position and pretended to be fast asleep.

Undeterred, the father crawled into bed beside her.

"Daddy, stop it, please!"

"Shh!" His alcohol-soaked breath nearly intoxicated Dalilah.

"Daddy, stop it," she said timidly. "Please!"

"Be quiet now!"

Dalilah struggled to free herself from his grip, but to no avail. As he slid his hand to the hem of her dress and pulled it up, her teacher's voice echoed in her head: *As girls, you should always say 'stop' loudly, clearly and confidently to stop annoying and unwanted catcalls, harassment and sexual advances. Don't say 'stop, please' in a nice way. Your timidity and shyness will not put these men off.*

"Daddy, stop!" Dalilah shouted, clearly and forcefully.

"Be quiet!"

„Daddy, stop!"

A repulsive stench assaulted her nose. Instinctively, she opened her eyes to see a terrifying stranger standing in the doorway. A figure in a skirt held a flickering candle behind the man. She heard her father muttering something, his voice a mixture of shock and disbelief.

"Get out of the house, Dalilah," the stranger said. "Don't look back. And don't forget your pen."

Dalilah didn't need to be told that again. Determined to get as far away from her father's torment as possible, her unshod feet pounded the unforgiving earth, the moonlight dimly illuminating her path. Stones and twigs dug into the tender soles of her feet, but Dalilah refused to let the discomfort slow her down. She ran without looking back. She ran without stopping to catch her breath.

Exhausted, she dropped to the ground. As she lay there, the nail-biting sounds of approaching nocturnal creatures rang out in the darkness. Clutching her talisman with protective fervour, she sang a gentle melody with trembling lips – a song of courage and resilience. She fell asleep.

With the first light of dawn, Dalilah's eyes fluttered open, her body protesting as she rolled onto her belly.

Raised as a believer, she knelt down and clasped her hands.

"Dear God, I'm scared, but I know You're with me. Please show me what to do, and keep me safe. Help me not to give up. In Jesus' name I pray. Amen."

Crawling forward on all fours, Dalilah licked the morning dew from the leaves and nibbled cautiously at anything that looked halfway edible.

A renewed sense of determination to put as much distance as possible between herself and her father drove her to run again. But the further she ran through the untamed wilderness, the more her strength waned and her thirst grew.

She stumbled upon a lone figure sprawled beneath a tree, eyes closed. When Dalilah spotted a bottle of water protruding from the woman's backpack, she took it as a sign of divine intervention.

She hid behind a tree, calculating her next move.

"Devil, you are a liar," she whispered, as the only move she could think of was to steal the water.

With cautious steps, she approached the backpack, her heart pounding and her mind racing with conflicting emotions, torn between survival instinct and breaking God's commandment not to steal.

She reached for the bottle and silently pulled it out.

"Thank you, Jesus," she murmured as she unscrewed the lid.

Greedily, she drained the liquid in one desperate gulp.

The young woman awoke and Dalilah reflexively dropped the empty bottle.

"I am sorry ... I'm sorry I took your water."

"No problem." The young woman sat up. "What are you doing here all alone?"

"I ... I ..."

"My name is Sharona. What is yours?"

"Dalilah."

"How old are you?"

"Eleven."

Her phone ringing brought Dalilah back to the here and now.

"Hey, sis, I was just thinking about you," Dalilah answered Sharona Warinda's call.

"Really? Then why haven't you called me back? When did you get back from Kisumu? How was the trip?"

"When will you learn not to ask a hundred questions at once?" Dalilah laughed. "We got back late last night. It's a long story; I'll tell you later."

"Now you've got me curious. Did you secretly marry Prince Charming in Kisumu?"

"Certainly not!"

"What was it like being by his side all day? Have you finally got the hots for him? He is very fond of you and seems like an eligible bachelor."

"Romance was not on my to-do list. And to be honest, I didn't see anything special about him after spending the whole day with him. If anything, some of his behaviour repulsed me."

"Your WhatsApp was daft. Just: 'Off to Kisumu with Musamali Demba.' Then you went offline."

"Forgot my charger at home, picked one up on the way back," Dalilah explained. "Just arrived at the doctor's. Catch you later."

"Doctor? Are you—"

"I'm fine. Sorry, I didn't keep you informed. Events overtook me. I'll fill you in later."

Born and raised in the slums of Muoroto, Mombasa, Sharona Warinda faced life's challenges when her mother died. She was 16 at the time, with no job and no outside financial support, yet she somehow managed to make ends meet and became the sole provider for her two younger siblings.

Four months after her mother's funeral, Sharona suffered another blow when she was evicted from her home for rent arrears. Her much younger siblings found refuge with a kind neighbour, but Sharona was not so lucky. She spent her nights on the street, huddled under a torn sack. Hunger gnawed at her insides on a regular basis, and every night was overshadowed by the threat of physical and sexual violence.

After being deceived by several men with false promises of work and shelter, Sharona learnt to navigate the streets cautiously. But her growing desperation made her vulnerable to drug dealers who took advantage of her situation, offering tranquillisers and stimulants in exchange for sex. It was during this time that she met Dalilah, seven years her junior, who soon became her closest friend, sharing her makeshift open-air shelter.

"Why did you run away from home, Dalilah?" Sharona asked for the umpteenth time as they huddled under the cover of a bus stop, sheltering from the pounding rain.

"My father was very ... very bad. He would come to my bed at night and ... and ..."

"I am sorry. That was really bad. How could you run away from home?"

"I shouted, 'Daddy, stop!' Loudly. I think the man heard me and came. He looked very scary. He told me to go away and not to look back."

"Wow! You shouted, 'Daddy, stop!' and a man came. So, Daddy Stop saved you?"

"I don't know."

"Yes, Daddy Stop saved you; I'm absolutely sure of it." Shaped by her superstitious upbringing, Sharona seemed absolutely convinced of her conclusion, and made Dalilah believe it too.

This superstitious belief became their lifeline, something they clung to with desperate resolve, and something Sharona exploited, especially when she was high. When sleazy, drooling men approached, offering money or drugs for a date with Dalilah, her voice cut through the drug haze with a firm, 'Daddy, stop!' Though 'daddy' was a buzzword, something men revelled in, her tone alone was enough to make them freeze. Eventually, they slunk away, and the girls giggled. Most importantly, Dalilah and Sharona believed that those two words – 'Daddy, stop' – kept the men at bay.

Years later, they set up a foundation to help children who had suffered similar physical and sexual abuse, as well as being deprivation. As they brainstormed names, their old superstitions resurfaced, and they called it *Daddy Stop Save Kids Foundation*. However, when it came time to register the foundation, they decided on a more formal name: *DS Savekids Foundation*. *Daddy Stop* was too informal for official records. While DS secretly stood for Daddy Stop, everyone else assumed it was an acronym for Dalilah and Sharona.

◆◆◆

Dressed in a chic, dark brown striped suit, Musamali sat in his office on the tenth floor of a high-rise building in Nairobi's central business district. In the left-hand corner of his desk was an old typewriter, and in the middle, a laptop with a picture of Dalilah Beale's business card on the screen.

He dialled Lucy Kosgey's number.

"Hello."

"Hey, Lucy, this is Musamali Demba from KNN. Long time no see. How are you holding up? And how are the twins?"

"Still trying to come to terms with the attack on Jared."

"I can't believe this has happened to him. I can't imagine what you're going through. But I want you to know that I'm here for you. Whatever you need – anything. You're not in this alone."

"Thank you, Musamali."

"Another reason I called is that there are rumours going around and I think it's best to set the record straight."

"What record do you want to set straight?"

"I know that you have a happy family. Such rumours could potentially damage your relationship, and it would be wise to address them immediately and nip them in the bud."

Lucy's huffing and puffing crackled through the receiver.

"What do you suggest?" she asked.

"Why don't we get together? Maybe at your place? I could bring someone who specialises in talking to traumatised children. It would help them a lot. The sooner, the better."

"Thanks for the offer, but I'm not sure it's a good idea. I don't want to make things harder for them. You know how people think you have to be crazy to see a psychiatrist?"

"I understand your concern, Lucy. But having a professional talk with your children might help them process what they're holding back," he said, his voice smooth, almost too polite. He was fishing for information, treading a fine line between professional curiosity and calculated manipulation. "She'll take things at their pace and make sure the kids feel comfortable every step of the way."

"Okay, it can't hurt to try. Tomorrow morning at seven-thirty? At my place."

"See you then. And keep your head up, Lucy."

The swivel chair let out a low squeak as he leaned back, fingers laced behind his head, staring up at the ceiling with a satisfied smile. The game had begun, and he was already several moves ahead.

CHAPTER 19

Tuesday, 20 March, 07:20

"The bastard's late again," grumbled DCI Dennis Mugo, seated across from his wife at their breakfast table.

"Typical Killian; I knew he wouldn't be on time," Virginia said, her words partly drowned out by the clatter of the breakfast dishes she was clearing from the table. "But Dennis, why did you ask him to pick you up in the first place?"

"I have a bone to pick with him. He put his hands on Sarafina again." The torment of his twin sister, Sarafina, who was married to DS Killian Bakari, was also his. Dennis protected her with a ferocity that could one day culminate in bloodshed and mayhem.

The roar of an engine made Dennis jump to his feet. He recognised Killian's battered red Peugeot 407 as it pulled up outside his fence.

With a face contorted like a bulldog bent on confrontation, Dennis yanked open the door of the Peugeot. His eyes darted between his much younger brother-in-law and the worn leather seat, his mind weighing whether to sit or take his own car.

"Don't you have a watch?" he exploded.

"There was an accident on the—"

"You are like a broken record, repeating the same lie over and over again."

He squeezed his large body into the cramped front seat, pushed it backwards and slammed the door shut with such force that Killian must have thanked God the windows were not shattered.

"Last warning," Dennis growled, wagging his index finger. "If you dare lay your paws on Sarafina again, you will pay dearly."

The gravity of his words hung in the air like a gathering storm. Killian opened his mouth, probably to make an inappropriate remark, but he seemed to catch himself in time.

"I'll keep that in mind," Killian huffed.

"Are you being sarcastic?" howled Dennis, giving Killian a look that made it clear that this would be considered insubordination. He had made it clear on more than one occasion that if his twin sister was in danger, he would throw aside any semblance of professional propriety and break the law if he had to.

"No, I'm not being sarcastic."

Dennis wrinkled his nose and rolled down the windows, trying to dissipate the lingering stench of nicotine. Just for this blatant disregard for his aversion to cigarette smoke, he could have used Killian's face as a punching bag.

Like an old married couple, jaded by years of living together and the monotony of routine, they drove in silence through the morning traffic to headquarters. Unbeknown to them, the situation with the Duo had taken an unexpected turn and was hurtling towards the brink of a potential state of emergency.

◆◆◆

Musamali parked his car at the gate of MP Kosgey's house.

In keeping with his calculated moves, Dalilah slipped on her oversized sunglasses before getting out of the car. Her casual pink t-shirt, tucked into tight jeans, gave her a deliberately girlish charm. The wig changed her appearance, and together with the sunglasses, she was utterly unrecognisable.

The maid opened the door and led Dalilah and Musamali into the living room, where Lucy Kosgey sat beside her daughter Rebecca. Her son Robert had steadfastly refused to join them. He had seen nothing that night. Basta!

As Lucy rose from her chair, Musamali Daudi seized the moment and made the first move before she had a chance to extend her hand for a handshake.

"Wow, what a lovely home you have, Lucy," he said, looking around in admiration. "Did you design it all yourself or did you hire an interior designer?"

His stratagem seemed to have achieved the desired result. A smile lit up Lucy's face and she seemed eager to answer Musamali before greeting them.

Dalilah presented Rebecca with a big-eyed plush raccoon.

"I've got one just like that," Rebecca gushed.

"Really? Show it to me."

Rebecca stood up and headed for a door.

"Can I come with you?" Dalilah called.

Rebecca looked at her mother to answer the question and Musamali Daudi chimed in casually, "Ah, she's the specialist I told you about on the phone, Lucy."

Lucy nodded, and Dalilah followed Rebecca upstairs.

Checkmate! Musamali smiled and sat down. His plan couldn't have worked out better.

"You have a lovely room," Dalilah said with a smile. She took off her sunglasses.

Rebecca smiled. "I recognised you at once. Your voice."

Dalilah had gained Rebecca's trust the previous year, following the DS Savekids Foundation's initiatives in many schools on issues related to sex and sexuality. Still, the girl had not found the courage to name her tormentor, but she had confided in Dalilah and asked her to keep it a secret. A few weeks later, Dalilah could not reach her on her mobile phone. When she returned to school, she found that Rebecca and her brother were no longer enrolled.

"I think I saw Scarface that night," Rebecca revealed. "But I am not sure."

"Where did you see him?"

"He was standing by the toilet."

"Had you ever seen him before that day?"

"No." Her eyes darted to her fingertips. "Did you ask the Merciless Duo to ... um ..."

"I had nothing to do with it, Rebecca. Ah, you wanted to show me your teddy bear?"

Rebecca reached into a box on a table. She took out three cuddly toys, and Dalilah noticed that the business card, which should have been attached to the pink and purple plush raccoon, was missing. The cuddly toys had been provided by a company based in the UK.

The flip-book business cards, sponsored by a local print company about two and a half years ago, featured a mini comic strip entitled 'Children are the Future'. This gave the cards a childlike feel and deflected suspicion away from what might otherwise have raised eyebrows – a child with a business card. Questions faded before they were fully formed. Dalilah's contact details and toll-free number were printed on the front of the cards.

"Do you still have the card that came with the teddy bear?" Dalilah asked.

Looking for the card that must have fallen off the teddy, Rebecca lifted her rucksack and emptied it onto her bed.

"I think I lost it."

No, you didn't, Dalilah thought. But how did the Duo get hold of the business cards? How do they keep track of my protégés? Some kind of tracking software on their phones?

"Will Dad be all right?"

Is she worried? Is she scared or just curious? Dalilah wondered, knowing that not all abused children suffer from a dysfunctional relationship with their abuser.

"He will be in hospital for a while." She patted Rebecca's left arm. "I haven't been able to reach you by phone since we last met at your old school. Did you lose your mobile?"

"No. Dad bought me a new SIM card with a new number."

Why? Because he found out that you were in contact with me?

"My dad once tried to take my phone away from me," Dalilah invented to draw Rebecca out. "I shouted at him, 'Daddy, stop!'"

Rebecca's smile suggested familiarity with the expression. Before she could speak, her bedroom door flew open. Her twin brother stood there, a PlayStation controller dangling from one hand, headphones slung around his neck.

His eyebrows shot up to his forehead, and his lips whispered, "Dalilah Beale."

Noticing the questioning look on his face, Dalilah cursed under her breath: *Bloody Internet. He's read what they've written about me.*

"Hey, you." Dalilah smiled at him. "What is your name, young friend?"

Seemingly unfazed by the implication that he was Dalilah's young friend, Robert stepped back. *I'm going to snitch on you both*, was written all over his face.

He ran to the stairs and shouted, "Mum."

Rebecca took a deep breath and whispered, "They're going to hate me when they find out what I've done."

Dalilah got down on her knees so they were at eye level. She then took a visibly shaken Rebecca in her arms and comforted her.

"It was not your fault, Rebecca. I'm going to talk to your—"

Lucy Kosgey, whose pride had always compelled her to protect her public image at all costs, painting a false picture of her world as one of order, appeared in the doorway. She noticed a subtle but unmistakable telltale expression on her daughter's face.

"Somebody tell me this is not what it looks like!" she cried, feeling like she had an ice cube stuck in her cleavage.

Sudden dizziness forced Lucy to brace herself against the door frame. She turned to Musamali, who had followed her upstairs.

"Is this ... is this ..." She lowered her voice. "Dalilah Beale's Foundation cares for sexually abused children. Is this why you brought her? You knew about Jared's—"

"No, I had no idea Jared was involved in anything like that."

Every breath felt like a struggle as Lucy wrestled with the now obvious reason for her husband's attack.

Nooo. Not Rebecca, a voice inside her screamed. When had this happened?

She watched helplessly as Rebecca walked shyly past her. She longed to protect her daughter, but the storm of emotions now sweeping through her confused her maternal instincts and froze her jaw.

Tears filled Lucy's once vibrant and confident eyes as she entered her daughter's bedroom and sat on the edge of the bed.

"Ms Beale," she began, her voice trembling, "what … when …" With the back of her hand, she dabbed away the mascara-stained tears and smeared them onto her carefully made-up cheeks. "How did the Duo find out …"

Her body convulsed as an avalanche of pain tore through her, igniting every nerve. Her fingers clenched into fists, manicured nails biting into her palms.

◆◆◆

Atieno-Masinde rested her hands on the back of her chair, her well-trained frame leaning forward. She waited for Mugo and Bakari to take their seats, then opened the meeting.

"Greetings, fellow investigators. Reports have reached us that the Duo struck twice last night: in Garissa around 9 p.m. and in Meru at 3 a.m. These two counties are four hundred kilometres apart and at least six hours by road."

"This means that the Duo must have moved on to the next victim immediately after their first crime," said DS Kebaso.

"The night before, on Sunday, a young, single, white Italian immigrant was attacked by the Duo in Tudor," Atieno-Masinde continued. "He does not fit the profile of their other victims, who are mostly middle-aged men with families. The Italian immigrant and the Garissa victim have the hashtag on their backs, while the Meru victim has an 'I'. Dalilah Beale's business card was only found in Meru."

The door flew open. Stepping in, laptop in hand, the Digital Sleuth delivered the news without hesitation.

"We have a suicide victim in Limuru. The funeral will take place this afternoon. The man hanged himself in his home three days ago. He left a handwritten suicide note asking that there be no autopsy or photographs of his body." He walked over to his chair and sat down. "When the funeral home staff were dressing the deceased this morning, they discovered a hashtag on his back."

"The suicide rate among these victims seems dubious," Bakari observed. "The suicide notes don't explain their decision to end their lives, but they stress their decision not to have photographs taken of their bodies and are against autopsies. Isn't that weird?"

"These men would rather take the cause of the attacks to their graves," said Kebaso. "What makes me wonder is how quickly they're being buried."

"There's something fishy about the hasty burials," agreed the Digital Sleuth, "but we must also consider that cultural or religious practices, or a decision not to embalm, may require a quick burial."

"We are on the brink of a state of emergency, and further attacks are very likely," said Mugo, rubbing his forehead and staring intently at the file in front of him. "We can't tolerate any more victims invoking their right to silence and refusing to cooperate."

"That's the hurdle we're up against, boss," Kebaso said. "These victims are prepared to take their own lives rather than cooperate with us for the sake of justice. I think that Dalilah Beale and the members of DS Savekids should be subject to much closer scrutiny."

"Speaking of Dalilah Beale, she was spotted at the Kisumu hospital where the village chief was found dead. The death is currently being treated as a suspected suicide," the Digital Sleuth reported. "Miss Beale was seen with KNN television presenter Musamali Demba. And here comes the kicker ..." He hit the spacebar, and his laptop came to life. A code was projected onto the screen on the wall.

msa_d3imo3y/g6s&edl-di3m12ylg59

“The first five entries msa_d could refer to Musamali Demba,” the Digital Sleuth elaborated. “A victim with the inscription ‘u’ could still be silent about his injuries. Or he could be one of those who died last year and were buried without an autopsy. The fifth inscription, ‘d’, could be the first letter of the surname Demba. He goes by the name Musa_D on social media.”

Mugo nodded in concurrence. “Contact him. Ask him to come for an interview.” He turned to Bakari. “Killian, get a partner. Gather any relevant information that Dalilah Beale may have dug up in Kisumu. Atieno-Masinde and I will go to Limuru. If the deceased was one of the Duo’s victims, we’ll interview the widower.”

“Dalilah Beale has been through two rounds of questioning and had that loudmouth lawyer Kizito with her,” Bakari interjected diplomatically. “We can’t expect much cooperation from her.”

“I expect results,” Mugo said firmly. “Everyone, get to work.”

As the team rose, Mugo gestured to the Digital Sleuth, who walked over and sat beside him.

“MP Kosgey indirectly hinted that it was his wife who suggested the detour to the public toilet,” Mugo said. “She may be in contact with someone connected to the Duo.”

“In other words, I need access to her recent text messages and call logs,” the Digital Sleuth surmised.

“How quickly can you do that?”

“If I bypass the usual channels, maybe four to six hours. If we go by the book … days.”

“We don’t have days. Get it done, whatever it takes. This could provide us with valuable information and perhaps lead us to the person in direct contact with the Duo. It’s probably her uncle, Jonathan Wasike. This could be the break we need – if we’re right.”

"And if we're wrong?"

Mugo exhaled sharply. "I need leverage to get Lucy Kosgey to lead us to Jonathan Wasike's hideout. If this man is the link, he will lead us to the Duo, willingly or not."

CHAPTER 20

Wednesday, 21 March, 11:30

The cosy dining room was decorated with colourful balloons, a large bouquet and a handmade poster that read, 'Happy 60th Birthday, Rose Beale'.

Rose Beale – Dalilah's adoptive mother – sat at one end of the long linen-covered table, laden with the used plates of the twelve guests. Rose wore a stylish, elegant outfit that exuded joie de vivre and contentment. Short, silver-streaked hair framed her face and accentuated her graceful ageing.

A mixture of happiness and sadness lingered in her eyes as her sister, who had to return to London, ended her farewell speech with the words, "I promise to keep up the tradition of regular visits and celebrations in the years to come. Distance may separate us physically, but it will not diminish our bond ..."

The shrill ringing of the doorbell made her pause.

"I'll get it," Dalilah called, rising to her feet. She turned to her adoptive father and asked, "Are you expecting anyone else?"

"Actually, no."

Dalilah walked across the immaculately manicured courtyard to the imposing black gate. Through the peephole, she saw two men in suits. Unable to shake the suspicion that they might be Jehovah's Witnesses or pesky journalists, she decided not to open the gate.

"How can I help you?" she asked.

Holding his service card to the peephole, Detective Sergeant Bakari introduced himself and Detective Sergeant Kebaso. His voice was urgent as he added, "We need to speak to Dalilah Beale."

Dalilah unlatched the small swinging door embedded in the wrought-iron gate and pulled it open. Her body language said, *Speak from outside.*

"We hope we have not caused you any inconvenience, Ms Beale," DS Bakari apologised. "We have some questions regarding the Merciless Duo."

"This is rather inconvenient, almost annoying. You could have called me."

"We tried. Unfortunately, we did not get an answer."

"That was a clear sign that I didn't have the time. Besides, I had promised to contact your colleagues if I had any information that might be relevant to the case."

"When would you have time for a chat, Ms Beale?" asked Kebaso. "The Duo had left your business card in the toilet after attacking MP Jared Kosgey."

"What is keeping you there?" Sharona's voice rang out.

"The CID."

"Are they following your every move now?"

"If they were, they wouldn't admit it."

Bakari smiled. "You mentioned in a previous interview that you only hand out your business cards to clients in your care. Could some of these clients have contacted the Duo and given them the business cards?"

"It's absurd to suggest that these children ... clients have had any contact with the Duo," Sharona replied, now standing next to Dalilah.

"When are you free, Dalilah Beale? The Duo are misusing your business cards, and we need to find out why."

Dalilah sighed theatrically. "Your colleagues have thoroughly interrogated all the members of the Foundation, haven't they? To question us again is, to say the least, brazen and shameless."

"In the course of the investigation, we come across new aspects that we have to take into account," Bakari explained. "Look, no one is pointing a finger at you, but we need your cooperation. A hacker may have infiltrated your servers and accessed client data."

"First of all, we don't publish the names of abuse victims on our network," Dalilah clarified. "Some clients only give us a first name, no address, no phone number. So if you're suggesting that the Duo somehow accessed their contact details on our computers and contacted them, you're way off the mark."

Shifting weight from foot to foot, Bakari said, "I suppose you keep a list of your clients, whether they give their real names or not. We would appreciate it if you could give it to us."

Something about Bakari bothered Dalilah, but she couldn't put her finger on it. "Aren't you aware of the professional ethics of confidentiality?" she bellowed with a touch of arrogance. "It requires us to protect the privacy of our clients."

"Therapists are sometimes required by law to report a client's information to the police. The Tarasoff duty requires you, as a therapist, to warn potential victims or inform the—"

"Are you saying I know of potential victims?" Dalilah interrupted Bakari brusquely. "That in itself would be serious defamation. Character assassination. I'm sure my lawyers will find other grounds for charges."

"Have a nice day, officer," Sharona called and slammed the gate shut.

◆◆◆

"We offer our deepest condolences on the tragic death of your husband," DS Atieno-Masinde said after introducing herself and her boss, DCI Mugo, to the widow in Limuru. They had stopped at the morgue and confirmed that the Duo had assaulted the alleged suicide victim before his death.

"We won't take up much of your time," Mugo said. "We just have a few questions about your husband's injuries before he died."

"This is not a good time," said the widow, wearing a black funeral dress. "Come in, but we must limit ourselves to thirty minutes at the most."

Inside the spacious house in the upmarket suburb of Tigoni, Atieno-Masinde admired an impressive aquarium teeming with various sea creatures. It stood elegantly next to a black piano.

"You have a beautiful home," Atieno-Masinde remarked, her eyes wandering over the wooden carvings that adorned the wallpapered walls, arranged with aesthetic flair.

The widow's youngest daughter burst into the room, glanced at the guests, then turned to her mother and said, "Zip it up."

"Please," said the widow, gently reminding her daughter to be polite. She zipped up her black dress.

"When are we going?" the little girl asked.

"Soon. I'll be there in a minute. Go to your sisters now."

The door closed behind the girl, and Atieno-Masinde said, "Your late husband was brutally attacked a few days before his death. Are you aware of this?"

"He was attacked by the Merciless Duo. It was a terrible ..." Her voice trailed off.

"How do you know the Merciless Duo attacked him?"

"My sister got married two weeks ago. My husband wasn't there. When I returned from the event the following Sunday morning, I found him lying naked on the floor, tied to the bed. He told me what had happened."

"When you found him after the attack, did you find anything beside him that didn't belong to the house?"

Atieno-Masinde paused for a moment. "A business card, perhaps?"

She shook her head. "No."

"Why is he being buried so quickly without an autopsy?" Atieno-Masinde asked.

"I'm respecting his last wishes. He said so in his suicide note."

"How was his relationship with you and your children?"

A wrinkle played at the corner of the widow's mouth, her eyes darting between the officers. She allowed a moment of silence to pass before speaking.

"We were together for eleven years. After the birth of our third child four years ago, he was again disappointed that she was not a son and heir. Due to complications during my pregnancy, I had an IUD inserted. I tend to think that this was the reason for his emotional coldness towards me, which he passed on to our children."

"How did your husband's coldness towards you or the girls manifest itself?"

"We hardly ever saw him. He always came home late and left for work very early. I have only worked night shifts for the past year to avoid him. My younger half-sister lives with us, and we have a nanny who looks after the children when I'm at work."

"Did he ever abuse you or the children in any way?" Atieno-Masinde inquired.

"He was always a quiet person. Never violent. But when he told me that the Duo had attacked him, I panicked because of what I had read about the Duo's motives. I immediately made an appointment with a doctor and had my children and my half-sister examined for signs of abuse."

"Do you have the doctor's report?"

"Not in writing, but I can give you her phone number." She reached for her phone, which lay on the sofa beside her, and looked at the time. "We don't have much time."

"We would be grateful if you could give us the doctor's phone number," Atieno-Masinde said. "One last question: did your husband ever say why he was attacked?"

"No. But as I tended to his wounds, he kept apologising. He said he was sorry for being a bad husband. He was worried that if people found out the Duo had attacked him, they'd judge him and think he deserved it." She shuddered. "I'm a surgeon; I've seen terrible things done to people. But what the Duo did to him ...it was beyond anything I thought a human could do to another human."

"Can you describe it?"

Her eyes darted away as if to escape the memory.

CHAPTER 21

Wednesday, 21 March, 14:20

Dalilah and Sharona left the few remaining guests upstairs and retreated to a windowless room in the basement, which Dalilah had turned into a sort of sanctuary. On one side of the wall was a large map of Kenya, criss-crossed with lines that resembled an asymmetrical spider's web. It was covered with various Polaroid photographs, illustrations, printed information and handwritten notes. Pertinent details were boldly outlined and highlighted in a variety of colours.

Using a black marker, Dalilah drew a circle around Kisumu Province and pinned a Polaroid of the village chief inside it. She then drew a line from the photograph to a large sheet of white paper with a list of names. She wrote: Beatrice (father - adopted daughter).

She pinned a Polaroid of the MP, drew a line from Nairobi and wrote: Rebecca (father - daughter).

"Can you see the forest for the trees?" asked Sharona, seated at a small table with a laptop.

Dalilah turned from the map to face Sharona.

"First, a child is abused. The abused child contacts the Foundation and is given a business card. The business card disappears. A man is attacked and the missing business card is left at the scene. In three cases so far, the child whose business card was found at the scene of the crime has a direct relationship with the man who was attacked."

She took a seat across from Sharona.

"I don't have to be a genius to put the pieces together and see the picture," Dalilah said. "The business card embodies the sexually abused child it was given to."

"The high suicide rate of assaulted men or the fact that they do not cooperate with the police reinforces your conclusion."

"But why are the Duo only using my business cards? Why not yours?"

"There must be something special about your business cards or the cases you handle."

"I think we need to contact Sonaya Printers," Dalilah said, turning the laptop towards her and pressing the power button.

"The sponsors?"

"Yes. Ever wondered why they changed the design of my business card but not yours? Yesterday, I had a weird feeling – like they contained some high-tech tracking device to trace whoever received them."

Sharona laughed. "You watch too many science fiction movies. But you're right, Sonaya Printers could give us some answers."

The partnership began two years ago with a phone call from Sonaya Printers, based in Ukunda, a coastal town south of Mombasa. The company representative had explained how they had decided to support the charitable work of DS Savekids Foundation by sponsoring basic office supplies. The Foundation was delighted with the offer. A few weeks later, Dalilah received an email with a ZIP file attached. It contained several designs for a new logo, business cards and stationery. Dalilah was asked to select one.

The board agreed on a design.

A month later, the office supplies arrived. Everything was perfect except Dalilah's business cards. They were a far cry from the original concept – the design was impressive, but also cheesy. It was more of a compact four-page mini-booklet, the size of a conventional business card. The inside pages featured a comic strip titled

'Children are the Future' – the Foundation's slogan. Dalilah decided to hand them out only to her young clients.

Unlike many companies that seek recognition and expect a return on their investment, Sonaya Printers wanted to remain anonymous as a sponsor. When asked about this decision, the representative had simply replied, "*Good wine needs no bush.*"

"I found the office number," Dalilah said, reaching for the landline. She dialled the number.

"Sonaya Printers," a female voice answered. "What can I do for you?"

"My name is Dalilah Beale, chair of the DS Savekids Foundation. I would like to speak to Mrs Sonaya."

"May I ask why you wish to speak directly to the managing director? Is it a complaint, or an order? We have different departments that deal with different issues."

"It's about the sponsored office supplies we received from the company two years ago."

There was no sponsoring department.

"Oh, I see. Just a moment, please, Mrs Beale."

Dalilah pulled a business card from her handbag and studied it curiously.

"Sorry to keep you waiting, Mrs Beale. Mrs Sonaya is unable to take your call at the moment, but she would be delighted to meet with you. She will be away on business for two weeks from Saturday. But if it's urgent, I can make an appointment before she leaves."

Dalilah held the receiver between her shoulder and ear and opened her handbag. She reached for her diary and scanned the entries up to Friday. The next day, Thursday, was the Foundation's general assembly to elect the board of directors.

"This Friday would be ideal," Dalilah said. "Let me check flight connections and call you back."

◆◆◆

"Good afternoon, ladies and gentlemen. This is your Captain Steven Wachira. On behalf of the entire airline crew, I would like to thank you for flying with ..."

The announcement jolted Oliver Morgan out of his momentary slumber. He shared a brief smile with Omari Sekibo, seated next to him, before turning his attention to the plane's window, which offered a captivating panoramic view of Mombasa.

The main task in the coastal province was to clear seven containers from the UK that were due to arrive at Mombasa port tomorrow.

Oliver's chauffeur was waiting in the car park. His fingers tapped on the steering wheel as he dreamily read the newspaper headlines.

> KSh 250,000 reward for information leading
> to the arrest of the Merciless Duo.

A faint smile tugged at the chauffeur's lips as he imagined extravagant plans for spending the money – apart from taking a second wife. Out of the corner of his eye, he saw a girl with a shoulder bag walking alongside a man with a hood pulled low over his head.

"The Duo?" he wondered aloud. Although he was a changed man, having stopped verbally and physically abusing his wife for fear of the Duo's wrath, he thought it would be sheer folly and recklessness to remain in the car park.

Hastily, he got out and hurried to the terminal. His eyes widened in disbelief as he overheard two men on their mobile phones frantically describing the unusual couple they had spotted in the car park.

He turned to a burly man beside him and asked, "How can an ordinary, average man and a schoolgirl plunge an entire nation into chaos like this?"

"Ma broda, dis country na wahala o!" the man said in a Nigerian pidgin accent. "Abeg, make you dey follow me go toilet. A dey fear the Duo well, well."

"Holy shit!" exclaimed the chauffeur. He could well understand the burly man's fear of going to the toilet alone.

CHAPTER 22

Thursday, 22 March, 17:00

"If everyone agrees, we'll move on to any other business," Dalilah announced. She had been unanimously re-elected as chair of the DS Savekids Foundation at the General Assembly. All 22 members were present, seated around a large table in a hotel conference room hired for the meeting.

The Foundation was established to provide vital support and care to children, young people, and women affected by sexual abuse and domestic violence. However, the all-female counsellors often grappled with the complex nature of these sensitive cases. Many victims were reluctant to fully disclose their experiences of abuse, name the perpetrators, or consent to medical examinations. The lack of medical evidence made it difficult to prove clear signs of abuse, often creating significant barriers to justice.

And now, the repeated appearance of Dalilah Beale's business cards at the crime scenes had begun to cast a dark shadow over the Foundation's reputation. Some sponsors had publicly distanced themselves from the Foundation, while others had withdrawn their financial support. As a result, the Foundation's resources were dwindling, threatening its ability to carry out its vital charitable work.

Esther Aoko, the re-elected treasurer, raised her hand before speaking – a practice that had become second nature to all members.

"I move that we change our name and slogan," she proposed. "We must make it clear to the sponsors ... and the nation that we have nothing to do with the Duo and don't want to be associated with their crimes."

"We all have nothing to do with the Duo and are exonerated," said a long-time member with no official role. "The fact that they left Dalilah's business cards after the attacks is none of our business. I am against changing our name or our slogan."

"Apart from the fact that it's difficult to continue our work without the support of sponsors, how many more men have to be dehumanised before we make a clear statement?" asked Esther. "Changing our name and slogan, because the Duo are using them for whatever reason, is the only effective way to deal with this situation."

"Personally, I couldn't care less about what the Duo do to those they victimise," said re-elected vice-chair Sharona Warinda. "In my opinion, the Duo are not indiscriminately hunting down innocent people. I oppose the name change. If anything, these attacks are invaluable publicity for us. We are constantly in the media, and it's only a matter of time before we get new sponsors."

"How can you be so indifferent?" Esther croaked. "It's the worst kind of publicity. I wouldn't be surprised if one of us fell victim to reprisals."

Betty Gitau, the oldest in the group and a dedicated member without an official title, spoke up: "Dear comrades-in-arms, I must say that there is some truth in the rumour spreading about 'an eye for an eye'. It pains me deeply to see countless women and children suffering the horrors of domestic violence in silence. Perpetrators often exploit legal loopholes and escape punishment. In any case, I am against changing the name."

"Have you completely forgotten what Mahatma Gandhi once said?" Esther asked, slapping her thigh in a theatrical gesture. "'An eye for an eye makes the whole world blind.' Even if the allegations were true, we have a functioning legal system; we don't need psychopaths for that."

"But that's the problem," said Dalilah. "Justitia is blind, but also biased. It always favours those who can buy their way out with their wealth and power, or influence and connections. If the Duo's actions are the most effective method, then amen."

Mike Chukwuemeka, a long-time member and the Foundation's webmaster, took a hearty gulp of beer. For him, as for most men in the country, the comfort of solitude had become a luxury of the past. He spent most nights in crowded public places, waiting for official information to confirm or deny the rumours circulating about the Duo's motives or targets. Whenever he was alone, his eyes constantly darted around, never resting in one place for too long, as if every shadow held a lurking threat. The slightest sound triggered his defensive mode, though he believed what they said about Scarface: "The man is indomitable." Now, with his health deteriorating due to these fears, Mike Chukwuemeka was seriously considering returning to his native Nigeria.

He raised his hand and said, "The slogan 'Children are the Future' is no longer appropriate as our mission has expanded to include the care of abused women. Although the name DS Savekids is well known, we need to express our solidarity against this barbaric torture by changing the name and the slogan."

With his hand raised, he took a sip of beer.

"I'm surprised, Esther," he continued. "You're great at quoting Gandhi, but you don't seem to know what's trending on the internet."

Esther frowned. "What are you talking about?"

"And don't make it any more tense, Mike," Sharona pleaded.

Mike opened his laptop, pressed the power button and let it boot up. After a few keystrokes, he turned it towards Esther, then Dalilah. Two photographs were juxtaposed on the screen: the assistant as in the sketches, and Dalilah's, digitally altered to make her look younger. The caption read: *Is Dalilah Beale the assistant?*

Dalilah felt the hairs on the back of her neck stand up.

"Say something," Mike urged Dalilah.

"What would you say to such nonsense if it were you," bellowed Sharona. She turned to Dalilah. "You'd better go now; you've got a plane to catch."

Dalilah's chair scraped the floor as she pushed it back and stood up.

◆◆◆

"What a pleasant coincidence, Mrs Kosgey," the familiar voice sliced through the evening air in the hospital car park where MP Kosgey had been admitted.

Lucy Kosgey, who had just stepped out of her Range Rover, turned to see DCI Mugo and DS Atieno-Masinde approaching her.

"Are you following me?" Lucy's sharp retort was laced with aggression and bitterness. "If you are, I'm suing the whole bloody department."

"Mrs Kosgey," Mugo said, "I'm giving you a choice. We can talk privately, or I'll have no choice but to handcuff you and take you in for questioning as a suspected co-conspirator. Which will it be?"

"What are you implying? It's absurd, and I don't have time for such nonsense."

Mugo held up a court order. "Our investigation has revealed that around the time you left the Golf and Country Club, you received a text message from your uncle Jonathan Wasike's number. He wrote, 'All set', to which you replied with a thumbs-up emoji. At 11:40 p.m., the same time your husband was attacked, you received a call from Jonathan Wasike's number. That's too much coincidence, don't you think?"

Lucy Kosgey's face contorted like someone who had bitten into a particularly sour lemon.

"When we asked you if you had any interaction with Jonathan Wasike that day, you skilfully dodged the question," Atieno-Masinde added. "It's not unusual to lie to protect a loved one involved in criminal activity. But is it worth the risk, Mrs Kosgey?"

Lucy snorted like an irritated bull. Without a word, she hurried to the entrance. Atieno-Masinde and Mugo trailed close behind.

Lucy burst into her husband's room, slamming the door behind her.

Trusting his police instincts, Mugo gently touched Atieno-Masinde's elbow and whispered, "Let's give them a moment of privacy. Looks like they need it badly."

"You disgusting bastard," Lucy's voice boomed. "You sick, filthy beast ... what have you done to Rebecca?" She unleashed a torrent of abuse, curses, and threats.

"Please lower your voice," the MP pleaded, his voice was uncharacteristically soft. "This is a misunderstanding. I swear—"

"Shut the fuck up! You swear, my ass! I swear on my life, you will pay dearly!"

Lucy stormed out of the room.

"If you still can't wait to handcuff someone, do it now," she barked, her steely gaze fixed on Mugo. She pointed to the room. "Cuff that rotten, depraved beast! He's of the vilest breed, far worse than the Duo you've been relentlessly hunting down."

"Don't leave, Mrs Kosgey, or you could be charged with fleeing the police," Mugo advised. He entered the room, followed closely by Atieno-Masinde.

"How dare you barge in here without my permission?" the MP snapped, his voice stripped of its usual authoritative tone.

"Apparently, you have no intention of helping us bring the perpetrators to justice?" Mugo said. "If you ask me, your wife's state of mind and her fits of rage have revealed more about the motives behind your attack than you're willing to admit."

"You are annoyingly arrogant and have no respect for a patient's right to privacy. Tell me your name again, Inspector. I suppose I have no choice but to have a serious talk with your superior."

"Detective Chief Inspector Dennis Mugo, Special Crime Prevention Unit. Just so you know, Mr Kosgey, I always deal with hardened criminals – those eager to take their secrets to the grave. I never let them get away with their crimes so easily."

"Did you just call me a hardened criminal, inspector?"

"No, I did not. But are you?"

If looks could shoot, DCI Mugo would be riddled with bullets by now.

"I suggest you keep your phone on," Mugo advised. "We'll be in touch soon with the proper warrant. You may see yourself as a victim here, but from my point of view, you are a key player in this game. That's what caught the Duo's attention, isn't it?"

The MP's fingers lingered at his temple, where a vein visibly throbbed.

"You might consider asking us to stay," Atieno-Masinde said, her tone calm and encouraging. "Wouldn't you like to know how the Duo followed you into the public toilet? Or how they dared to attack you so boldly, apparently confident that your men would not intervene until their mission was complete?"

CHAPTER 23

Thursday, 22 March, 20:20

"Dalilah Beale, I'm Malombo from the Coast Leo newspaper. I'm sorry to bump into you so awkwardly."

Dalilah ignored the reporter. With her luggage in tow, she made her way to a shuttle van with a banner reading 'La Dasara Beach Resort'.

"Just one question," the reporter shouted, following closely behind Dalilah. "How do you respond to the allegation that you are Scarface's assistant?"

The shuttle driver approached Dalilah and helped her with her luggage.

"Dalilah Beale, do you denounce the crimes of the Duo?" the reporter asked.

Dalilah jumped into the air-conditioned van. After the driver loaded her two bags, they drove south through the city with soft music playing in the background. Dalilah looked out the window and marvelled at the remarkable transformation of her hometown. It had been eighteen years since the Beale family had adopted her, and she hadn't returned to the Coast Province until now.

The van rolled onto the Likoni ferry, which then glided across the channel. An hour's drive later, Dalilah arrived at Diani Beach, where endless stretches of white sand and swaying palm trees greeted her.

As the driver unloaded her luggage, Dalilah's eyes swept over the imposing façade of La Dasara Beach Resort.

"Good evening, Dalilah Beale," a man of Asian descent called out as she approached with hurried steps. "I'm Raprul Singh, the hotel manager," he added, extending his hand for a handshake, his thick Indian accent unmistakable. "Please follow me to my office. I won't keep you long. The concierge will take your luggage to the reception desk."

In the manager's office, Dalilah sat in the visitor's chair, Raprul Singh in his black leather executive chair.

"I'll get right to the point, ma'am," the manager said, tapping his feet nervously.

"Call me Dalilah, not ma'am. Or Ms Beale."

"Yes, ma'am." His feet were tapping even more vigorously. "You know, most of our guests value their privacy very highly."

"I also value my privacy."

"I heard about the incident with the journalist at the airport. Pretty soon, they will be poking their noses into this hotel and snooping around because you are here." His head bobbed from side to side with every word. "On behalf of ... in the interest of our valued guests, I would like to ask you to leave the hotel. You will, of course, be given a full refund. I will also arrange for our hotel taxi to take you to your next hotel free of charge."

He gave Dalilah his business card.

"About the hotel taxi, I'll get back to you," Dalilah said as she slipped the card into her purse. "As for the trouble with the journalists, I'm sure you're well prepared for such scenarios, aren't you?"

"Indeed, ma'am, we can certainly tackle the issue of the snoopers. The only problem is that your name is associated with the Merciless Duo. Our institutions firmly distance themselves from all forms of violence and from those who practice or condone it. I hope I have made myself clear."

Dalilah's breath caught as she processed what she had just heard.

"This is a shameless slander," she thundered. "How dare you?"

"I'm sorry, ma'am, if you feel I've offended you."

"Get in the habit of calling me by my name. You're far too old to call me ma'am."

"Yes, Ma... Ms Beale."

With a loud sigh of disbelief and a shake of her head, Dalilah rose from her chair.

"Unless you pull strings to have me thrown out, I expect to be treated like any other worthy guest. And rest assured, you will live to regret this slander."

"How will I regret this?" Raprul Singh's voice was barely a whisper, so low that only he could hear it. "Are you going to attack me?"

◆◆◆

On the fourth floor of La Dasara Beach Resort, Bahati was on the verge of exhaustion. The relentless bouncing on the box spring had taken its toll, and his eyelids felt like lead. Lying on his back, struggling to keep his eyes open, he entertained himself with the remote control for the LED lamp – each time he pressed it, the room lit up in a different bright colour.

Oliver and Omari sat in the adjacent lounge, eyes glued to the TV, barely blinking as the final minutes of the UEFA Champions League match played out. They were nervous about the corner kick the other team was about to take.

A triumphant smile spread across Omari's face as the final whistle blew. He and Oliver leapt to their feet in triumph. They high-fived each other in celebration of their team's 1-0 victory.

"What a game!" Oliver exclaimed. He grabbed the remote and turned off the television.

"I'm going to meet Lynnette. She's already waiting eagerly," said Omari, raising his glass in a final toast. "See you tomorrow for breakfast."

"Have fun."

Omari left.

Oliver retired to the bedroom to find Bahati sound asleep. He tucked the mosquito net under the mattress, turned down the air conditioning and opened the windows.

Too engrossed in his thoughts to enjoy the soothing rhythm of the waves breaking gently on the shore, he walked away from the window and climbed into bed next to Bahati. With a click of the remote, he dimmed the LED lights to a faint blue glow.

Lying on his back, he stared at the ceiling, contemplating his next move. He was used to callboys, street urchins and whoever else Omari procured for him – boys whose feelings meant nothing to him. Boys whose mouths he would shut with callous force when they screamed. After all, he had paid for them – the twisted rationalisation he whispered to himself over and over again, like a prayer.

Excited and with slightly trembling fingers, he stroked Bahati's back.

The LED light went out.

As he fumbled on the bed for the remote, a foul stench hit him and made him chuckle. He sniffed Bahati, trying to determine if he was the source of the air pollution.

The sound of a throat being cleared pierced the darkness.

"Omari?" called Oliver.

"Shh!"

Oliver's pulse pounded in his ears. Instinctively, his eyes darted in the direction of a bedside table, where a room telephone lay in the dark. All he had to do was pick up the receiver, press zero and shout, "Help!" Security would be in his room in a heartbeat – that much he knew.

"I've disconnected the phone, white boy," the voice said.

"*Sijaona uso yako.*" Oliver's first survival instinct was to assure the intruder that he had not seen his face. The same instinct had led him to speak in his passable Swahili, even though the intruder had addressed him in English.

"Are you an American or an Englishman?" the barely recognisable face asked in a soft, almost unenergetic tone, sticking to English.

"Englishman."

"Then speak to me in your mother tongue. I speak almost perfect English. It would be a terrible pity and a great disadvantage to you if we had any linguistic misunderstandings."

"I welcome the suggestion. Much appreciated." Oliver's second survival instinct was to avoid his distinctive colloquialisms lest there be any misunderstanding.

Silence reigned.

"I have money in my safe. You can take it and go. I will give you the code and not alert anyone." Oliver's next survival instinct was bribery. Pragmatically, he understood that bribery was woven into the fabric of society. After all, he had used it before to avoid legal trouble and disaster.

"First, take the child into the other room and watch your step. Leave the lights off. Come back, and we will have a little chat. Nothing to get excited about."

Hesitantly, as if afraid that the floor beneath him would give way, Oliver climbed out of bed.

"A word of advice, Englishman – don't try to be clever if you want to live to see tomorrow. If you pinch the boy to wake him up, I will give you a few minutes to regret it and then slowly slaughter you."

"I won't do anything stupid."

Afraid of waking Bahati, Oliver cautiously reached under the boy's body, lifted him and carried him into the second bedroom. There, he laid him gently on the bed and covered him. As he returned to the invisible intruder, he heard the windows being closed.

He entered the room and pleaded, "Please, just take the money and go. The code for my safe is 2020."

The door was locked.

"Please allow me to leave without seeing your face." Oliver's survival instinct told him that seeing the face of such a criminal was tantamount to sealing his own death sentence.

"Unlike you, I have nothing to hide, Englishman. I always show my face."

A candle flickered.

The sight sucked the air out of Oliver's lungs, and his breathing became shallow.

"*C'est la vie*, Englishman!"

The Englishman's heart pounded to the rhythm of an Isukuti drum, the fast-paced, passionate beat of western Kenya.

He drew a deep breath. "As I said, I've got British pounds, cash, here in the safe, the equivalent of a million shillings." His typical soft Oxfordshire accent became more pronounced and tinged with a tremor. "That is four times the reward for information leading to your capture."

"I'll take you up on your offer."

The words calmed Oliver's pounding heart.

"I guess we don't need to introduce ourselves, do we?" Scarface said, placing his metal toolbox down.

"Not necessarily. You're Scarface." Oliver plucked up courage and forced a smile. "Maybe your last name?"

Hands behind his back, Scarface walked over to Oliver and stood at arm's length. He placed his hand firmly on Oliver's shoulder and pressed his thumb down on the area just above the collarbone, near where the neck joins the shoulder.

A sharp, searing pain shot down Oliver's left arm, causing severe numbness and loss of movement. Self-defence was out of the question. A haunting memory swept through his mind like a tsunami: the tragic story of a burly muscleman and revered former village wrestler. Physical and mental anguish, persistent sleep and metabolic disorders, and even the relentless phantom scent of Scarface were said to have driven him to despair after his encounter with the Duo. In the end, the only way out seemed to be taking death into his own hands.

"Let's get one thing straight, Englishman: I don't tolerate wiseacres, liars and deniers. I also despise loudmouths and those who want to show off their martial arts. They end up miserable."

Oliver, unable to stand the pain and fearing that the unbearable stench was affecting his lungs, whimpered, "I'm not an abusive husband."

Scarface let go of Oliver, reached into his kangaroo pocket and pulled out a business card. He stuck it in Oliver's face and ordered, "Read the title."

"Children are the future."

"This is the smoking gun, Englishman – proof of your guilt."

Oliver swallowed hard.

"You have been found guilty on four counts, Englishman. One: sexual abuse of a child. Two: physical abuse of a child. Three: emotional abuse of a child. Four: defilement and rape of a child."

The words were a dagger, cutting deeper with each syllable.

"How do you plead, Englishman? Guilty or not guilty?"

"Bahati ... This boy, I haven't done anything to him. Look at him. Talk to him. Let a doctor examine him. This is not fair, Scarface. Who ruled me guilty without due process?"

"We are not here to answer such smart-aleck questions, Englishman. We are here to carry out your sentence. Failure to answer my question will have dire consequences. Lying will have brutal repercussions."

Oliver dug his fingernails into the palm of his hand, his mind racing: who could have sold him out? Only a handful of people knew his itinerary. Only Omari knew of his shady business dealings. Had someone been shadowing Omari?

"One last time, Englishman, do you plead guilty or not guilty to all four charges?"

CHAPTER 24

Friday, 23 March, 07:30

Apart from a few grey clouds lazily romping around the sky, tempting some laymen to predict rain, the sun shone in all its glory. The weather forecasters had predicted high temperatures of up to 37 degrees and a light south-southeasterly breeze.

Dalilah stood in front of a large mirror, assessing her outfit – a three-piece kimono made of light, breathable fabric, perfect for the weather. Satisfied, she unplugged her phone from the charger, retrieved the hotel manager's business card from her handbag, and called him.

"Raprul Singh," he answered.

"Consider yourself lucky. I'm checking out. Prepare the refund and have the taxi ready, as you said last night."

"Who am I talking to?"

"Dalilah Beale. Send a concierge to my room immediately."

"You can manage that without a concierge."

The free line tone at the other end signalled the end of the call.

Did he hang up? Dalilah wondered and dialled again, but the call was immediately rejected.

Pulling her suitcases behind her, Dalilah took the lift down. The lift doors opened on the ground floor and she saw a gurney and two paramedics in their distinctive uniforms. Next to the lift were Raprul Singh and a police officer.

"Dalilah Beale, I am Sergeant Meshak Kioko. I'm—"

"How rude of you to hang up on me, Mister Singh," Dalilah snapped, interrupting the officer.

"I'd be stressed too if I were the manager, Mrs Beale." There was no hint of humour in Sergeant Kioko's face or tone.

Dalilah's gaze shifted to the adjacent lift, where the doors had parted to reveal a figure being wheeled out on a collapsible stretcher. She watched as the bloodied man with the swollen face barely had time to get his bearings before Sergeant Kioko stepped forward and leaned in to whisper something.

Dalilah met the gaze of the man on the stretcher, his right eye fixed on her, the other lost beneath the swelling. His auburn, bushy eyebrow arched upwards as he pointed at her. He opened his swollen mouth as if he wanted to say something, but all that came out of his strained expression were signs of breathlessness.

That seemed to be enough for Sergeant Kioko. He walked over to Dalilah.

"Mrs Dalilah Beale," the sergeant began, "you've been positively identified."

Dalilah took it in good humour, her eyes fixed on the lift opposite. It had opened, and a female police officer stepped out, hand in hand with a small boy – Bahati.

"What happened?" Dalilah blurted out.

"Nice try," Sergeant Kioko purred. "We are placing you under temporary arrest, Mrs Beale. You are suspected of involvement in an assault on a hotel guest."

"Is this a joke, officer?"

"Not even close," he hinted smugly. "Mrs Dalilah Beale, you are under no obligation to say anything. But concealing anything during questioning could hurt your defence. Anything you say can and will be used against you in a court of law."

Dalilah's sigh froze halfway through, giving way to a shock-induced paralysis.

The sergeant pulled out a handcuff and reached for Dalilah's right hand, but she yanked it away.

"Mrs Dalilah Beale, I refer you to Section 253b of the Penal Code. Any person who resists or wilfully obstructs a police officer in the proper discharge of his duties is guilty of an offence and is liable to imprisonment for up to five years."

The metal closed tightly around her wrists. As she was led to a waiting police jeep, recent horror stories flooded her mind – police brutality, lynchings, kidnappings.

A question suddenly flashed through her mind: Will this ride really end at a police station and not in a perfidious ambush on a deserted street where no one will hear my screams?

◆◆◆

A police search party, divided into teams, meticulously combed the area around La Dasara Beach Resort and its environs. The lynchpin of the manhunt was a dirty white Nissan pickup truck. The driver, seen by several witnesses, was described as wearing a dark sweatshirt with a hood over his head and carrying a blue toolbox. The sighting had prompted a flood of calls to police.

The first call had been received at the police emergency centre at 5:23 a.m.

"There's a man here who looks like the wanted Scarface. He's wearing a dark hood over his head and carrying a bluish toolbox," the caller had reported.

"Where are you, ma'am?" the emergency dispatcher had asked.

"I am sitting in my car, about 200 metres from La Dasara Beach Resort. The man got into his car. I think he's going to leave."

The second call had been received at 5:36 a.m.

"I am following an old white pickup truck. Scarface is driving it," the caller had reported. It wasn't the first time he'd called the police, so he knew the drill: he'd started by giving his name, the location he was calling from, and that he could be reached at any time on the number he was using. Like many ambitious citizens, he felt a responsibility to help catch the Duo and was always on the lookout for suspicious-looking couples. However, getting his hands on the reward money was the driving force behind his great ambition.

"How do you know this man is Scarface?" the dispatcher had asked.

"I saw him before he got into the car. He had his dark hoodie over his head and his blue metal toolbox, just like on the Most Wanted posters."

"Scarface is dangerous and ruthless. Don't go anywhere near him," the dispatcher had warned. Then, after a pause, he asked, "Is he alone or with the assistant?"

"He's all alone."

"Do you have the car's registration number?"

"Yes, I have it." The sputtering of the engine had been a sign that the fuel was running low. "Oh no, I might lose him. I'm running out of petrol."

"Where are you now, and which way are you going?"

"I am on the Diani Beach Road, heading north-west. By the way, I get the reward for the tip and the information about the licence plate, don't I?"

The crucial phone call that led police to the suspect Dalilah Beale had been made at 7:10 a.m.

"I am Raprul Singh, the manager of La Dasara Beach Resort. I want to report that the Merciless Duo has left a victim in my hotel. The accomplice is still inside the hotel."

"I am dispatching help for the victim right away. Uh ... how do you know that the accomplice is still in the hotel?"

"A boy called, crying and saying, 'he is bleeding, he is bleeding!' The receptionist and I rushed to the room. I found a note with the accomplice's name and asked the victim, 'Dalilah Beale'? He couldn't speak, but he nodded. As a matter of fact, she had threatened me last night when she checked in."

"Who checked into the hotel?"

"Dalilah Beale."

"What name did she check in under?"

"Under the name of Dalilah Beale."

"How and why did she threaten you?"

"I told her she was not welcome because her name was associated with the Duo. She gave me a threatening look and told me I would regret what I had said. Up close, I could have sworn she was the assistant on the sketches."

CHAPTER 25

Friday, 23 March, 14:40

Oliver Morgan felt trapped, invisible clamps pinning him to his hospital bed, tightening with every word the doctor spoke.

"We'll perform a colonoscopy and a gastroscopy with tissue sampling," the doctor continued.

Oliver's right eyelid twitched as he struggled to focus through the haze of sedation that clouded his mind.

"We'll take anal swabs to test for rectal gonococcal and chlamydial infections. With your consent, we'll also carry out blood tests for hepatitis and HIV. The detection window for hepatitis and HIV in the blood is at least two weeks after exposure. Early detection is crucial for the timely management and treatment of these infections."

The invisible clamps tightened, biting relentlessly into Oliver's psyche.

"Your treatment will require more than conventional methods. Given the severity of your injuries, we've called in a specialist. She's highly regarded for her unique ability to deal with the deep psychological trauma suffered by victims of violent crime. Her approach is compassionate and focuses on healing the invisible scars – the ones that often resist traditional treatment."

A thick tear slid down Oliver's cheek, soaking the light blue plaid pillow. The spectre of possible terminal illness loomed, casting a grim uncertainty over his future. The nappy that managed his incontinence only deepened his humiliation, while the phantom stench of Scarface clung to him, suffocating and inescapable.

He shook his head in disbelief, remembering how he had taken the rumours circulating on the Internet with a pinch of scepticism – but now he was living proof that they were true.

His body convulsed violently at the haunting memory of the Duo's dirty, blood-stained instruments – grim tools of torment that had etched pain into his flesh and deep into his soul.

◆◆◆

An old, white, plastered, rusty Nissan pickup truck approached two traffic police officers on the Ukunda-Ramisi road. One of the officers held up a stop sign.

The man at the wheel, wearing oversized sunglasses and a hooded sweatshirt, was the subject of an intensive search in the area. He slowed down on the gravel road, stopped a few metres from the officer and flicked his cigarette butt out of the window.

The officer cautiously approached the car, his hand on the standard police weapon – a German-made G3 rifle.

"Get out slowly and keep your hands where I can see them," the officer shouted.

Tyres squealed as the Nissan pickup sped away, leaving a billowing cloud of dust in its wake. Oncoming traffic reacted quickly to avoid an accident, making dangerous swerving manoeuvres and honking incessantly. Pedestrians and hawkers screamed, cursed, and scattered hysterically from the roadside, making the two rifle-wielding officers reluctant to fire at the fleeing car.

The two policemen sprinted to their vehicle to take up the pursuit. They radioed their colleagues with details of the Nissan pickup and its registration number.

The high-speed chase tore through the busy road, with both vehicles recklessly swerving over speed bumps and dodging potholes. As they approached the Ukunda-Diani junction, the tension peaked with a hair-raising moment. A head-on collision between the pickup and a packed *matatu* – a minibus – was only averted by the *matatu* deftly swerving to the right. But it spun out of control and collided with an overloaded lorry. The lorry's tyre burst with a deafening explosion. It overturned, blocking the entire intersection. The screams of commuters echoed through the air as the *matatu* crashed into a lamppost.

The police car screeched to a halt just short of the overturned lorry.

"Why did you stop?" shouted the policeman in the passenger seat. "We're losing Scarface."

"We have to help the victims of the accident."

"Scarface is a great threat to the country. Drive on."

The radio hissed, then a voice broke through: "Nissan pickup sighted. Passed our patrol opposite Equity Bank. In pursuit."

The driver of the Nissan pickup saw the patrol car in his rear-view mirror, its red and blue lights flashing and sirens wailing as it approached. He rounded a corner. Two hundred metres ahead, a Maasai man in a traditional Kanga dress was leisurely leading a herd of goats across the road. He honked angrily and swore at the top of his lungs as he took his foot off the accelerator.

"Get those damn animals off the road," he shouted, desperately manoeuvring behind the herd. But he veered too far off the road and accidentally hit a fire hydrant. All attempts to get the car back on track failed.

The man jumped out of the car and took off with the agility of a cheetah, gaining valuable ground. He scurried through the tangled undergrowth of a wild, overgrown patch, weaving around clumps of sisal and leaping periodically over thickets of prickly roses. The scorching sun seared his skin, draining his strength with each step.

"Fucking flowers," he cursed as thorny branches clawed at his trousers, slicing across his skin. Like the big cat, his Achilles' heel was endurance. He eased his pace and threw a glance over his shoulder. The patrol car barrelled towards him, tyres screeching as it came to a halt beside his pickup, its path blocked by the animals. The doors flew open. Two uniformed officers jumped out, AK-47s at the ready. Seconds later, another police car pulled up beside the pickup, and four officers got out.

Gasping for breath, he staggered to a halt under the sheltering canopy of a colossal baobab tree, its massive branches arching over a two-metre-high brick fence. The oppressive humidity clung to his skin and seemed to test his resolve with every breath. As he considered his next move, he dropped low, the dense foliage hiding him. From his makeshift hideout, he watched the police fan out in a grid pattern, combing through the thicket and peering under fallen branches.

He saw an officer's hand shoot up and point directly at his hiding spot. This jolted him into action, and like a leopard dragging its prey up a tree to hide it from scavengers, he scaled the baobab. He reached the top of the fence and jumped into the yard of a farm, where he took an unfortunate fall and dislocated his right foot.

The rustle of dry leaves and snapping twigs told him the police were closing in. With a surge of desperation, he fought through the pain of the dislocation to get to his feet. Every step was a struggle as he dragged his injured limb, determined to avoid arrest.

"Freeze!" shouted a policeman from his perch in the baobab tree, his G3 rifle pointed at the suspect.

He ignored the order and limped away, heading for the corner of the farmhouse ten metres away.

A single shot tore through the man's left thigh. He fell to the ground, screaming.

"Suspect down!" the policeman reported.

◆◆◆

An initial search of the Nissan pickup uncovered several illegal items, including several grams of marijuana and a dozen counterfeit Viagra pills. The most striking find, however, was a rusty blue metal toolbox.

CHAPTER 26

Friday, 23 March, 16:30

Dalilah's fingers drummed an impatient rhythm on the metal bench. To her pleasant surprise, the small cell was remarkably clean. But the oppressive smell of sweat and urine burnt her throat, and every breath felt shallow and unsatisfying.

There were six other women in the cell. One in particular made Dalilah uncomfortable: a woman with angular cheekbones and a steely gaze. She kept pacing back and forth, her movements jerky and restless. The telltale signs of drug use were etched into her dilated pupils and erratic mood swings.

"I recognise you," a cellmate with heavy make-up and a raspy voice growled as she approached Dalilah. "You are the assistant. Is that right?"

Dalilah hesitated, her throat constricting.

"Answer that," the woman with the steely gaze barked, giving the impression that she was bracing herself for trouble.

"Why the hell are you attacking tourists now?" the raspy-voiced woman fumed. "We're all just tryin' to pick up the pieces after the last terrorist hit, and here you are stirrin' up trouble in our coastal hood. You got any clue how much danger you're putting us locals in? Tourism keeps us alive, for fuck's sake."

The bulging pouch at the front of the woman's dress turned Dalilah's unease into a cold, palpable fear. And to twist the already deeply buried knife, the woman had been brought in less than fifteen minutes ago.

Has she got something illegal to stab me with? Or, God forbid, a dirty dildo? Dalilah wondered, an icy current rippling through her. She had heard all sorts of strange stories.

◆◆◆

Superintendent Gordon Kalonzo's office in Kwale was cold and impersonal, dominated by a large L-shaped desk draped in a dark blue tablecloth. A grey metal cabinet stood at the far end of the room, next to a white portable air conditioner that hummed as it cooled the room.

He rose from his seat, saluted the higher-ranking Detective Chief Inspector Dennis Mugo, and extended his hand for a handshake.

"Welcome to Kwale," said the superintendent, beaming. He wore a khaki police uniform with silver insignia and a navy blue field cap.

Sergeant Meshak Kioko entered the office with a file in his hand. He greeted DCI Mugo and asked, "May I offer you something to drink? It's a record-hot day."

"Let's cut to the chase. Under what pretext was Dalilah Beale arrested?" Mugo asked impatiently, taking the visitor's chair. This was no time for pleasantries; urgency demanded immediate attention. His superiors and prominent figures were breathing down his neck. The nation was on tenterhooks, and each new case that came to light added to the growing sense of panic.

The superintendent flashed a smile. "Several reports came in about a suspicious man in the area who looked like Scarface. While reviewing the calls, the hotel manager at La Dasara Beach Resort alerted us to the female suspect. He had found a piece of paper in the assaulted guest's room while administering first aid. The victim had confirmed to the manager that he had written down the name of the perpetrator – Dalilah Beale." He opened a file and handed Mugo a piece of paper with a handwritten name on it. "Sergeant Kioko arrived just in time to intercept Dalilah Beale in the hotel lobby."

"She wanted to check out, even though she'd booked a three-day stay," the sergeant informed with a confident half-smile. "When the victim was brought into the lobby, I asked him if he could identify the perpetrator. He pointed to Dalilah Beale. He was about to say something else, but a medical emergency stopped him."

"So far, all the staff and some hotel guests have been questioned," the superintendent said. "Nothing concrete yet."

"Are the photos ready?" asked Mugo. Over the years, he had learnt that a line-up didn't always guarantee a more accurate identification than a simple set of photographs. And that sometimes the truth could be distorted by the tension of a face-to-face confrontation.

"Yes, of course." The superintendent slid a file across the table to the DCI. "We have mug shots of both suspects."

Mugo flicked through the pages of photographs, shaking his head in clear disapproval.

"Are you aware that these photos contrast starkly with the composite sketches of Scarface and his assistant?"

"Dalilah Beale's is not far off," Sergeant Kioko observed.

"I need a vehicle and a driver to take me to the hospital immediately where …" Mugo looked down at his notebook, "where Oliver Morgan is being treated."

"I'll take you there myself," Sergeant Kioko offered.

◆◆◆

DS Bakari and DS Atieno-Masinde entered the windowless interrogation room. The suspect sat handcuffed to the table, his thigh wrapped where a bullet had torn through the flesh. His face was relatively unremarkable, the scalp covered in thick tufts of hair, and he bore no resemblance to the sketch of Scarface. The information already known about his background further exonerated him. He worked as a caretaker at a holiday resort and moonlighted as a gigolo. On the night in question, he had claimed to have been with a tourist he had met in a nearby hotel. The woman had corroborated his statement that he had been with her all night until 5:20 a.m.

A minute-long eye-to-eye duel ensued between Bakari and the man.

"Are you Scarface, the ringleader of the psycho Duo?" Bakari broke the silence.

"Is that why I got shot in the leg?" The man gave a mirthless laugh. "That's an absolute scream! Can you imagine I stopped drinking in the evenings when I heard that the Duo were up to their mischief again? I don't want to be ambushed like the MP when I pee at night."

"Why did you flee from the police?" asked Atieno-Masinde.

"Out of fear. The Duo allegedly posed as police to ambush the men."

"Where did you hear that?"

"The Duo are on everyone's lips." His eyes darted nervously between the two officers. "Some people say, the Duo are not just posing as police … they are the police."

CHAPTER 27

Friday, 23 March, 17:40

A doctor in a white coat with a stethoscope around his neck changed course when he saw the famous detective chief inspector approaching the hospital reception, accompanied by a uniformed police officer. He approached the officers and held out his hand in greeting.

"Good afternoon, chief inspector. I am Dr Sharma. I can guess why you're here."

Mugo maintained his serious, matter-of-fact expression. "I'm here to speak with Mr. Oliver Morgan. Is he able to answer my questions in his current condition?"

"If the questions require a simple yes or no, I think he'll be able to answer them with a nod or a shake of the head. His mouth and gums are too damaged for him to utter a single word."

"A nod or a shake of the head will do for now. Show us to his room, please."

"Follow me," the doctor said, leading the way. "His condition is critical. He suffered severe trauma. We've stabilised him for now."

They got into a lift.

"How severe are the injuries?" Mugo asked.

"The preliminary examination revealed an anal fissure—"

"What's that?" asked the sergeant.

"This is a painful tear in the anal mucosa caused by overstretching of the sphincter muscle. We removed a viscous, purulent fluid and particles from the rectum. They are being examined. We are in the process of running a series of scans to try and get a more detailed picture of the internal damage he has suffered."

They exited the lift, walked down the corridor and entered the opulent private hospital room, conspicuously free of the typical hospital odour. Mugo's eyes scanned the luxurious amenities – individually controlled air conditioning, a DVD player, an oxygen supply and even a mini-bar. Oliver Morgan lay in bed, surrounded by medical equipment that kept beeping and watching over him. His left eye was bandaged. Tubes snaked out of his arm, and a nasal cannula delivered oxygen.

"Here I am again, Mr Morgan," Dr Sharma greeted as he checked the readings on the medical equipment. After a cursory glance at the IV level, he explained, "These gentlemen from the police are here to investigate your assault. They need to ask you a few questions. I'll give them ten minutes at the most."

"Mr Morgan, I'm Detective Chief Inspector Mugo from the CID, and this is Sergeant Kioko. All I'm asking for today is a simple thumbs up. If you understand what I mean, go ahead and give me one."

Oliver raised his right thumb.

"If you need help, Mr Morgan, just press this button," Dr Sharma said, pointing to the button.

"I'm going to ask you a few questions about last night's attack," Mugo said, casting a fleeting glance at Dr Sharma as he headed for the door. "Then I'm going to show you some photographs to see if you can identify your attackers."

The door softly clicked shut behind the doctor as he left the room.

"Were you attacked last night by a man and a young woman?" Mugo asked.

With a pained expression, Oliver raised his thumb.

"Did you get a good look at their faces?"

Thumbs up.

Mugo opened his file and moved closer to the head of the bed.

"I'm going to show you a series of photographs that may help you positively identify the individuals involved in the attack."

Mugo flipped through the pages, giving Oliver time to examine each of the men's photographs.

After the last photograph, Oliver shook his head.

Without a word, Mugo continued, flipping through the photographs of the women one by one. When he reached the fifth, that of Dalilah Beale, Oliver raised his right eyebrow, a look of shock on his face.

After the sixth and final photograph, Oliver shook his head.

"You hesitated on the fifth photo," Mugo remarked, showing Oliver the photograph again. "Take another look. See if something clicks."

Oliver shook his head.

"Don't you recognise the woman in the photo?" Sergeant Kioko blurted out, taking an unprofessional, threatening step towards Oliver. "Isn't that the perpetrator who attacked you?"

Oliver looked at the sergeant in confusion, as if his heavily accented English was difficult to understand.

"Mr Morgan, let me jog your memory," the sergeant suggested. "First of all, do you remember me?"

Thumbs up.

"Do you remember being wheeled on a stretcher from your room?"

Thumbs up.

"When you were lying on the stretcher in the hotel lobby, did you see a woman with two suitcases in front of the lift?"

Thumbs up.

"Do you remember when I leaned over and asked you a question?"

No reaction.

Sergeant Kioko repeated the question. When no answer came, disbelief flickered across his face.

"Mr Morgan, I did ask you if you could identify the perpetrator," Sergeant Kioko said, his tone calm but insistent. "You responded by pointing to the woman standing by the lift. She was the only woman in the vicinity. Can you recall that moment now?"

Oliver clenched his fist, his knuckles white, revealing his tense reserve.

"Come on, Mr Morgan," Sergeant Kioko fumed, "do you want to be uncooperative now? I'm telling you, you're not getting off that easy." He flicked through his file and showed Oliver the open page. "Is this your handwriting?"

Thumbs up.

"You wrote down the perpetrator's name, didn't you?"

Oliver's swollen lips twitched as he reached for his mobile phone on the side table. With slow, unsteady fingers, he unlocked it, typed something and handed it to the sergeant.

"Are you kidding me?" Sergeant Kioko thundered, his face etched with disbelief.

◆◆◆

Superintendent Kalonzo hunched over his desk, a pen in one hand, a clipboard tilted towards him in the other. His slight nodding suggested that he was diligently taking notes. But the paper on the clipboard told a different story. Each stroke of the pen sharpened the caricature he was sketching, humorously capturing the lousy mood of the impeccably dressed middle-aged visitor seated opposite him. It was Jeffrey Kizito, Dalilah's celebrity lawyer, known for his scathing criticism of the police and his tireless advocacy for justice and human rights. A man lauded by the media and with a legion of loyal followers who hang on his every word during his numerous televised legal clinics.

"An arrested person has the right to speak to a lawyer or anyone else who can assist them," lawyer Kizito reprimanded.

The superintendent curled his lips, adding an overly dramatic quality to his sketch – the strands of hair spiked upwards, and tiny droplets of saliva sprayed from the mouth, spreading like fine mist from an aerosol can.

"It's a travesty that all those who could have provided Dalilah Beale with much-needed support or advice had to learn of her arrest from the press."

"I asked you to be patient," the superintendent said, adding a tie to the caricature. "The sergeant should be here any moment and will give you the details of the arrest."

Without so much as a knock, the door swung open. Sergeant Kioko marched in, his expression filled with concern, only to darken further at the sight of the lawyer.

"This is Sergeant Kioko," the superintendent introduced his subordinate.

The lawyer was immediately in his element. "Denying a detainee their constitutional right to a telephone call is a violation of human rights. Are you aware of this, Sergeant Kioko?" His symmetrical face, framed by round, vacant eyes and a feminine softness in the cheeks, contorted into a mocking grin.

"Dalilah Beale will be released immediately without any charges being brought against her," the sergeant said, his words partially drowned out by the unpleasant squeaking of the chair he was pulling. "We are just finalising the paperwork."

The door opened and a policewoman led Dalilah into the office. The toll of the last eight hours was etched on Dalilah's face. She reeked of urine and sweat that had seeped from the cell into her pores and clothes. Yet relief seemed to wash over her, and she took a long breath, obviously appreciating something she had taken for granted – the precious gifts of freedom and boundlessness.

"Did you come all the way from Nairobi so I wouldn't have to sleep in my new accommodation?" she quipped as she sat beside her lawyer.

The lawyer flashed an artificial grin. "A last-minute business trip like this is part of the job when my clients' lives are at stake."

Mugo, who had been on the phone, entered the office and took a seat next to Dalilah.

"You are free, Mrs Beale," growled Sergeant Kioko. "But isn't it an interesting coincidence that you and the victim were in the same place at the same time?"

"Coincidences have led to the harassment of many innocent citizens," the lawyer rebuked, his tone sharp and accusatory. "Civil rights are constantly being violated. This habitual search for scapegoats to expedite the closure of cases can no longer be tolerated."

"Let's not blow this out of proportion, Mr Kizito," Mugo intervened. "A mistake has been made, and I will personally launch an investigation."

"What mistake?" snapped the lawyer, his astonishment unmistakable.

"Due to the ongoing investigation, I cannot disclose the sequence of events leading to the arrest of Ms Dalilah Beale."

"I see. But was there a reasonable suspicion that my client had committed the crime? I don't need a stratospheric IQ to realise that you were simply following the unsubstantiated rumours on the internet – public opinion, not evidence, seems to determine the truth."

The sergeant rolled his eyes. "Mr Kizito, I'd rather inconvenience an innocent person than let a wanted criminal slip through the cracks of justice."

"I am extremely concerned that you see things so tyrannically—"

"Suffice it to say that we are under enormous pressure to catch the Duo," the superintendent interrupted the lawyer. "Let's not make a mountain out of a molehill."

"Ms Beale, I need to speak to you urgently, preferably before you leave the province," Mugo said, pulling his business card from his wallet and sliding it across the table to Dalilah. "Make sure you call me."

The lawyer pulled back the sleeves of his designer coat and glanced at his gleaming gold-plated watch – a chronometer worth more than the annual salaries of the superintendent and the sergeant put together.

"Off the record or not, never speak to a police officer without your lawyer present," he advised his client. "A desperate officer could use your words against you."

"Please contact me, Ms Beale," Mugo insisted. "The man who was attacked at the hotel can't speak at the moment. But he could type on his phone. He wants to speak to you urgently. He has an offer for you from Scarface."

CHAPTER 28

Saturday, 24 March, 07:30

Mugo joined Atieno-Masinde and Bakari for breakfast at their hotel restaurant. The new day had arrived with a bright blue sky and a light veil of clouds, heralding a humid, warm, tropical climate.

As Mugo poured himself a hot coffee, his phone vibrated in his trouser pocket.

He pulled it out, flipped it open and answered, "Detective Chief Inspector Mugo."

"This is Dalilah Beale. I intend to return to Nairobi soon. It would be helpful to know when I can speak to the man who has an offer from Scarface."

"I'm waiting for the doctor to tell me when he'll be able to speak without too much difficulty. How about a private conversation while we wait?"

"Provided you don't try to interrogate me."

"My priority is to fight the terror that is wreaking havoc in our country. I'll have to interrogate you sooner rather than later, Ms Beale."

"Just call me Dalilah, Inspector."

"Chief Inspector," Mugo corrected.

"I'm free from half past three. We can meet off the record, anywhere but in a police station."

"Perfect. I'll call you back in an hour and tell you where," Mugo said and hung up.

Bakari snorted. "Will it be one-on-one, or will her loudmouth lawyer accompany her?" he asked rhetorically. "Speak of the devil," he shouted, turning to the television on the wall, which showed the lawyer. The news ticker read: 'Jeffrey Kizito takes legal action against police harassment.'

"Can you turn up the volume?" Mugo asked a restaurant worker.

Lawyer Jeffrey Kizito was speaking:

"... Since the emergence of the Merciless Duo, cases of abuse of power and wrongful arrest of innocent people have skyrocketed across the country. There has also been a disturbing increase in cases of unjustified or unlawful house searches, often carried out without any visible criminal activity or evidence."

The cameras focused on Musamali Demba.

"What advice would you give our viewers who may encounter such harassment?"

Lawyer Jeffrey Kizito's face filled the screen.

"I would like to remind the public that you have the right to inform a family member, friend or lawyer of your arrest. In some situations, you may not be allowed to make the call yourself. However, it is important to stress that you have a constitutional right to inform a relative or lawyer of your arrest."

The camera panned to Musamali Demba.

"What are your views on the arrest and detention of your client Dalilah Beale yesterday? How do you intend to respond?"

The lawyer's face appeared on the screen.

"We will file a civil suit and prove that the officer acted in bad faith. He either knew or deliberately disregarded the fact that there was no legal basis for the arrest and detention of my client. As a result of this unlawful action, my client has suffered considerable inconvenience and distress."

◆◆◆

A warm sea breeze ruffled Dalilah's hair. She adjusted her sunglasses on the bridge of her nose as she crossed the road on her way to the region's largest psychiatric hospital. Her biological father, Mwasima Majimbo Junior, had been readmitted with a diagnosis of bipolar disorder.

"How did you decide to visit Majimbo Junior?" asked Sharona on the other end of the line.

"It was a spur-of-the-moment decision. I thought I'd make myself productive while I bided my time to talk to that assaulted hotel guest."

"What do you think Scarface wants or has for you?"

"I have no idea. I'm really curious."

"Me too," Sharona said. "Couldn't you reschedule your meeting with the manager of Sonaya Printers? Ah, forget I asked. She's leaving today for two weeks. Well, let's hope Majimbo Junior comes clean. He owes you some answers."

"By the way, I tried to call Sammy, but he didn't answer."

"Which Sammy? The street kid?"

"Yes. I have a bad feeling."

"I will call him and go and see him. Send me his number."

Dalilah cradled the phone between her ear and shoulder, slowing her pace as she fumbled through her bulging handbag for her ID.

"I'm already at the hospital. Keep your fingers crossed that the old man answers my questions."

"Fingers crossed. Remember: fortune favours the brave."

In a corner of the half-filled visiting room, a bald man with grey stubble and rough skin sat on a white plastic chair. His crumpled, stained hospital gown and the gaping hole in his trousers on the right thigh bore witness to hard days.

Dalilah walked over and greeted him with a simple "Hi."

With dry, chapped lips, Majimbo Junior sneered, "You ... you finally c-c-come to see me." The dark brown, sunken skin under his eyes – the result of countless battles within his body – seemed much thinner, the blood vessels more pronounced.

Dalilah sat down on a white plastic chair opposite the man.

"Er ..." The rehearsed opening speech had slipped her mind. She took a deep breath and looked around. Seeing a guard with a watchful gaze and two nurses in white coats and headscarves seemed to help calm her nerves. She took two bottles of Coke from her shopping bag and handed one to Majimbo Junior.

"Just a b-b-bottle of Coke?" he stammered, accepting the soft drink.

"I d-debated whether to g-get you anything at all." The tension had irritated a nerve, causing Dalilah's vocal cords to quiver.

Majimbo Junior clucked his tongue, unscrewed the bottle with difficulty, took a swig and burped loudly.

"I s-s-saw you on TV. Th-this false pomposity th-that you c-c-carry around with you ... th-that you flaunt here ... th-that is just a f-f-false front, girl."

"My name is still Dalilah, not girl." Her voice was sharp, her tone biting and laced with a hint of venom. "*Girl* is the helpless minor that you ... that you ..."

"Wh-where are your m-m-manners?" he whispered, his dainty fingers clutching the bottle belligerently. "Have ... sh-show respect f-f-for your elders."

"Respect must be earned. So start earning it by telling me what you did to Lucinda and Mum."

"M-M-Mum?" he mimicked her, using air quotes – his arthritic fingers made it look like he was waving, so Dalilah cocked her head to the side to see who it was.

"Yes, Mum. What happened to her?"

"I'll t-t-tell you what: i-i-if that-that whore you call M-Mum … i-if she hadn't-hadn't been whoring a-around with the who-whole n-n-neighbourhood …" He gestured wildly. "I d-did time … I d-did time for her disappearance, b-but the whore ran off with her l-l-lover."

Dalilah's mind catapulted back to that fateful night over two decades ago. The vivid memory of the last time she had seen her mother flashed before her mind's eye: She could see her mother screaming as her father's insults and tirades escalated into fisticuffs …

"How s-s-stupid I was to r-r-raise you."

"Abusing your little children is what you call parenting?"

"You are not m-m-my children. And you were n-no longer children." He looked around, then lowered his voice. "If a g-g-girl starts bleeding down there, she c-can … she c-c-can … y-y-you know it."

Dalilah clenched her jaw, fighting the rising bile that threatened to choke her. Every fibre of her being screamed to pounce on the man, to tear at his leathery, wrinkled skin. But an unseen force wrapped around her wrists and held her still.

"Who is my biological father?"

"Your f-f-father? You c-carry the de-devilish blood of the witch – the M-M-Midnight Dancer of Dakacha."

"Midnight Dancer of Dakacha? What's his name?"

The man's hand trembled as he raised the bottle to his lips. He took a sip, burped croakily and whispered something.

"What?" Dalilah squealed. "That's not a name, is it?"

"You are g-g-getting on my nerves." He propped his hands on the armrest and struggled out of the chair. "I have to t-t-take a shit."

"Sorry, I didn't catch the name," she said, her right hand quickly disappearing into her handbag, past packets of tissues and crumpled receipts, before emerging with a pen and a small leather-bound diary. "Would you spell out the name for me, please?"

Without warning, he grabbed Dalilah's wrist, his eyes locked on hers with steely intensity.

"You know him, d-d-don't you?"

"No, I don't. This is the first time I have heard this."

"You l-liar. You d-d-do know him."

"Why should I lie? Why should I deny it?"

Majimbo Junior began to spell out the name, each letter stretched by his stutter.

No sooner had the letters of her supposed biological father's name formed into a coherent word than Dalilah gasped.

"You've got to be kidding me! This must be some ridiculous prank."

She scrutinised the man, but found nothing frivolous about him.

CHAPTER 29

Saturday, 24 March, 18:45

Mugo sat alone on the terrace of a beach hotel. Colourful light bulbs flickered around him, scattering insects with a crackling sound. Miriam Makeba's "Pata Pata" played softly in the background, blending with the rhythmic hiss of the waves kissing the shore. The location had been meticulously selected – a secluded celebrity retreat nestled in lush greenery and fortified by a vigilant security team that left nothing to chance. The paparazzi stood no chance.

He took a sip of his Guinness and watched as the setting sun bathed the endless expanse of azure water in golden light. A gentle but persistent breeze swayed the coconut palms, filling the air with the salty scent of the Indian Ocean.

After a moment's hesitation, he rose to greet Dalilah. Wearing a wig and large sunglasses, she was almost unrecognisable. A waiter arrived and placed two menus on the table.

"Shall we order first, Ms Beale? I'll foot the bill."

"Good idea. I'm starving. And please call me Dalilah. A little less formality would help keep the conversation from feeling like an interrogation."

"Fine, on a first-name basis."

They leafed through the menu in silence until the waiter returned to the table.

"I'll have kakori kebab with mint sauce to start," Dalilah ordered. "Then number twenty-seven with croquettes instead of fried potatoes."

"Twenty-seven with croquettes," the waiter noted on his slip. "What would you like to drink?"

"Ginger ale, with a slice of lemon and plenty of ice."

"Cheese balls with hot chilli sauce for starters," Mugo said. He leafed through the menu. "Then spare ribs with roast sweet potatoes."

The waiter picked up the menus and disappeared.

Mugo laced his fingers together and rested his elbow on the arm of his chair. He leaned forward slightly, his gaze steady but not overtly confrontational.

"It's none of my business, I know," he said, his voice low and measured, "but what brought you to the same hotel as the Duo's victim?"

"Dalilah's lips curled into a sneer. She took off her sunglasses and placed them on the table.

"Pure coincidence. I came to the coast in search of answers to the question of what role my business cards played in the attacks."

"Have you been able to get any answers yet?"

"I was arrested before I could attend the meeting that brought me here."

"The victim's name is Oliver Morgan. Do you know him?"

"Never heard of him." She paused for a moment. "If I may ask, a little boy was escorted out of the lift that day. Was he found in Oliver Morgan's hotel room? If yes, may I know his name?"

"His name is Bahati Balozi."

Dalilah reached for her smartphone. Navigating to her Excel app, she opened her extensive list and searched for Bahati and Balozi using the 'find and replace' function.

There was no match.

"I'd like to contact the boy and his family," she said, watching the waiter weaving between the tables with their starters.

Mugo thanked the waiter, waited until he was out of earshot and asked, "Why do you want to contact the boy and his family?"

"I have a hypothesis that every single one of these men who have been attacked is a child molester."

The cheese ball that Mugo had speared with his fork floated in the air, frozen on its way to his mouth. His full attention was now captured.

"Every business card I give out has a unique handwritten number. They are case numbers that correspond to the abused children in my care. I affectionately refer to them as my 'protégés'."

"Protégés," he repeated, putting the cheese ball back on the plate.

Dalilah took a bite of the kakori kebab and spoke through her half-full mouth: "Suppose a man called Jack is attacked, and a business card with case number 1 is found at the scene. I would hypothesise that Jack was targeted because he sexually assaulted my protégé, who is assigned case number 1."

"In other words, you are saying that the attacks and the business cards left behind were not random but calculated retribution?"

"Hypothesis, I said. But I firmly believe that the Duo's mission is to give these sexual predators a taste of their evil. To make them feel a physical and psychological torture similar to the one they inflicted on the child sex victim."

"These are grave allegations, Dalilah."

"Yes, they are. I have recently received confirmation that my protégé, case number seventy-six, was sexually abused by MP Kosgey. Unless I am entirely mistaken, the business card found after his attack should bear the number seventy-six."

Mugo didn't waste a moment. He reached into his pocket, pulled out his phone and called the Digital Sleuth.

"Hi, boss," he answered.

"Access MP Kosgey's evidence file," Mugo ordered. "Specifically, the business card ..." He turned to look at the waiter who had returned to the table.

"Is everything all right with the food?" the waiter enquired.

"Everything's fine. We are slow eaters," Mugo assured him. "Another Guinness for me, please." He turned to Dalilah. "Would you like a glass of wine?"

Dalilah nodded. "Red wine. Merlot or Cabernet Sauvignon."

The Digital Sleuth's voice boomed in Mugo's ear: "Got it!"

"I need the number on the business card," Mugo instructed.

"The mobile or landline number? There's also a toll-free number."

"I said number," Mugo emphasised, "not phone number."

"My bad. You mean the red handwritten number? It is seven six, seventy-six."

"Seventy-six," Mugo repeated. "Thank you."

He snapped the phone shut and let the beer run down his throat. Then he tried to refill his glass, but there were only drops left in the bottle.

"When did you find out there was a connection between the victims and the business cards left at the scene?" he asked.

"Recently." She took a sip of her ginger ale. "It's important that this boy, Bahati Balozi, is examined soon for signs of physical and sexual abuse."

"The boy and his mother spoke highly of Oliver Morgan. The mother said there were plans for an informal adoption."

"Some children who are abused by someone they trust and love may think it's normal. They may not understand that the abuse is wrong."

"Your assumption may be supported in some cases, but business cards are not always left behind after attacks. For example, no business card was found in Oliver Morgan's hotel room."

Mugo's phone vibrated on the table.

"Hello," he answered Atieno-Masinde's call.

"Hi. Just a quick update," her voice came through. "The Italian immigrant, Francesco Lombardo, seems to have left the country. He is nowhere to be found."

"Get hold of the boy, Bahati Balozi, who was found in Oliver Morgan's hotel room. He should be examined by a doctor for sexual abuse immediately."

"Are you saying Oliver Morgan abused him?"

"The Duo's motive is beginning to emerge. It seems they knew about Oliver Morgan's shady dealings and unleashed their twisted vigilante justice on him." He fixed his gaze on Dalilah, his words dripping with a deliberate drawl as he continued, "The question is, how did they know? How could they trace him back to the hotel he had checked into just two days ago?"

◆◆◆

The shrill chirping of a bird pierced Oliver Morgan's room. It was the designated ringtone for an incoming call from his mother.

Oliver mustered the last of his strength to force the words past his cracked, swollen lips: "Hi, Ma."

"Oh, Oli, I can't believe this has happened to you?" Panic laced his mother's voice. "Charlotte said you were attacked in the hotel. How bad is it?"

"It's ... um ... I'm ..." His voice trailed off. Bone-deep exhaustion had gripped him, his energy sapped by the unrelenting pain that, despite painkillers and sleeping pills, disturbed his sleep and overwhelmed his nervous system.

"Please, tell me you'll be all right, Oli." Her voice broke with emotion. "Are you in a decent hospital ... I mean, a reputable one?"

Oliver turned his phone's camera towards his opulent room.

"Lots of amenities, I see. Do they work? Are the doctors competent?"

"Ma ... we'll ... chat later."

"What are you hiding from me, Oli? Why don't you look into the camera?"

Oliver sighed and held the camera in front of his face.

"Oh, my goodness!" The silent struggle against the suffering he didn't want to express, but couldn't hide, was evident in the tense lines around his eye and the stiffness of his jaw. "I'll book a flight—"

"No!" Oliver growled.

An involuntary groan escaped his lips. He ended the call abruptly and clawed desperately at the sheets as he waited for the sudden pain to subside. After what seemed like an eternity, he managed to send a text message to his mother.

> It was all my fault. I cocked it up proper.
> First of all, I've got to square things with the blokes who roughed me up.
> None of you are to set foot here.

CHAPTER 30

Monday, 26 March, 11:45

Dalilah Beale, accompanied by DCI Mugo and DS Bakari, entered the private hospital room.

Oliver reached for the remote control and raised the headboard of his bed. Every movement was an effort, and he felt it in every muscle.

"We already know each other," Mugo began. "This is Detective Sergeant Killian Bakari. And Dalilah Beale, the person you wanted to speak to."

Oliver nodded.

Dalilah and Mugo sat on the two bright, white leather visitors' chairs. Bakari stood beside them, phone in hand.

"I don't want to be recorded," Oliver said.

"You will not be recorded," Mugo assured him. "And for the record, I am officially instructing Dalilah Beale to keep your name and any information you give us confidential." He pulled a pen and notebook from his pocket. "Let's get started. State your name, age, country of origin and reason for visiting Kenya."

"I doubt that's relevant," Oliver countered, raking a hand through his dishevelled hair. His fingers caught briefly on a knot of matted strands and dried blood. "Actually, I have information that only concerns Dalilah."

"And we have some questions about your attackers, Scarface and the assistant," Bakari explained. "Suffice it to say, this is not an official police interview."

"But let me be clear, Mr Morgan," Mugo said, "If I detect the slightest hint of dishonesty in your answers, I will not hesitate to take you to the police station for a more thorough interrogation."

"I won't tolerate any threats from you," Oliver ventured. "I know my rights. Everyone, please leave my room."

There was a click as Dalilah opened her handbag. She pulled out her smartphone and unlocked it with a pattern swipe. Tapping her mobile, she stood abruptly, stepped closer to the bed and held the phone in Oliver's face.

"I know exactly why you were attacked," she hissed, her voice cold and venomous. "So don't you dare talk about your rights in my presence."

Thunderstruck, Oliver remained still, his swollen lips half-open. His hands trembled like aspen leaves in a storm.

"You can stay," he murmured, his chest rising and falling in uneven, laboured breaths. "But it still has to be a non-protocol conversation."

"Only if you answer all the questions." Dalilah's tone was stern.

"You can't expect me to answer every private question."

"This isn't a wish-fulfilment concert," Dalilah retorted sharply.

Mugo stood up, touched Dalilah lightly on the shoulder and said, "Can I talk to you outside for a moment?"

Gritting her teeth, Dalilah shuffled to the door behind the two detectives.

Mugo shut the door behind him.

Legs apart, arms crossed, he said, "I don't like being surprised like this. Why didn't you tell me you had incriminating information on him?"

"What's on the phone?" Bakari asked somewhat imperiously.

"Stuff you keep on your mobile," Dalilah said with a sneer, her tone sharp. "Next interrogation."

Bakari dug his teeth into his lower lip.

Dalilah looked at Mugo and whispered, "That was wild speculation. It was based on the hypotheses I explained yesterday. I showed him a picture of one of my protégés."

"Do you have any other surprises up your sleeve?"

"Expect surprises from Oliver Morgan," Dalilah shot back, "but not from me."

Oliver watched as the door opened, and the three people returned to his room.

The two officers remained standing. Dalilah sat down, crossed her legs and laced her fingers on her thighs. She looked ice-cold – almost like the assistant, Oliver thought.

"I'm listening," she said curtly.

"I was in bed when I heard a voice in the dark," Oliver began, his eye fixed on a spot on the ceiling. "I thought it was a burglar and begged him to take the money from my safe without hurting me. The assistant lit a candle. I tried to negotiate with Scarface, offering him the equivalent of a million shillings from my safe. Scarface said, 'I'll take your bribe. But perhaps you should reconsider because you cannot buy your way out of your impending doom'."

A searing pain coursed through his back, almost making him howl. He grimaced, squeezed his eye shut and clenched his teeth. For a moment, he writhed in pain. He swallowed two painkillers before he continued feebly.

"I begged Scarface not to take my offer as a bribe. He said, 'OK. Now I've got a million shillings. I will give it all to a children's charity'. I spontaneously mentioned the DS Savekids Foundation, which I had seen on the news. Scarface agreed. Then he warned me that if his donation did not reach the Foundation, I would face dire consequences for cheating him out of a million shillings. That's why I wanted to talk to you, Mrs Beale."

"This is a matter between you and Scarface. I want nothing to do with it," Dalilah blurted out gruffly. "Did Scarface tell you which child you were being punished for?"

Oliver swallowed hard, his throat as dry as a bone.

"Let's make this easy," Dalilah said. "Scarface told you why they had to punish you. What was the reason?"

Was Dalilah a co-conspirator, someone I shouldn't lie to? he wondered. What exactly did she know?

"Scarface listed the four charges of which I had been found guilty. Then he asked me if I pleaded guilty or not guilty. I ... I ..."

A knot of unease formed in his stomach, and his throat tightened, forcing him to hold his breath. He waited a moment for the unease to subside.

"I was scared to death of that man." He scratched the tip of his nose nervously. "That's why I pleaded guilty."

"Would you list the four charges," Mugo asked, jotting down a quick note on his pad.

His voice, when it came, was strained and uneven, somewhere between a whisper and a plea: "Sexual abuse of a child. Physical abuse of a child. Emotional abuse of a child. Defilement and rape of a child."

"Did you plead guilty out of fear or because you are guilty?" Dalilah asked.

"I had consensual sex with young prostitutes. I paid for their services. If they were underage, it was because they had lied about their age."

"Were they girls, or boys, or both?" Dalilah's face was a vivid mask of disgust.

Just before Oliver could say, "Does it matter?" an inner voice warned him: Watch your tongue, son. Homosexuality is not tolerated in these African countries.

"I'm straight," he replied succinctly.

"Did Scarface tell you how they found out about your paedophilia or how they managed to track you down?" asked Mugo.

"No. But he said that their persecution will not stop until the last victim of paedophilia has been rescued and rehabilitated. And when the last paedophile has been punished, either by themselves or by the law."

"What is your relationship with Bahati Balozi?" Dalilah wanted to know. "And how did you meet him?"

"Bahati is like my own child. I met him through an agency that places children for adoption abroad."

"Do you have children of your own?"

He avoided Dalilah's gaze. "Yes, two."

"How long have you had these paedophilic tendencies?" Bakari asked. "And how did it start?"

"My sex drive has always been strong. About ten years ago, I came across child pornography on the Internet. That's when I started to feel the urge."

"I doubt that you just stumbled across such illegal material. You chose the paedophile way," Bakari put it into perspective.

"Excuse me! You don't choose to be a paedophile; you are a paedophile," Oliver corrected. "It's a mental disorder."

"Therapy can help control urges and prevent abuse," Dalilah rebuked sharply. "There must be several institutions and psychiatrists or therapists in Europe you could have turned to."

Olivers shook his head. "Unfortunately, the British health system is not yet equipped to deal effectively with such a mental disorder. Every time I sought treatment, I was turned away. It seemed that no one wanted to be associated with a paedophile. Later, I saw a psychologist.

But he had no experience with such cases. I was his guinea pig. This only made my situation worse."

"I don't believe that, but I'll give you the benefit of the doubt. Scarface usually leaves my business card during the attack. Where is it?"

There was a knock at the door. Two nurses entered, the younger carrying an IV bag.

"How are you feeling, Mr Morgan?" the older nurse asked as she drew blood from a cannula in the back of his hand.

"Very uncomfortable," Oliver whispered. "My nappy ... I think it's slipped off."

Turning to the visitors, the nurse said, "I'm afraid you'll have to go out while I attend to my patient."

"Can you answer my question first, Mr Morgan?" Pure disapproval filled Dalilah's narrowed eyes, and Oliver felt its weight press down on him. His face contorted, and a raspy, guttural sound escaped his throat.

"I need to attend to my patient now," the nurse said imploringly. "Come back in the afternoon, but check with the doctor in charge before you leave. Dr Sharma."

◆◆◆

His pleas to be spared this ordeal were brushed aside. He sat in a rigid chair, his wrists and feet raw where the cable ties had bitten into his skin.

As his eyebrows were removed with hot wax that had seeped into his right eye, the pastor's son let out a piercing scream – a cathartic release that echoed throughout the room. The same ominous room where he had been held for over three weeks was lit by a rusty gas stove, its blackened surface hinting at its grim secrets. Above the open flames, a pile of iron bars and rods of various sizes glowed red.

"Perfect," said Scarface. The assistant had removed all the hair from the pastor's son's head and face, including his eyelashes, nose hairs and even the fine hairs in his ears.

With slow, deliberate movements, Scarface dragged a chair over, placed it beside the pastor's son and sat down.

"The assistant will now make you look like me," he revealed, pulling down his hood.

A shiver ran down the pastor's son's spine as he looked at Scarface's head, a patchwork of blisters and scars, looking raw and fresh. His heart began to beat like a drum against his ribs. He knew what was coming.

"You ... You're one of a kind, Scarface," he stammered, cold sweat soaking his vomit-stained shirt. "The last thing you'd want is someone else walking around with your face ... I mean, you don't want anybody else to look as unique as you do, do you?"

He watched Scarface's protruding Adam's apple bob.

"Nice try, pastor's son."

"Please, Scarface, do not disfigure my face."

"Trust me, you'll thank me later. This procedure is nothing compared to what your kind endure once I'm done with them."

"Please, Scarface, I beg you."

"You will be able to hide the physical scars with make-up or surgery. I'll spare you the mental anguish, the emotional and spiritual strain – the ones that leave permanent marks. You've probably read about it, right?"

The assistant put on a glove and took an iron rod from the stove, but Scarface stuck his index finger in the air. She nodded, placed the rod back in the fire, and took a glass ampoule and a hypodermic needle from her rucksack lying on the floor.

Scarface tilted the pastor's son's head, patted him lightly on the neck and said, "We'll give you an extra dose of adrenaline and antibiotics. We can't afford to have you screaming to death in our custody. We're not criminals."

"Yes, you are! You two are the most wanted criminals in the history of our country. And you, Scarface ... the Bible, which you keep quoting, says in no uncertain terms: 'Do not repay evil for evil'."

"You are absolutely right, pastor's son. The Bible says, 'Do not repay evil with evil, but with blessing. What we are going to do with you will be a great blessing to others. The Lord says: 'It's mine to avenge; I will repay'."

"This God complex is blasphemy, Scarface. I suggest we close our eyes and pray together for the forgiveness of our sins."

Scarface pursed his lips.

"Alright, pastor's son, I'll cover my eyes so you can pray. But pray only for your soul, for my soul is not like yours; it's undefiled."

"This is hypocritical. Delusional. You are not Mary, the mother of Jesus—"

"Speak, but do not raise your voice."

"Why do you want to disfigure my face? You never did this to your victims."

"I have great plans for you. Obey me, and you will live a normal life. But if you defy me, a punishment worse than death awaits you."

"I will obey. Just ... spare me this ordeal. Please, I beg you."

"Didn't you want to pray? Or have you lost your faith?"

"Yes, I'll pray," said the pastor's son, his voice trembling. "What are your plans for me?"

"You will soon find out. If everything goes according to plan, they will be amazed. And you, pastor's son ..." Scarface leaned closer, "you will laugh."

CHAPTER 31

Monday, 26 March, 15:40

"The number you have dialled is currently unavailable. Please try your call again later."

Dalilah's fingers tightened on her phone. The silence on the other end gnawed at her – the same creeping dread she had once felt in a deserted, dark alley, with the chilling certainty that she was not alone. She sought shelter from the scorching sun in the shade of a tall coconut tree and dialled the number of Sammy's supposed brother.

"Heelloo."

"Hi, Mickey, this is Dalilah. Do you remember me?"

"Waas uup?" he slurred.

"Are you high, Mickey?"

"You maa mothaa now or waat?"

"Hey, Mickey, Sammy's mobile is off. Is he with you?"

"No."

The connection broke.

A simmering ember rose inside Dalilah, ready to erupt like a volcano in the depths of her belly. She feared the worst had happened to Sammy and knew she was directly to blame. She leaned back against the coconut tree and let her mind drift back to that day in her office after Sammy had been examined.

"I have a present for you, Sammy," she said, handing Sammy a phone. "It's yours from today."

"Thank you."

"Press this button and then press one," she instructed him, demonstrating how to do it.

Sammy did so. Her phone rang. She took the call, and Sammy smiled as they spoke briefly on the phone.

She hung up and said, "That's easy, isn't it?"

"Yes."

"Try it again."

Sammy made the call.

"Great! You can always reach me this way."

"Okay."

She took her business card from her handbag and wrote the next case number on the card and her list: 1993.

"Sammy, I want you to keep this card in your trouser pocket at all times."

"Okay."

"You must never lose it or give it to anyone."

"Okay."

"When you put on a new pair of trousers—"

Sammy cut her off with an infectious laugh. When she joined in the laughter, Sammy ended it by saying, "I only have this one pair of trousers."

She turned in her swivel chair and looked out the window at the building across the street.

Sharona's conviction from the past echoed in her mind: *Daddy Stop saved you; I'm absolutely sure of it.*

The urge to protect Sammy with every fibre of her being overwhelmed her. She rose from her chair and walked over to the boy on the other side of the table. More like a sworn companion than a loving caregiver, she put her arm around his shoulder.

"Sammy, I want us to practise something together today."

"Okay."

"Say, 'Daddy, stop'."

"Daddy, stop."

"Say it louder, like you're screaming." She demonstrated.

Sammy repeated her words in a similarly shrill tone.

Am I really doing the right thing? her rational mind asked, and the feeling that she desperately needed psychiatric help gnawed at her.

Her more restless thoughts screamed in the background: Help this shy boy, who has no one to turn to, to find the courage to stand up to those who torment him. Confidence will get you through; cowardice will be taken advantage of.

"Sammy, I want you to listen to me very carefully."

"Okay."

"This *mzungu,* or any other man, will not hurt you if you shout 'Daddy, stop' as we have practised. If the *mzungu* wants to touch you, shout, 'Daddy, stop', just like we have practised."

"But he is not my daddy. I don't have a daddy."

"If you shout like that, my friends will hear and come and stop him."

"Okay."

Dalilah turned her back to Sammy, pressed her palms together and closed her eyes in silent prayer: *Dear Father in Heaven, don't let Sammy's cry of 'Daddy, stop' end in a tragedy …*

◆◆◆

Mugo, Atieno-Masinde and Bakari took their seats in the hotel's modest six-seater conference room, now reserved exclusively for their use. Laptops, mobile printers, crime scene toolboxes and water bottles were spread out on the table.

The familiar chime of an incoming video call sounded on the laptop before Atieno-Masinde, the nickname 'Digital Sleuth' flashing on the screen.

"Right on time," Atieno-Masinde answered the call. "We are gathered in our new incident room. Shoot."

"One of MP Kosgey's aides turned up here today and spilt the beans," the Digital Sleuth reported. "The MP is said to have admitted that the Duo attacked him."

Mugo huffed indignantly. He scratched his forehead and thundered, "That's nothing new, even if he never admitted it to us."

"The MP is said to have told them about something strange that happened that night," the Digital Sleuth continued. "Scarface had pinned him against the wall with one hand around his throat and holding the DS Savekids Foundation business card in front of his face. Each time Scarface tightened his grip, the initials 'D' and 'S' moved further apart, and the space between them was filled with letters. Finally, the card read: Dahdi Stoppa Savekids."

Mugo chuckled. "I had a confidential oral report. The MP was drunk and stoned that day. That statement should be taken with a pinch of salt."

"We have a victim on record who made a similar claim last year," the Digital Sleuth said. "Remember?"

"Now that you mention it. Try to work out the meaning of this phrase—"

A knock at the door made Mugo stop. Bakari got up and opened it.

Dalilah, standing in the doorway, turned to Mugo and asked, "May I have a word with you in private?"

"Ms Beale, we are a team," Bakari said firmly. "If it's relevant, say it here. Saves time and keeps us all on the same page."

Mugo met Dalilah's eyes, then gave a slow, deliberate nod towards an empty chair opposite him. Dalilah walked into the room and tripped over an extension cord that snaked out of an awkwardly placed socket next to the door, powering the devices on the table. She steadied herself and sat next to Atieno-Masinde.

A flip phone buzzed on the table. Mugo picked it up and answered the call. He pushed back his chair, stood up and walked to the window.

"I have read your affidavit," said the prosecutor on the other end of the line. "But I don't understand why you think the victim tampered with evidence at the crime scene."

"Dalilah Beale hands out her business cards to victims of sexual abuse, mostly minors," Mugo explained. "The Duo somehow got hold of these cards and left them behind after the attacks as incriminating evidence of child sexual abuse. We have reason to believe that these attacked men are guilty of child abuse and were aware of the implications of the cards. This may explain why business cards aren't always found at the scene of an attack."

"How is this evidence relevant to the investigation? You're not after paedophiles, are you?"

Mugo rubbed his chin thoughtfully. "The victim, Oliver Morgan, cooperated and stated that Scarface had accused him of raping a minor. But he insisted it was consensual sex with a young prostitute. Finding the business card will help Dalilah Beale confirm that Oliver Morgan is a child molester. And that would underline the motive behind the Duo's attacks."

"If Oliver Morgan is as cooperative as you say, why didn't he give you the business card voluntarily?"

"This further confirms that he knows the business card will expose any lies he has told. As he was taken straight to hospital, the card could still be somewhere in his hotel room, or he may have it with him in his hospital room."

"You didn't make that part clear in the affidavit."

"I'll rewrite it and send it to you right away."

"Good," came the reply. "The warrant should be ready within the hour."

"Thank you."

No sooner had Mugo hung up than Atieno-Masinde turned to Dalilah and said, "Bahati Balozi, the boy found in Oliver Morgan's room, was examined yesterday. There were no signs of physical or sexual abuse."

"How long has this man been in the country?" Dalilah wanted to know.

"He arrived in the country via Nairobi on the 13th of this month, flew to Mombasa on the 21st and took a flight to Diani on the afternoon of the 22nd, where he was attacked that night."

"Where did he stay in Nairobi?"

"We don't have that information yet. He may have stayed in private accommodation. He has a multiple-entry visa."

"My youngest protégé is an eleven-year-old street boy. He was sexually abused by a white man in Nairobi. When we were at the hospital, I showed Oliver Morgan the photo of the boy. Only then did he open up to us, but not without reservations. I can't nail him without the business card."

"Speaking of business cards, some victims reported strange things that happened when Scarface showed them the cards. I won't go into details now. The name Dahdi Stoppa allegedly appeared on the business card." Atieno-Masinde spelt out the name.

Suddenly, Dalilah stood, eyes wide open, mouth slightly agape, obviously processing what she had heard.

"Sorry, I need some time alone," she breathed as she headed for the door.

CHAPTER 32

Monday, 26 March, 18:15

Omari Sekibo sat spellbound at the bedside of his friend and boss, Oliver Morgan. With every word of the harrowing account of the attack and its devastating health consequences, Omari's chest tightened like a drumskin stretched in the heat.

"If Scarface told you that the business card was proof of your guilt, that means either Dalilah Beale is connected to the Duo, or she's the assistant, as is now rumoured."

Oliver pressed his lips into thin lines and clenched his hands into fists, his knuckles chalky white as if the blood had abandoned them.

"Get my trousers from the wardrobe," Oliver said. "The business card is in the pocket."

"You can't be serious, boss. Why are you walking around with it? Do you want to end up in our prisons? Do you have any idea what the inmates will do to you if they find out why you are in there?"

"How could I've gotten rid of it in my condition? I can't even get outta bed without a hand, can I?"

Omari stood up and grabbed Oliver's trousers from the wardrobe.

"Fuck!" he wailed, pulling out the business card with trembling hands. "I'm just as guilty, maybe worse. I made false promises to the parents of these kids."

"I'm sorry for getting you mixed up in it. Might ease your mind a bit to know you're not guilty of what Scarface accused me of. Doubt they'd be after you."

Omari felt his heart pounding in his ear, drowning out the reassuring words. The creeping feeling of being watched tightened like a noose around him, forcing him to step to the window and scan the manicured garden below.

"I also need you to get rid of the hard drive from the hotel safe," Oliver instructed. "The code is 2020. Burn the thing until it's ashes. You got the spare key, right?"

"No, I had given it to Scarface. Of course, I have the key. But will they let me in? It's a crime scene."

"You'll have to spin them a yarn about fetching my meds from the safe."

"Fuck, fuck!" He slipped the business card into his trouser pocket.

"Relax, mate. Can you give Vitória in Malindi a ring? I need to chat with her before she talks to my mum."

"Your ex Vitória García?"

"Yes, her."

"Boss, the fewer people who know about this, the—"

A knock at the door silenced Omari. He felt the contents of his stomach turn to an uncontrollable consistency as the two familiar faces, Dalilah Beale and DCI Dennis Mugo, entered, followed by a man and a woman, each carrying a black hard plastic case. Two doctors were close behind.

"See you tomorrow, boss," Omari called.

As he made for the door, Mugo grabbed his arm and said, "Not so fast. First, may I know your name and your relationship to this man, Oliver Morgan?"

Omari's nostrils flared, each breath a struggle to get air into his lungs.

He forced a smile and replied, "Omari Sekibo is my name, sir. Oliver Morgan is my boss."

No sooner had Dalilah heard the name than the electrician's words echoed in her head: The man I followed is called Omari. I think he was an errand boy for someone who lived in the luxurious aparthotel.

Convinced that this was no coincidence, Dalilah rummaged through her handbag, yanked out her phone, and tapped frantically on the screen as she rushed to the door.

"Oliver Morgan, we have reason to believe you tampered with the evidence left in the hotel room after your attack. That's why we're going to ..."

She closed the door, cutting off Mugo's words, and dialled the electrician's number.

"Pick up, pick up, pick up," she urged telepathically as the dialling tone rang in her ear.

"Hello, Dalilah," the electrician's voice rumbled from the other end.

"Please give me the full name of that man who took the street kid Sammy to the apartment hotel."

"I can barely hear you, Dalilah. Hang on, I'm going to a quieter area."

"Shit," she cursed as she saw Omari Sekibo leave the room and hurry away.

Oliver shuddered. The snap of latex as DS Atieno-Masinde pulled on her gloves sounded like a distant gunshot.

"Your trousers look a bit out of place, Mr Morgan," she said, pointing to the trousers wedged between the wardrobe doors. Without hesitation, she grabbed the trousers and felt them from top to bottom. Then she searched the nearly empty cupboard and drawers. "No business card."

"Did the man who just left the room take the business card from your trousers, Mr Morgan?" Mugo asked.

Oliver tried to mask the answer with a cough.

The door burst open, and Dalilah shouted, "Omari Sekibo is the man!" She strode to Mugo and whispered in his ear.

Mugo's reaction was not long in coming. "DS Bakari, stop this Omari Sekibo."

Bakari stormed out of the room.

"Mr Morgan, you flew to Mombasa via Nairobi." Mugo's gaze was cold, piercing. "Where did you stay in Nairobi?"

"I ... ah ..." Oliver kneaded his temple, where a tension headache had made itself felt. "Don't I need a lawyer?"

"Of course, you have the right to legal representation," Atieno-Masinde replied.

"But you're going to need an excellent lawyer," Dalilah hissed. She stepped closer to Oliver's head, leaned forward and lowered her voice. "Omari Sekibo is a pimp with absolutely no scruples. Was the eleven-year-old boy he brought to you a prostitute who claimed to be of legal age?"

Without warning, unseen hands wrapped around Oliver's neck and wrists, pinning him relentlessly to the bed. A stench hit him, suffocating and familiar, like that of Scarface. His legs jerked involuntarily, as if he were sitting on a live electrical wire. Overwhelmed, he turned and collapsed to the floor.

As Mugo and the two doctors helped Oliver back into bed, Dalilah moved sideways, her phone angled just right. With muted clicks, she snapped three pictures of Oliver's face.

"Hyperventilation syndrome," one of the doctors announced.

Mugo took the doctor aside and challenged him in a low voice: "I don't think so, doctor. Looks like a staged stunt to me."

"People unconsciously react to stress, panic or excitement by taking deep, rapid breaths," the doctor lectured. "This causes an increased exhalation of carbon dioxide, which leads to a lack of calcium in the blood. The result is increased nerve and muscle excitability, which can lead to muscle spasms and, in extreme cases, hyperventilating tetany. That's it for today, chief inspector."

◆◆◆

Dalilah walked through the hospital's double doors, so engrossed in a text message that she only noticed DS Bakari when she almost bumped into him. A sigh of frustration escaped her as Omari Sekibo was nowhere to be seen. She stepped out into the scorching sun, heading for the shade of a secluded corner as she dialled Sammy's number.

The out-of-service message played, and her stomach clenched. With trembling fingers, she dialled Mickey's number.

"Hello."

"Mickey, it's me, Dalilah. Please don't hang up this time."

"What do you want?"

"Is Sammy there?"

"Samiii," Mickey shouted, "come here. The chips masala biatch is on the phone."

That was such a load off Dalilah's mind. She was so relieved that Mickey's insolence sounded like a compliment.

"Make it snappy, homie," she heard Mickey say in the background.

Sammy's voice came through: "Hello."

"Hi, Sammy. How are you?"

"Good."

"Hey, Sammy, I told you to leave your phone on all the time."

"My battery is dead. There is nowhere to charge it."

The boy's low voice prompted her to dip the tip of her index finger into her free ear to block out the traffic noise.

"Hurry up, homie," Mickey called in the background.

"Sammy, do you still have that card I gave you?"

There was a moment of silence at the other end of the line.

"No," Sammy breathed. "Are you mad at me now?"

"No, Sammy, I'm not mad at you. Tell me, were you taken to the *mzungu* again—"

"Enough!" Mickey's voice interrupted her flow of words.

Shaking her head, Dalilah stared at her phone screen, which had returned to the home screen.

Did Sammy lose the business card? Or was it taken from him to appear at the scene of an attack? she wondered as she walked to the waiting car – Atieno-Masinde at the wheel, Bakari in front and Mugo in the back.

She got in. The car had barely started when Mugo tapped the centre console of the back seat and announced, "Dahdi Stoppa."

"Dahdi Stoppa," Dalilah echoed. "The other day, I went to see my father, Majimbo Junior. He told me that my biological father was a Midnight Dancer from Dakacha called Dahdi Stoppa."

Almost simultaneously, Atieno-Masinde looked in the rear-view mirror; Bakari turned to the rear; Mugo to the side. Dalilah watched the astonishment on their faces.

She detonated the next bomb: "DS, in the name of my foundation, DS Savekids stands for 'Daddy Stop', which is pronounced almost exactly like the name Dahdi Stoppa. Officially, DS stands for Dalilah and Sharona."

"I doubt it, but we'll see if the business card we found in the toilet has a lenticular animation effect," said Mugo.

"What is that?" asked Dalilah.

"It's the flip effect, where an image changes or flips into another image when viewed from a different angle," Atieno-Masinde explained. "Would you mind telling us why you chose such a strange name for your foundation?"

"How can I best describe it? A firm belief. A superstitious delusion. I was convinced that shouting 'Daddy, stop' could save a child in the clutches of a sexual predator. Somehow, I still believe it."

"There must be a good reason why you cling to such a strange superstition or belief," Bakari speculated. "Has it directly influenced you?"

Dalilah couldn't quite pinpoint the source of her aversion to Bakari. Was it his raspy voice or the prominent scar on his cheek that gave him a rough appearance? Or was it her innate moral compass that made her uncomfortable around those who were fundamentally immoral?

"Why I hold on to a superstition, strange or not, is none of your business," she barked, a little harsher than she'd intended. "End of discussion."

"Then let's summarise what we've gathered so far," Bakari said with a wry grin. "The Duo are leaving behind the business cards you gave your protégé. They are acting based on the judgement you have passed on these men, and I dare say some of it may be unjust. The basis of my argument is this: you issued the business cards after hearing and unconditionally believing the testimony of your clients. In doing so, you incriminated the alleged perpetrators without any substantial evidence. For instance, you say Oliver Morgan is guilty of child molestation. Where's the evidence?"

"Wow! Your talk about injustice is so powerful. Where were you to talk about my unjust arrest? Do you know what your dear colleague, Sergeant Kioko, who arrested me, said? He said, and I quote: 'I'd rather inconvenience an innocent person than let a wanted criminal slip through the cracks of justice'."

"I'm sorry for your wrongful arrest," Bakari said. "But every decision made during an arrest is based on the information available at the time."

"This Oliver Morgan, the MP, and the rest of the despicable bunch are receiving round-the-clock care and medical attention. Yet most of the real victims have to endure their physical and psychological torture in silence. They are never medically examined, receive no therapeutic treatment, no help ..."

Bakari's snobbish look made Dalilah pause.

"What?" she snapped. "You expect me to condemn the Duo's actions? I won't. The main purpose of my information is to expose the perpetrators of child abuse who are falsely portrayed as victims. They are by far the worst criminals."

"I'm sure you are familiar with our country's legal system and norms," Bakari said. "Everyone—"

"Do you have any idea what these young victims of sexual exploitation and abuse go through?" Dalilah cut him off. "They endure anxiety, struggle with low self-esteem, face challenges in forming and maintaining relationships. They develop eating and sleeping disorders, depression and a host of other problems. So let's not get bogged down in discussions about our country's legal system and standards. The welfare of these children is a far more important issue to discuss."

The guard at La Dasara Beach Resort opened the gates. Atieno-Masinde drove in and found a shady spot in the open car park. She left the engine running, the air conditioning still on, and turned to face Dalilah.

"It's safe to assume that the Duo will use your business card in their next ambush," Atieno-Masinde said. "How many have you handed out, if I may ask?"

Dalilah laced her fingers together, rested her chin on them and squinted at Bakari, who was looking at his vibrating phone.

"I have given out almost all of my 2,000 business cards."

"What?" Bakari's phone dropped from his hand. "You gave out 2,000 cards?"

"What surprised you more: the number of men who could be targeted or the fact that 2,000 cases of child abuse are just a drop in the ocean?"

Bakari snorted.

"Let's get back to Dahdi Stoppa," Mugo said. "You seem convinced that shouting 'Daddy, stop' can save a child from a tormentor. I assume you have a good reason – perhaps even a justifiable one. Would you care to enlighten us?"

Dalilah stared ahead, her eyes unblinking, betraying nothing of the storm raging within. She felt her throat constrict painfully, but she forced the words through the tightening knot.

"Daddy Stop saved me – from the clutches of a child abuser."

"Who or what saved you?" asked Mugo. "Dahdi Stoppa, the Midnight Dancer of Dakacha, or the cry, 'Daddy, stop'."

"That," Dalilah whispered, "is a good ..." Her voice faded. Without another word, she opened the door and slipped out, disappearing into the moonless night.

Bakari exhaled sharply. "This woman is so full of secrets."

"What exactly do you think she's hiding?" Atieno-Masinde's voice barely rose above a whisper as her gaze swept the darkness, searching for any trace of Dalilah.

CHAPTER 33

Tuesday, 27 March, 11:45

"Looks like two different people to me," Atieno-Masinde said into her headset, seated in a six-seater police helicopter between Bakari and a retired OCPD (Officer Commanding Police Division), with Mugo in front of them. They were on their way to Dakacha.

Atieno-Masinde compared the two pictures again. One was the more than twenty-year-old mug shot of the Midnight Dancer of Dakacha, Dahdi Stoppa, born Daudi Ratego. The other was the sketch of Scarface, digitally retouched for comparison – the deep scars smoothed out and the right eye protruding from its socket reconstructed.

For hours on end, a team at the Dakacha police station had hunched over dusty and frayed files, painstakingly combing through the non-computerised archive. Eventually, the weathered documents had come to light, revealing faded mugshots and fingerprints of Dahdi Stoppa. The documents had been scanned and emailed to the task force.

"It's one and the same person," Bakari remarked. "In the sketch, the man looks more like a cold-blooded psychopath. In the mug shot, he looks sad and reserved, almost shy. You could be forgiven for thinking, 'This man can't hurt a housefly'."

"Dahdi Stoppa was known as the man with two faces," said the retired OCPD, a native of Dakacha and an old close friend of Mugo. "People described him as threatening and intimidating, especially when he was up to no good at night. Those who met him during the day described him as shy and reserved."

"Why is he called the Midnight Dancer of Dakacha?" Atieno-Masinde wanted to know.

"Dahdi Stoppa comes from a clan where witchcraft is passed down from generation to generation. The ceremonies took place at midnight."

"In other words, he is a night runner?" Bakari deduced. "They are said to be possessed by demonic spirits and terrorise their fellow villagers and neighbours at night."

"The Midnight Dancer of Dakacha was no night runner," said the OCPD. "This man was revered, even respected, for his supposed supernatural powers. People believed he could cast or lift curses, not just on individuals, but on entire families. Those afflicted with a disease or possessed by evil forces sought him out. He had a large, almost fanatical, following."

"Is this midnight madness still going on?" asked Mugo.

"The man has been inactive for many years. Rumour has it that one of his sons is being groomed to take over his nocturnal activities. Once he has taken up his calling, or vocation, he will be given an appropriate name. Daudi Ratego became Dahdi Stoppa."

Atieno-Masinde adjusted her headset and asked, "What was Dahdi Stoppa's vocation?"

"The role of the Midnight Dancers of Dakacha was to help the weakest and most vulnerable in society, mostly children and women. They helped the physically and mentally disabled, the poor and desperate, the neglected and abandoned. Dahdi Stoppa was said to be dedicated to helping children in need. But I don't know how he did it – or if he did it all."

"Would you have thought that Scarface was the Midnight Dancer of Dakacha?" Mugo asked.

"Never. In the sketch, Scarface doesn't even look human."

"We are coming in for a landing," the captain announced.

◆◆◆

Dalilah, back from Mombasa, emerged from her house, her smartphone pressed to her ear.

She jumped into the back of an Uber and said, "Hi."

"Hello, Dalilah," the driver replied with a smile.

Dalilah closed the door and turned her attention to the voice on the other end of the line.

"Yes, Mickey, I'm back in town."

"We're starving. Me and Sammy. And our sister Shiro."

"How about we meet in an hour? For masala chips and sausages."

"Now you're talking! See you."

"Wait …"

Mickey had hung up.

Just as her finger hovered over the green button to call Mickey back, her phone vibrated and the name DCI Dennis Mugo flashed on the screen.

"Hello, Dennis."

"We have mug shots of Dahdi Stoppa," Mugo said, standing a few metres from the helipad, his finger pressed to his other ear to block out the sound of the helicopter's propeller. "I'm sending them to you as promised. It's a mug shot from about twenty years ago. I'll need your email address."

"I'm sending it to you right now via WhatsApp."

"I don't use WhatsApp. Send it via regular SMS service."

Unlike his younger colleagues, who had a plethora of apps on their smartphones, Mugo clung to an old flip phone that was on its last legs. Once, when a colleague teased him about his outdated device, he argued, "*What can a smartphone do that my flip phone can't? I make calls and send messages – what more do I need? As long as an old cat can still catch mice, it's good enough for me.*"

Like the proverbial cat, Mugo seemed to have made a good catch with Dalilah.

"One more thing, Dalilah, I will also send you a series of codes made up of numbers and letters. Look at them and try to decipher what they mean. You may swap the letters and numbers from one code to the next, but the original sequence must be maintained."

◆◆◆

In a police jeep, with the OCPD at the wheel, the task force drove down a country road without signs or landmarks.

"Dahdi Stoppa would be around fifty years old," DS Atieno-Masinde initiated a brainstorming session. "If he is Scarface, how can he be kicking butt like he's in his prime?"

"Dalilah's a wildcard," Bakari said bluntly, leaving no doubt that he was critical of his boss's decision to involve Dalilah extensively. "There's something calculated about her – unpredictable, maybe even manipulative. She could lead us down the wrong path with a fib."

A quizzical look crossed Atieno-Masinde's face. "Give her the benefit of the doubt."

"Why don't we get a court order and question her clients ... or her protégés, as she fancifully calls them?"

"Come on, Killian," Atieno-Masinde said, shaking her head. "That would be a waste of time and energy. For a start, Dalilah's protégés are unlikely to give us any information. Even if they did, we'd need to carefully assess the credibility of their statements before taking any decisive action."

Bakari scratched his head. "We're allowing her too much control over the pace of the investigation. She only talks to us on her terms."

"An informal conversation with Dalilah would get more out of her than any legal threat," Mugo said, impatience flickering beneath his dismissive tone. "I make the decision. Period."

"Here we are," the OCPD called out, parking the jeep in front of a tree-lined compound that looked more like a forest retreat. "Home and last known address of the Midnight Dancer of Dakacha."

A middle-aged woman greeted the officers at the bamboo gate.

Mugo wrinkled his nose – the smell emanating from the compound was unbearable. He introduced himself and his team, his voice calm despite the unpleasant distraction.

"Can you state your name and describe your relationship with the Midnight Dancer of Dakacha, Dahdi Stoppa?" Atieno-Masinde asked.

The woman smiled warmly. "My name has an interesting and significant backstory. My mother was creative through and through. She could find inspiration in the most unlikely places, or when the going got tough. Such was the case when a plague of locusts swept through our neighbourhood many years ago." The woman paused for a moment. "My mother said it was the worst she'd ever seen. The sky was filled with the sound of swarms of locusts flapping their wings. They ate every blade of grass and every leaf in just a few days. I was born on the second day of the locust invasion, and my mother named me Ndiema. This name will forever be associated with the year and month when nature really let loose—"

Mugo raised his hand. "Enough. I want a simple yes or no," he said in a cold, commanding voice. "Is the Midnight Dancer of Dakacha, Dahdi Stoppa, at home?"

Ndiema's eyes widened, the whites standing out clearly against the dark pupils. She hesitated and took a breath before answering, "No."

"What is your relationship with Dahdi Stoppa like?" Atieno-Masinde's voice was warm, with a certain charm that encouraged openness.

Ndiema's face lit up like a sunrise. "Working for the Midnight Dancer is an honour beyond words. Many would like to take my place in this homestead. My fellow villagers, my friends, my family – they all share this incredible honour. They look at me with admiration, knowing that I am part of something so revered. They say that my hands help to maintain the sanctity of the Midnight Dancer, especially when Mama Daudi is away. They—"

"Who is Mama Daudi, and where is she?"

"Mama Daudi is the mother of the Midnight Dancer. Her return usually depends on how quickly she sells her herbs at the bazaar in Mombasa. She usually returns on Monday or Tuesday, but sometimes on Wednesday. She rarely comes back on—"

"Enough!" Mugo thundered. "Does anyone else live here apart from Mama Daudi?"

"No." She was chewing on her fingernails.

Atieno-Masinde's voice carried a note of reassurance as she asked, "When did you last see Dahdi Stoppa?"

A smile spread across Ndiema's face. "I was young when I first saw the Midnight Dancer. It was also the last time I saw him. It was a night I'll never forget." She giggled, her whole expression radiating a sense of pride and fascination. "The villagers had gathered in a clearing under a full moon, ready for the ceremony to begin. Drummers were singing. I was in the centre of a circle, holding a white rooster we'd brought as an offering. Then the Midnight Dancer appeared, decorated with feathers and pearls."

Just as Mugo was about to order Ndiema to cut her long story short, he noticed a subtle shift in her posture. Her eyes sparkled, and for a brief moment, her hand trembled as if on the verge of some crucial revelation. Mugo forced himself to be patient.

"When the Midnight Dancer came to me, I knew it was time. With a swift movement, he took the life of the bird and collected its blood in a sacred bowl. Then he dipped his fingers in the blood and smeared it on my forehead. He chanted in tongues. I felt connected to something much greater." Ndiema's voice grew louder and more energetic. "The Midnight Dancer exorcised the demons of dyslexia and dyscalculia from my head. Then he summoned the spirits of the great scholars who had died, and they surrounded me. They allowed their knowledge and wisdom to penetrate my mind. From that night on, I was a different person. The confusion that once clouded my thoughts was gone. I was pretty much the best in my class, every single year—"

"Yet you didn't do well enough at school to become a doctor or a lawyer," Bakari cut in, his tone questioning.

Ndiema fiddled nervously with the hem of her blouse as she grumbled, "I could have been a lawyer or a professor. Everything changed after my father got into a heated argument with the Midnight Dancer. To teach him a lesson, the Midnight Dancer put a curse on my father and our lives were turned upside down. The curse brought poverty and hardship, and—"

"Give me the number to reach Mama Daudi," said Atieno-Masinde.

"Like me, she has never owned a phone. Not that I'm complaining," she quickly added. "I don't long to own one. Menya makes all the arrangements. Ah, of course, the name means nothing to you. Menya is the herdsman and the one who organises my work schedule. He is out at the moment. He has taken the animals to the stream to drink. When he returns, he will tell me if I should stay until tomorrow, or if—"

"Enough," Mugo ordered. "We are going to look around the house and the grounds."

"I am not allowed to let anyone in here at all ..."

A flock of birds flew overhead, and Ndiema's face suddenly darkened.

"This isn't a coincidence, it's a warning," she growled, her voice full of conviction.

"What are you talking about?" Mugo asked, his patience wearing thin.

"Didn't you hear the birds that just flew by? They didn't sound happy. Birds and wild animals in this area react with joy or anger, depending on the mood of the Midnight Dancer."

"Rubbish."

"If I allow you to inspect this property without permission, it could be worse than the curse that tormented my father. It would be no different from ... from the red-skinned prince of darkness stalking me with his pitchfork."

CHAPTER 34

Tuesday, 27 March, 12:15

Sammy, Mickey, and Shiro, a thirteen-year-old street girl, sat in a fast-food restaurant enjoying a feast of masala fries, sausages and refreshing milkshakes – all at Dalilah's expense.

Mickey burped loudly, making Shiro laugh.

Dalilah was infected by the laughter, which seemed to encourage Mickey to repeat his act. But his paper cup was empty, so he reached for Shiro's milkshake, only to find that it was empty too.

"You guys want more?" Dalilah asked.

Shiro's face scrunched up, her pupils dilated. She held out her slightly trembling hand to Dalilah and said, "Give us the money. We'll buy some food later."

With a mixture of compassion and caution, Dalilah pulled a handful of coins from her purse and handed them to Shiro.

Almost in unison, Shiro and Mickey jumped out of their chairs, clearly in a hurry to leave.

"Bring Sammy later," Mickey said. "He always takes so long to eat."

Dalilah nodded, and the two slipped out of the restaurant.

Sammy took a bite of the sausage. With his mouth full, he said, "I shouted 'Daddy, stop' to the *mzungu*. Two times."

Dalilah felt every muscle in her body tense. "Was it the same *mzungu*?"

"Yes."

"When was that?"

"The other night."

"Which night, Sammy? Monday, Tuesday, Wednesday?"

A honking car seemed to have caught Sammy's attention. He turned and looked out the window.

"Sammy, on what day were you taken back to the *mzungu's* house?"

"I don't know."

"Was it the same man who took you to the *mzungu*?"

Sammy nodded and stuffed chips into his mouth.

"What happened after you shouted 'Daddy, stop'?"

"He said, 'Shut up'," Sammy replied, his mouth still full, so Dalilah wasn't sure she'd got him right.

"Shut up?" she asked. "The *mzungu* told you to shut up?"

Sammy nodded.

"What happened then?"

"He wanted to hit me."

"He wanted to ... so he didn't hit you?" Dalilah asked carefully.

"Yes."

"Yes? Did he hit you?"

"No."

"What happened then, Sammy?"

"I covered my face because he wanted to hit me."

Dalilah instinctively placed a comforting hand on his shoulder and stroked him gently, careful not to stir his emotions too much. She had seen many victims break down in tears. Some even shut down completely, erecting an impenetrable wall around the subject.

"What happened after you covered your face?"

Sammy shrugged and sipped at his milkshake. Each sip made the drink disappear a little more, and that seemed to worry him.

"Try to remember, Sammy."

He stuffed a handful of chips into his mouth and mumbled, "The man came and ..." His words became muffled as he chewed noisily.

Dalilah didn't need a fox's keen sense of smell to pick up on the words Sammy had left unfinished. Whatever he was about to say felt like a prelude to something crucial.

She clenched her hands into fists, trying to suppress the restless trembling, but the sensation only intensified.

Sharona's superstitious belief echoed in her mind: You shouted 'Daddy, stop', and a man came. Daddy Stop saved you; I'm absolutely sure of it.

"Sammy, the man who came, what did he look like?"

Sammy slurped down the last drops of his milkshake, the hollow sound signalling that the cup was empty. The distorted expression on his face showed that he was sad about it – which seemed to be all that mattered to him at the time.

◆◆◆

Exigent circumstances had led the task force and the OCPD to enter Dahdi Stoppa's expansive front yard and proceed to the living room. Framed newspaper articles and black and white photographs hung on the walls, capturing moments of Dahdi Stoppa's outstanding achievements in various disciplines. Sports trophies and medals, now badly faded, lined a shelf.

"Looks like our man was an outstanding athlete," Bakari remarked, placing the black hard plastic case he was carrying on the floor. It contained various crime scene tools.

"The first thing I notice is his crooked smile," Mugo said, his gaze lingering on a portrait on the wall. "It radiates an almost palpable cynicism."

"Please don't touch anything," Ndiema called to Bakari, who had opened the door to an adjoining room.

Bakari entered the cramped, dark room, which looked more like a cluttered stall in a Maasai market. The only window was cracked and held in place with brown tape, letting in minimal daylight. He switched on his torch, its glow sweeping across an assemblage of animal skins of various shapes and sizes that covered almost every inch of the walls. Opposite, stretching from wall to wall, was a dilapidated doorless cupboard, sloppily painted black with inferior paint. It contained a disorderly collection of small animal skulls.

Bakari crossed the room and unlatched a wrought-iron door. As he pushed it, the hinges squeaked, sharp and grating, almost as a warning. Then it hit – a suffocating stench of decay.

Wrinkling his nose, Bakari stepped out into the backyard, where the partially eviscerated remains of wild animals in various stages of decomposition hung from the posts of the bamboo fence. The overwhelming stench seemed to emanate from a bloated hyena carcass dangling from a tree trunk, its entrails hanging like some macabre decoration.

"What have you found, partner?" shouted Atieno-Masinde, coming out with a handkerchief to her nose.

"The reason Scarface stinks, I think." Bakari moved closer to the hyena carcass. "Judging by the decomposition, this beast has been dead for no more than four weeks."

"How the hell do you catch a hyena?" Atieno-Masinde wondered aloud.

"Probably a sacrifice to the gods and ancestors to protect the inhabitants of the house," the OCPD surmised as he and Mugo stepped into the courtyard.

"What's that?" Bakari muttered. He approached the maggot-ridden carcass and examined it closely. "There's a glass jar stuck inside the hyena," he shouted. "Someone put it in there and did a shoddy job of stitching the animal up."

Bakari returned to the house, grabbed the hard plastic case and went back into the yard. He opened it and took out a disposable overall and a pair of latex gloves, which he put on. Then he reached into the case again and took out a pair of pliers and a scalpel.

"You might also want to wear a protective suit," he told Atieno-Masinde. "I'm going to need help getting the glass jar out of the poor hyena."

"I won't touch the carcass," Atieno-Masinde said, picking up a branch from the ground. She used it to push the carcass aside to give Bakari enough room to work. "Hurry up," she urged, looking away. She was accustomed to death, but mutilated animals were another matter entirely.

Bakari set to work, cutting the first few seams. As he cut the next seam, an unexpected eruption occurred, spewing maggots and putrid fluids at him and his partner.

Atieno-Masinde dropped the branch and clutched at her stomach, her features contorted in disgust at the mess that had spread over her face and dress.

"Hey, don't throw up here; I can't stand puke."

She gave Bakari a cold, piercing look. "Did you do this on purpose?"

"No. The Midnight Dancer of Dakacha is to blame for everything."

"It's not funny, just stop!" She dashed away.

Bakari pried open the carcass, reached inside and carefully pulled out the glass jar.

"We have human teeth here," he shouted. "They were probably knocked out of the victims as trophies. Or for sexual gratification."

"No, no, no, I don't think so," the OCPD countered, shaking his head. "The Midnight Dancer of Dakacha had an ego as boundless as the night sky. Thought he was a mastermind. When I was after him, his followers swore I'd never nail him. They praised him, said he was always several steps ahead." His voice dropped to a near whisper. "This? Looks like he left us some subtle telltale clues. I'll even bet he set up the board for a twisted game of chess."

◆◆◆

A waitress brought another vanilla milkshake and two sausages for Sammy.

Sammy reached for the sizzling sausage, but quickly pulled his hand back as the searing heat bit into his fingers. He smelt the sweet aroma of fried pork clinging to his fingers and licked them clean, one by one.

Dalilah smiled at him. "Taste good?"

"Yes."

"Tell me, Sammy, the *mzungu* said, 'Shut up'. He wanted to hit you, and you covered your face. Then a man came into the room."

"Yes."

"What did this man look like, Sammy?"

Sammy shrugged his shoulders, sipping at his milkshake.

If Scarface had turned up just as the mzungu was about to hit Sammy, wouldn't there have been reports of an attack at the aparthotel? Dalilah wondered. She reached for her phone and opened the gallery. Photographs of Oliver Morgan appeared alongside three other white men – faces she had randomly downloaded from the Internet.

Unable to find a suitable picture of Oliver Morgan online, she had resorted to using the one she had secretly taken of him in hospital. The digitally retouched image of Oliver Morgan showed him looking normal, with no bandage over his injured eye and no swollen lips.

"Sammy, look at this photo." She showed Sammy the doctored photograph of Oliver Morgan. "Is this the *mzungu* who told you, 'Shut up'."

Sammy's eyes darted across the white man's face for a split second before returning to what was most important – the thick, creamy milkshake in his hand.

"Is this the man, Sammy?"

"I don't know."

Dalilah tapped on one of the randomly downloaded photographs. The man's grey hair, pale skin and chubby cheeks contrasted sharply with Oliver Morgan's, making the comparison almost absurd.

"Is this the man?" she asked, showing Sammy the photograph.

Sammy looked at the photograph and asked, "Can I have another milkshake like the one Mickey had when I finish this one?"

"Chocolate milkshake?"

"Yes, chocolate."

"Yes, you will."

Sammy's eyes lit up with anticipation, obviously thrilled at the prospect of a chocolate milkshake. He pointed enthusiastically at the phone and said, "Yes, this is the *mzungu*. Can I have the milkshake now? I answered you."

"But you haven't finished your milkshake yet. When you finish, I will buy you a chocolate milkshake."

"Okay."

Dalilah flicked through the photographs and showed Sammy the one of Oliver Morgan. She asked, "Is this the man who said to you, 'Shut up'?"

Sammy looked disinterestedly at the phone and sucked almost greedily at his milkshake.

"Sammy, after the *mzungu* said, 'Shut up', you covered your face, and a man came. Is that right?"

"Yes."

"What did that man do?"

"The driver?" Sammy asked. "He took me back."

◆◆◆

DS Bakari, now resigned to the likelihood that the elusive Scarface was the mysterious Midnight Dancer of Dakacha, let his mind wander over the tangled threads of his career. He had encountered countless cunning and ruthless criminals. Together with his colleagues, they had hunted down cold-blooded bandits and hardened terrorists, individuals whose abrasive reputations instilled fear and terror in all who crossed their path. But anyone who had relevant information about these criminals either volunteered it or cooperated fully with the police to bring these dangerous individuals to justice. The case of the Merciless Duo proved to be far more unusual than anything they had dealt with before. It was as if the entire village had made a pact with the Midnight Dancer of Dakacha. A heavy, unnerving silence hung over those who seemed to know him; their palpable fear barely assuaged by the promise of police protection. The few who spoke chose their words carefully; their voices tinged with genuine awe and reverence for the Midnight Dancer.

About three kilometres beyond the Midnight Dancer's homestead, three young men sat in the shade of a baobab tree next to a thatched mud house. One of them matched the description of the herdsman Menyas. In front of them was a bottle of a yellowish traditional brew and a small FM radio with its antennas outstretched, broadcasting a reggae song. Next to one of the men was an open plastic bag containing a bundle of khat, the stimulating leaves and stems of which they chewed incessantly. As the khat was neither swallowed nor spat out, the bulges in their cheeks had grown to the size of tennis balls.

Bakari introduced himself and DS Rahab Atieno-Masinde, then asked the men for their names.

Menya took a sip of the brew – a drink that often brought a sense of grandeur to his otherwise mundane life. He then introduced himself and the others by their first names.

"We're looking for Dahdi Stoppa," Bakari said with a slight air of authority, "the Midnight Dancer of Dakacha. Where can we find him?"

"*Kpigadomohataa*! *Hivjushinilskia mzeemwashikikasekatambuakeli*," one of the men mumbled. His words were slurred, and Bakari couldn't understand him.

"Can you open your mouth properly and speak clearly?" Bakari thundered. He turned to Atieno-Masinde and asked, "Or did you understand the mumbler?"

"Not a word."

The so-called mumbler spat green saliva, the result of chewing khat. What he said next sounded like his tongue was numb.

"Menya, can you translate what your friend said into an understandable language?" asked Atieno-Masinde.

"You know ..." Menya began, followed by a hiccup, "in our community ...." He hiccupped again. "Snitching leads to ...." Another hiccup. "It's a bad omen if ...." He hiccupped.

Bakari subtly pushed his jacket aside to reveal the handcuffs, adopting an imposing posture designed to instil fear of the police in the young men.

Seemingly unfazed by the attempt to intimidate them, the men casually sipped their home-brewed liquor and passed the bottle around.

Atieno-Masinde cleared her throat emphatically and said, "Menya, how long have you been working for the Midnight Dancer?"

"Who, me?" Menya asked. He hiccupped.

"You, of course," Bakari shrieked. "Or is your name no longer Menya? Answer the question: How long have you worked for the Midnight Dancer?"

"I ..." He hiccupped. "I ..." Another hiccup. "I ..." Hiccup. Hiccup.

"Menya, when was the last time you saw the Midnight Dancer?" asked Atieno-Masinde.

"Who, me?"

"Yes, you, Menya. Dammit!" Bakari spat venomously, certain that one more provocation from Menya would shatter his restraint and compel him to drag the men away for aggressive interrogation.

Menya had a hiccup. And another.

The mumbler said something that sounded like a tongue twister, and his friends laughed.

"These lunatics would rather rot in prison than talk about Dahdi Stoppa," Bakari whispered.

Atieno-Masinde crouched down, unfolded the sketch of the Duo and held it up to the men.

"Look closely," she said, her tone soft but commanding. "Do any of you recognise these two?"

The silence was heavy, broken only by Menya's hiccup.

"Speak, and you could be 250,000 shillings richer," Atieno-Masinde said, her eyes scanning their faces like a hawk. "Imagine what you could do with that kind of money."

Menya's fingers fiddled with the hem of his tattered jacket. His eyes betrayed a flicker of unease.

"I want to talk to you alone, Menya," Atieno-Masinde said, straightening up to her full height.

Menya hesitated, then followed the two officers a few paces away.

"You know them," Atieno-Masinde pressed, showing Menya the sketch. "You're not as good at hiding it as you think. Who are they?"

Menya hiccupped. Then, barely above a whisper, he said, "Scarface."

"I need his real name, Menya."

Menya's mouth opened, but no words came out. He glanced over his shoulder at his two comrades, their hard stares boring into his back like a warning. A shadow crossed his face, fleeting but unmistakable. Like someone afraid of a snarling dog, he flinched and took a step back.

Bakari closed the gap between them and breathed, "Don't try my patience, Menya. I could have you locked up for years for withholding information from the police."

Menya's nostrils flared. "I know nothing!" he snapped. His voice trembled with fear, but there was an undertone of defiance in it.

"Yes, you do, Menya."

Menya's expression hardened. He turned abruptly and walked away with quick, stomping steps, the hiccups echoing behind him like a taunt.

Holding the bottle, the mumbler got to his feet, spat out the khat and poured the brew onto the ground as if paying homage to his ancestors, or the gods or some unseen force.

"We know nothing," the words tumbled from his mouth like an oath, each syllable clear and distinct. "We know nothing."

Then he turned to the officers. The carefree cheerfulness that had flitted across his face just a moment ago had disappeared and been replaced by something sombre, almost ominous.

CHAPTER 35

Wednesday, 28 March, 20:20

"I'm tired of having to constantly update the public on the status of the investigation, especially when there's no tangible progress to report," Mugo grumbled as he washed his hands in the toilet at CID headquarters in Mombasa. He wore a navy corduroy uniform with three military stars on the shoulder and a navy blue cap. As a detective, he usually wore civilian clothes, reserving the uniform for special occasions such as press conferences.

"There's one burning question on everyone's mind right now," Bakari mused, gently smoothing his hair with the palms of his hands to make sure every strand was perfectly in place. "Is the Midnight Dancer of Dakacha the infamous Scarface?"

"It's too early to jump to conclusions without solid evidence," Mugo stressed, wiping his hands with a paper towel. "First, we have to confirm that the teeth found on Dahdi Stoppa's property belong to the victims. Then we have to find out how they got there."

"That won't be easy. No one in that damned village was willing to talk. Menya, the shepherd, knew something. Then his mumbling friend was suddenly able to speak clearly. He came towards us, almost menacingly at first. Then he softened and begged us to leave. After that, he answered every question we asked like a broken record: 'We know nothing'."

Mugo's phone rang in his pocket. He pulled it out and answered, "Hello, Dalilah." With a last glance at his reflection, he asked, "To what do I owe this pleasure?"

"In three days it will be 31 March."

"I'm well aware of that, Dalilah."

"Ouch! That's harsh of you."

"This is no time for a tête-à-tête," he said as he stepped out of the bathroom. "What are you getting at?"

"I think I cracked the code you sent me."

"I'm listening."

"The first fifteen numbers and letters reminded me of a date of birth."

"Hang on."

Mugo wedged the phone between his head and shoulder and reached for his notebook and pen in his breast pocket. He turned to the page where he had written down the five codes he had sent to Dalilah and walked to the end of the corridor, where it was quieter.

"You may proceed now, Dalilah."

"Look at the second code."

msa_d3imo3y/g6s&edl-di3m12ylg59

"Replace the letter 'i' with the number 1 from the fourth code."

Mugo noted the changes. Then he said, "Next."

"Replace the slash with the number 1 and the 'g' with the number 9."

Mugo did as he was told and whispered, "Okay."

"Replace the 's' with 5, then look at the first fifteen numbers and letters."

Mugo swapped as instructed, then counted the first 15 entries and crossed out the rest.

msa_d31mo3y1965~~&edl-di3m12ylg59~~

"Doesn't that look like a date to you?" Dalilah pointed out. "The 'd' could stand for day, 'm' for month and 'y' for year. This leaves the date: 31.03.1965."

"That's a fascinating observation," Mugo admitted. "Does the date mean anything to you?"

"I know someone who was born on that day in Mombasa. That is why I pointed out that 31 March is in three days. The first letters, 'msa', could be the initials of Mombasa. I am sure Google will spit out many other celebrities who were also born on that day in Mombasa."

"That's a good start. Which celebrity do you think of off the top of your head?"

"My lawyer, Jeffrey Kizito. It's customary for him to throw a lavish party on that day."

Jeffrey Kizito? Mugo's mind raced. The lawyer and human rights activist, notorious for his scathing and unsparing criticism of the local police's handling of the Merciless Duo case.

Given that Dalilah had proven to be an invaluable source of information, her suggestion deserved serious consideration, perhaps even unquestioning attention. But Mugo shook his head resolutely, his instincts rejecting the temptation to connect dots that might not exist.

"Actually, the main reason for my call is this," Dalilah jolted him out of his reverie, "I can give you the names of the next possible victims. All four of them live in and around Nairobi."

"How do you know this?"

"Seven of my protégés have recently lost their business cards. They could have misplaced them—"

"Or they could be on their way to the next crime scene," Mugo finished in a monotone. "You say that seven of your protégés have lost their business cards. How come you only have four names?"

"Three protégés refused to name their tormentors."

Mugo couldn't contain his impatience. Without hesitation, he blurted into the phone, "I need the names of the next possible victims."

"Don't get so bossy with me, Dennis. Before we can move forward, I need assurances that those who have committed these heinous crimes against children will be held accountable."

"You know better, Dalilah. The law always requires evidence, not hearsay."

"Then make sure these men don't hide the business cards like Oliver Morgan did. That's evidence enough."

"If the business cards turn up, I will do everything in my power to see justice done," Mugo promised.

"I will not reveal the names until you give me written assurances that you will take legal action against these sexual predators. Another thing: the public is becoming increasingly concerned about who might be the next target. It's time for the true motives behind these attacks to come to light."

"Are you making demands in exchange for the names? I strongly advise against it. It can be construed as obstruction of justice"

"Oh, please, Mr DCI, if we're talking about obstruction of justice, Oliver Morgan and his ilk should be under the microscope, not me."

"I understand, but what you are asking for is not possible in such a short time. Lives are at stake here."

"I'm sure you're familiar with the expression, 'It's my way or the highway'."

"Very well, Dalilah, we'll proceed on your terms. Expect to hear from me as soon as I have finalised my travel arrangements for my trip to Nairobi today. We should meet in my office this evening upon my arrival."

"What has been decided regarding Oliver Morgan?"

Mugo adjusted his cap. "We can only open an investigation if there's enough evidence to build a case. We believe that Omari Sekibo emptied the hotel safe, probably to destroy evidence that could incriminate him and Oliver Morgan. An arrest warrant has been issued for Omari

Sekibo and the apartment hotel in Nairobi is under investigation."

◆◆◆

Omari Sekibo's ears pricked up as his eyes darted between the rear-view mirror and the dark road ahead. Every sound, every stretching shadow fed his paranoia – was it the police closing in, or worse, the Duo? "*The police are after you, rafiki*," Oliver Morgan had warned him. "*Ditch the SIM card and leave the country before trouble closes in on you. It's only temporary; I'll sort everything out.*"

Omari reached for his vibrating disposable phone on the passenger seat. Vitória – Oliver's ex-fiancée – flashed on the screen.

"Vitória?" he asked, his voice low and taut with urgency.

"Yes, it's me. Where are you?"

"Near Bamburi Cement," he whispered. "Did you get everything?"

"Yes. Your passport, laptop, and the files. I also packed some clothes, like you said. In return, I expect details of what happened to Oliver."

"You'll get them."

"Should I come to Bamburi Cement?"

"Let's meet at the Nyali City Mall ..." He held his breath, thinking he heard footsteps crunching on dry twigs. He hung up and threw the phone back on the seat. His heart pounded painfully against his ribs as he fumbled with the ignition.

◆◆◆

The steady roar of a police helicopter's turbines grew louder as it approached the helipad at Wilson Airport, rousing the driver from his doze in the front seat of a Subaru Forester. Yawning, he watched as the aircraft's searchlight pierced the pitch-black, starless sky that enveloped the capital.

He got out of the car, opened the boot and watched as three figures emerged from the side door of the helicopter, each carrying a duffel bag and a briefcase. They hurried towards him.

Atieno-Masinde and Bakari slipped into the back seat. Mugo had just closed the passenger door when the phone in his pocket rang. He took the call and put it on speakerphone.

"We have a new victim," said the caller, DS Henry Kebaso. "Lawrence Zakayo, the music producer popularly known as Silver. The attack took place at his residence. I'm still at the scene and won't be able to get to the meeting in time."

"Was there a business card left?"

"Yes. The business card was on the floor when I arrived. It's a gated complex. When the guards opened the gate for a visitor, Zakayo's car shot through at an unusually high speed. They did not see the driver. One of the guards then went to the house to check that everything was all right. He found Zakayo brutally beaten and stripped. I've put out an APB on the vehicle."

Mugo ended the call and picked up a waiting call.

"Hi, Dalilah," he answered, "are you there yet?"

"We're waiting in the car park. Sharona Warinda is with me. How much longer do you need?"

"We are just around the corner. Sorry for the delay. We had a technical issue with our helicopter."

"Any information on Oliver Morgan's stay at the Nairobi aparthotel?"

"The aparthotel reservation was made in the name of Omari Sekibo. Oliver Morgan has categorically denied ever having been there. Hotel staff were unable to identify him."

"I hope he has travel restrictions. I strongly suspect that he is the man who abused my eleven-year-old protégé."

"Dalilah, all we have are theories, nothing concrete. Oliver Morgan has no travel restrictions because he's not under investigation. He is not linked to any activity that threatens national security, nor has he broken any immigration laws."

"Thank you, you made that very clear to me." Sarcasm dripped from every one of Dalilah's vowels.

The Subaru drove through the gate.

"We are here," Mugo said. "Please come to the entrance."

◆◆◆

"Dalilah Beale, chair of the DS Savekids Foundation, and Sharona Warinda, vice-chair, are attending the crisis meeting tonight," Mugo began, sweeping his eyes over the nine members of the task force seated in the incident room. "Dalilah Beale has names, possible next victims, but she will not name them until I have given her written assurances that we will prosecute these men. She is convinced that both those already attacked and those still on the Duo's list are guilty of child abuse. She sees the business cards left behind by the Duo as incriminating evidence. Each business card has a unique case number and is assigned to a specific abused child in her care."

"Miss Beale, there have been other cases where business cards were left behind," Bakari said. "Why haven't you urged us to take legal action against these men, as you are now asking us to do? And if we're going to investigate them for child abuse, we need your full cooperation – that means telling us everything you know about this case."

"I can only help directly if the victim of sexual abuse is willing to cooperate. Sadly, many are reluctant to relive their trauma, especially after the Duo have delivered justice and left the perpetrators in the misery they deserve."

Dalilah's words hung in the air like a dense fog, causing the room to sink into a muffled murmur.

Mugo opened a folder on the table before him. He slid it over to Dalilah and said, "My written assurance."

Dalilah and Sharona studied the document. Satisfied with the contents, they affixed their signatures.

"You also have my word that nothing you say here will be quoted or recorded," Mugo said, adding his signature to the document.

Sharona held up the document. "This is a formal commitment. You agree to abide by the terms of our working relationship. We will provide four names of the Duo's possible next victims. In principle, we would classify these people as perpetrators rather than victims."

"Monsters is the right classification," Dalilah interjected. "There's a good chance my business card will be left behind if these monsters I'm about to name are attacked. The business cards need to be secured before these child abusers have a chance to tamper with them."

The question of how best to use this information made Mugo's head spin.

Dalilah unlocked her phone and read out the four names and their addresses. Among the names was that of music producer Lawrence Zakayo.

"Lawrence Zakayo was attacked a few minutes ago," Mugo said. "They found a business card."

Dalilah looked at her phone and said, "If it has the number 477, the man is as guilty as sin."

"And he deserved it," Sharona added.

"I fully understand that child abusers should face justice," croaked the Digital Sleuth, who had typed the names and addresses into his laptop in record time. "But the Duo's apparent vigilante justice is illegal. Where do you stand on that?"

Dalilah shifted in her seat.

"If you saw the painful scars and bruises on the genitals and buttocks of children who have suffered the trauma of sexual abuse, you would not question my stance on these cases," Dalilah answered. Her voice was heavy, her emotions spilling across the room like a broken dam. "If you heard their terrifying nightmares, or learnt of the diabolical threats that force them to endure bestial abuse in silence, your tone would be less callous, less jaded."

"Thank you, Dalilah Beale and Sharona Warinda," Mugo said as he got to his feet. "Let me walk you to your car." In the same breath, he thought with conviction, *Finally, we are one step ahead of the Duo.*

◆◆◆

Streams of data flashed across the three monitors on his cluttered desk. The Digital Sleuth worked with machine-like precision, tunnelling through servers and databases to mine data, trace digital footprints and compile a comprehensive dossier on the potential victims Dalilah had named. This included photographs of the three men, vehicle registrations including make and colour, places of work, home addresses and aerial maps of their surroundings.

Finally, he took off his glasses, rubbed his eyes and reached for his mobile phone to make a call.

Mugo was on the line.

"Job's done," the Digital Sleuth reported.

◆◆◆

Standing at the front of the incident room, holding a remote control, Mugo addressed the assembled task force, augmented by officers from other units.

"Thank you all for coming so quickly and on such short notice. We have the photos, names, home addresses, and places of work of three men who may soon fall victim to the Duo. We'll be watching them around the clock."

Mugo turned sideways and pressed the remote control. The monitor on the wall came to life, showing images of three men.

"Our priority isn't to protect these men, but to use this opportunity to set a trap for the Duo. This is our chance to catch them in the act." He paused, letting the weight of his words sink in. "The men we'll be observing will be designated as Target-1, Target-2, and Target-3."

He clicked on one of the three images and zoomed in on the middle-aged man's face until it almost filled the screen. He was bald, had a thick moustache and a goatee.

"This man will be Target-1. Two-person team Alpha-1 will observe Target-1's house discreetly from the front. Two-person team Beta-1 will watch the house from the rear. Two-person team Charlie-1 will observe Target-1 at his place of work and other locations outside his home. Any deviation from his usual route home will be reported immediately to the on-call team Backup-1. Backup teams will be deployed as necessary to reinforce the surveillance effort."

Mugo clicked on the next image – a man with a well-groomed beard whose age was difficult to estimate.

"This will be Target-2," Mugo said. "Two-person teams, Alpha-2, Beta-2 and Charlie-2, will be watching him."

He clicked on the last thumbnail, and the full-size face of a man in his forties appeared on the screen.

"This will be Target-3. Two-person teams, Alpha-3, Beta-3, and Charlie-3, will be watching Target-3. No one goes into the target's house alone during the stakeout. And don't waste time trying to get the Duo to surrender – take them down by any means necessary. Remember, negotiating with psychopaths is a losing battle. The sheer unpredictability of their minds is like walking a tightrope at dizzying heights – one misstep and a catastrophic fall is inevitable." He scanned the faces of the officers bolstering his team, gauging their expressions to ensure they were all on the same page. Then he announced, "We take a twenty-minute break. After that, the teams will be formed, and the strategic and tactical plans will be worked out."

CHAPTER 36

Friday, 30 March, 20:35

A nanny's unease deepened as strong gusts of wind lashed rain against the window of a five-bedroom house in Athi River, 30 kilometres from Nairobi. She cast a worried glance outside before checking her watch for what felt like the hundredth time. It was her long-awaited night off this month, and her boyfriend was waiting at a nearby bus stop, his impatience evident in the stream of WhatsApp messages he kept sending. The three children, giggling at the Tom and Jerry antics downstairs in the living room, were too young for the nanny to leave alone. Their mother usually came home late, if at all, as she ran a busy bed and breakfast on the outskirts of town. Their father, who was supposed to be back by now, was more than an hour and a half late.

DS Atieno-Masinde, the leader of Team Alpha-1, sat unseen with her teammate in a nondescript car parked about 70 metres from the house. She watched as the front gate opened, LED lights flaring brightly as a silver-grey Toyota Vanguard SUV pulled into the courtyard.

"Target-1 has arrived. Over," she radioed.

"Copy that," came the reply from DS Bakari, the Beta-1 team leader. They were watching the house from the back.

◆◆◆

Alpha-2 team's radio crackled: "Charlie-2 here. Target-2 has left the office. Over."

"Copy," Alpha-2 radioed back, sitting in a civilian vehicle about 150 metres from Target-2's country house. The man lived about 45 kilometres north-east of Nairobi in Kiambu County. He was married with two teenage children. He also looked after the two adolescent children of his single sister, who had left the country to pursue further studies.

"Charlie-2 reporting. Target-2 has diverted to a local pub. Over."

"DCI Mugo here. Any sign he's staying put? If affirmative, forward the location to Backup-2."

"Roger."

Team Charlie-2 entered the bar and found seats in a secluded corner. Target-2 was in animated conversation with five men at a table laden with drinks. The festive atmosphere suggested that Target-2 had settled in for an extended stay.

"Friday night, weekend at last," the team leader murmured to his partner.

"Besides, it's the end of the month, everyone's out partying. Target-2 isn't going anywhere, is he?"

"Target-2 is here for the long haul," the team leader agreed.

To blend in and avoid arousing suspicion, Charlie-2 ordered drinks and sent Backup-2 the name and address of the bar.

◆◆◆

Target-3 lived a short drive from the algae-choked shores of Lake Nakuru, where tens of thousands of flamingos transformed the landscape into a shimmering sea of pink. The house was tucked away 160 kilometres north-west of Nairobi, deep in the heart of the Great Rift Valley.

Not far from the house, Target-3's wife lay isolated in a psychiatric ward.

"I will make you pay dearly," she screamed, vowing revenge on her husband. The man had once been the centre of her world, but that had rotted into something far darker – an all-consuming loathing that festered inside her like a poisonous wound. Her every thought was distorted, tainted by a rage so fierce that it made her a danger to herself and anyone who approached her. She had to be sedated and tied to the bed. But the intense hatred she felt for her husband pierced the fog of the sedatives and twisted her every thought into a cold, calculated plan for an act of gratifying revenge.

Little did she know that her husband was trapped in a diabolical nightmare of his own – one far worse than the revenge she had imagined.

A few metres from the house, Constable Okocha, the Alpha-3 team leader, was urinating against a tree behind their undercover car.

His eyes wandered from the puddle of urine to Target-3's fenced house across the road. A faint, flickering light behind a window with a semi-transparent curtain caught his attention. It looked like the flickering of a matchstick.

The assistant? Constable Okocha wondered. According to the information they had, Target-3 was a non-smoker.

The constable zipped up his trousers, walked back to the car and got into the back seat.

"Hey, partner," he began, "mind if I take a look around?"

"Go ahead, player. Holler if you see the Duo," joked his colleague, engrossed in a mobile game. "From my vantage point, not a single couple would slip by, especially that weird Scarface with his blue toolbox and his cute little girlfriend."

Superstitiously, Constable Okocha planted a kiss on a talisman hanging from a chain around his neck. He jumped out of the car and crossed the road towards the house. Sure that no one was watching, he disappeared around the side of the fence, overgrown with hibiscus and lantana.

With the agility of a klipspringer, he scaled the two-metre wall in one fluid motion and landed on the inside, crouching on a freshly mown lawn. He held his breath for a moment and pricked up his ears.

The coast was clear.

With a stun gun in hand, he switched off his radio, silencing the crackle of voices and static that could betray his trespass. Moving like a shadow in the still darkness, he slipped through the narrow side wing between the building and the fence and, after a few steps, entered the back garden.

His instincts triggered an internal alarm when he noticed the half-open patio door. Cautiously, he approached and stole a peek inside. A dim floor lamp burnt by the stairs, revealing a tidy room with several oil paintings on the wall.

Tacky, he thought as he concentrated on the faint sound. It seemed to be coming from upstairs.

After careful consideration, he swapped the stun gun for his Glock pistol. Inside the house, he tiptoed to the stairwell and quietly climbed the steps. On the top step, he looked down the long corridor with several closed doors. The one at the end was ajar.

Pondering his next move, he leaned against the wall of the stairwell.

There was a muffled moan.

Okocha curled his lips in disgust. Shit. I hope I'm not hearing Target-3's moaning and groaning as he jerks off.

He pricked up his ears.

Could he be moaning in pain? he wondered, pulling out his phone to communicate with his partner before taking any further steps.

The floor lamp on the ground floor went out. Before he could react, a figure materialised in front of him, its face unrecognisable in the darkness. In one fluid motion, the stranger's hand reached for his pistol while the other slammed into his wrist with brutal precision.

Pain shot up Okocha's arm. His grip failed and the weapon slipped from his grasp, leaving him defenceless. In a knee-jerk, desperate attempt to scramble to safety, he jerked around. But he slipped on the spiral staircase, his body tipping dangerously backwards towards the tiled foyer, ready to claim him. At the last moment, his hand shot forward and grabbed the railing. As he tried to stabilise himself, he teetered dangerously over the edge with his back to his attacker.

He felt the stranger's boot slam into his spine with ruthless force, sending him hurtling down the stairs.

He took the hard fall with a gasp and reached for his radio.

The attacker beat him to it, kicking his arm and sending a searing pain through his now dislocated elbow. A stinking shoe sole pressed over his mouth, cutting off the scream before it could escape his lungs.

A flickering candle revealed the Merciless Duo, and his intuition instantly warned him that the situation demanded a careful balance of calm, assertiveness and caution. But the unyielding foot pressing down on his face robbed him of his breath, forcing him to struggle to break free.

A kick to the groin sent his hands instinctively flying to his scrotum, clutching the painful area.

"Resistance is futile, flatfoot," Scarface taunted, his voice dripping with disdain. "The more you try, the more parts of your body get hurt, torn or broken."

In a desperate attempt to signal total surrender, the constable raised his hands in the air, palms open and facing up. Scarface bent, grabbed the man by the throat and pulled him to his feet.

"We're now going up. We need to keep an eye on your friend in the car."

Okocha tried to make sense of the situation: The Duo are aware of the teams stationed outside. Therefore, their intention must be to use me as a hostage to facilitate their escape plan.

"By the way, flatfoot, I've just lost a thousand shillings to my assistant," Scarface revealed as they reached the stairs. "I had bet that you wouldn't fall for our ruse to lure you here. But she believed you would, because you have an ulterior motive beyond your official hunt for us. Is that true?"

"I am a policeman; my duty is to protect and serve. The man in the car is also police. This house is under surveillance."

"Then I guess we'll have to hurry with you. I hate to rush things, but as the French say, *c'est la vie.*"

Scarface pulled a business card from the kangaroo pocket of his hoodie and said, "This card is for you, flatfoot."

Constable Okocha felt the colour drain from his face.

"Just out of curiosity, flatfoot, did you ever suspect we had you on our radar?"

◆◆◆

"DCI Mugo," he answered the call in his office.

"Beta-3 here, sir. We have two victims. Constable Okocha and Target-3. The Duo got away, sir. No sign of forced entry, and we can't track their escape route."

Mugo clenched his right hand into a fist and pounded it on the sturdy wooden desk that dominated the room, rattling the neatly stacked files next to an old rotary telephone.

His eyes lingered on his narrow bookshelf, crammed with criminal procedure manuals, before he asked, "How did the Duo get away right under your noses?"

"We are still investigating what happened. Constable Okocha is in a pitiful state. He is barely alive. His partner is coming out of unconsciousness. He was drugged in the car."

"Did the Duo leave a business card?"

"Yes, sir. We have secured two business cards."

"I'm on my way," Mugo said, feeling a throbbing headache settle in his skull. "I expect a preliminary report before I arrive and a detailed one first thing in the morning."

"Yes, sir."

With a yawn and a glance at his watch, Mugo hung up.

"Fuck!" he cursed as he dialled the number of the Digital Sleuth who was working the night shift in his office.

"Hello, boss." The voice sounded enthusiastic. "Let me guess: you're calling it a day, right?"

"Target-3 and Constable Okocha have fallen victim to the Duo."

"What?"

"You heard it right."

Expecting caffeine to lift his spirits and boost his circulation, Mugo made his way to the kitchenette.

"Is there any trace of the Duo?" the Digital Sleuth asked. "Did they leave any business cards?"

"Two business cards were left behind. Get the dog squad."

"The canine unit is already asleep at this time of night."

"Get them out of bed with your bare hands if you have to." Mugo's voice rose a decibel, and his tone left no room for procrastination. "I'll wait for them here. We'll leave for Nakuru immediately."

Mugo ended the call, swung open the kitchenette door and was greeted by the tantalising aroma of freshly brewed coffee.

As he filled his thermal travel mug, he heard the voice of his immediate superior, Senior Assistant Inspector Gitonga, call out from behind him: "Look who's finally graced us with his presence. When did you get back?"

Mugo cocked his head. "Last night."

"The pressure is mounting, and all I get from you are reports with no positive progress."

"The situation has just reached a critical point. I'm about to leave for Nakuru, just waiting for the canine unit to arrive."

"Give me the key points."

"As we speak, we have two victims at the same scene. One of them is our agent on the surveillance team."

Mugo watched as his superior raised his hands in a helpless gesture before lowering them to his sides in defeat.

"The two victims may have been involved in child abuse, as two business cards were left behind," Mugo added.

"Now we've fed the press exactly what lawyer Kizito is spreading against us. I can already see the damning headlines: 'Police incompetence'."

The thought made Mugo's stomach churn. He picked up his travel mug and screwed the lid on.

"We are not going to let the press sniff at this yet," he said. "And speaking of lawyer Kizito, we have reason to believe that the code may have something to do with him."

"When and how did you crack the incomplete code? And when was I supposed to know about this masterstroke?"

"We haven't cracked it. I asked Dalilah Beale to look at the code."

Mugo took a sip of coffee and winced – the coffee tasted like molten lava on his tongue.

"I want to keep a close eye on lawyer Kizito," he said.

"How do you plan to do that?"

"By both physical and electronic means."

"Out of the question," he gushed with a decisive shake of his head. "We don't have the budget for such an operation without substantial evidence. Explain why you don't think it's necessary to get a court order for Dalilah Beale to provide information about her ... what was it called?"

"Protégé," Mugo helped him out. "Finding the 2,000 children she gave her business card to would be like looking for a needle in a haystack. Secondly, we don't have the expertise to interview sexually traumatised children."

"Does she still give out her business cards?"

"No. They're all used up, and she has no plans to reprint them."

"What do we know about how the Duo tracks down these suspected sex offenders?"

"Still piecing it together. Looks like the Duo first broke in to steal the business card, then went back to carry out the attack."

"How could the Duo break into the same house twice without leaving a trace?"

"There are always traces left behind. But they're usually compromised by the time we get there. Sometimes, evidence is deliberately destroyed. In Nakuru, we got very close. The scene is not contaminated. We should find something concrete."

CHAPTER 37

Saturday, 31 March, 09:10

With a wary glance over his shoulder, Target-2 slipped through the iron gate of his house, one hand gripping the handle of a briefcase, the other dragging a suitcase behind him. His wife followed with a handbag slung over her shoulder and keys dangling from her fingers. She slid into the driver's seat of a white Toyota Camry as Target-2 hoisted the suitcase into the boot.

About 90 metres away, the two-person Alpha-2 team watched in silence from the back seat of a nondescript Honda Accord, its tinted windows obscuring their presence.

As the Toyota's reverse lights came on, the team leader's hand shot to the centre console and grabbed the radio. He pressed the push-to-talk button and radioed, "Target-2 in motion. Passenger side. Toyota Camry. Repeat, Toyota Camry, passenger side. Over."

"Copy that," came Charlie-2's reply, loud music in the background making his words barely audible. A pause, then the shuffling of boots on the tarmac. "We're in position, ready to intercept."

Charlie-2's team leader gripped the steering wheel as the white Toyota Camry veered sharply onto the main road. The team eased into the flow of traffic, the Toyota's tail lights glowed about 200 metres away, separated by four cars.

The road wound through narrow bends, roundabouts and speed bumps. Eventually, the suburban sprawl thinned out as the traffic joined the Kenyatta Highway.

Without signalling, the Toyota pulled into a petrol station, taking Charlie-2 by surprise. The team slowed down and pulled over to the side of the road. Pretending to have broken down, they opened the bonnet and watched Target-2 through binoculars.

A few minutes later, the Toyota Camry pulled out of the petrol station and continued along Garissa Road towards the Embu-Nairobi Highway. Charlie-2 caught up with it at a calculated, inconspicuous distance.

"Charlie-2 here," the partner radioed. "Target-2 probably en route to Nairobi. Current location: Embu-Nairobi highway. Over and out."

◆◆◆

The black Mercedes Benz 280 SE took exit 10 towards Bunyala Road. Behind the wheel, Mugo stifled a yawn and reached for his third mug of coffee from the cup holder. Fatigue, frustration, and exhaustion clung to him like a second skin.

"Could you repeat that, Dalilah?" he asked, speaking into a pair of white headphones.

"One of the two case numbers you sent me last night belongs to a protégé whose phone number has since been assigned to someone else."

"Is there any other way to reach him or her?"

"If she doesn't contact me, I can't reach her. She only gave a first name and no exact address."

Mugo shot a brief side glance at the Digital Sleuth in the passenger seat before saying, "The victim was one of ours – he was guarding the house in Nakuru. He is single and has no children. Could he have inadvertently got in the way of the Duo?"

"Was he tortured in the usual way?"

"More or less the same way. Probably worse, he is in a pitiful state."

"Why else should he suffer the same torment as the guilty?" Dalilah argued.

"I see your point."

"Squeeze the truth out of him," Dalilah said with finality.

Mugo yawned, shifted down a gear and eased off the throttle as a traffic jam loomed ahead.

"I'll call you back later, Dalilah."

He ended the call and dropped the headphones on the centre console, his mind reeling with the aftertaste of defeat. The trip to Nakuru, which he had hoped would yield damning evidence, had come up empty. Every possible clue and lead had been thoroughly and comprehensively investigated. Neighbours had been questioned at length, and the dog squad had combed the area extensively. Despite all these efforts, there was not a shred of evidence to suggest how the Duo had managed to go undetected. A neighbour across the road had seen a couple walking away with a bag. At the time, a recurring blackout had plunged the neighbourhood into darkness, so he had no description of the people.

Mugo shook his head. "I was pretty sure we'd find at least the assistant's screwdriver still wet from the crime."

"The Duo are proving to be in a league of their own," said the Digital Sleuth. "Their criminal skills are on a whole other level."

Mugo gave him a disapproving look. He could feel the weight of exhaustion in his dark, sunken eyes, a reflection of sleepless nights and mounting pressure.

"This is Charlie-2," crackled the radio in the Digital Sleuth's hand. "Request instructions. We are at Jomo Kenyatta Airport. Target-2 has checked in. He's flying to Germany via Amsterdam."

Mugo yawned for the umpteenth time as he thought of the equally exhausted and sleep-deprived members of the task force.

He grabbed the radio and ordered, "All the teams observing Target-2 are to relieve the teams observing Target-1." That would give Atieno-Masinde, Bakari and Kebaso a few hours' rest.

◆◆◆

Target-1 sat across from his wife at the breakfast table strewn with half-empty cups and scattered crumbs. His bald head gleamed in the harsh sunlight, his jet-black goatee and moustache contrasting sharply with his dark brown eyebrows.

To avoid his wife's direct gaze, he looked out the window and watched his three children playing in the backyard.

"We promised the children we'd take them to the national park. You can't just cancel that at the last minute," she complained, her disappointment lingering like a thundercloud about to burst.

Target-1 pressed his lips into a thin line, feeling the weight of his unfulfilled promises crushing him. He glanced furtively at his watch and cursed under his breath. He was late.

"I don't understand why you have to go to Patrick's funeral," she said, her voice rising. "You two had drifted apart and were barely in touch."

"I abandoned him when life hit him hardest. The least I can do is pay my last respects."

"You're hardly ever around at weekends these days."

"Come on, babe! Business trips are important. The compensation I get for travel expenses covers most of our luxuries."

He saw how his words resonated with her. The realisation was reflected in her face, albeit like the brief flicker of a match.

"I'll make it up to you and the kids," he added. "How about an Easter holiday trip? Remember our last one?"

"That was four years ago."

"We had such a great time – swimming in the sea, sipping caipirinhas, and watching the sunset."

A faint smile twitched at the corners of her mouth, but it quickly faded as she said, "The time is ripe for a repeat performance."

"We will. As soon as I get back tomorrow, we'll book a trip. Check out some destinations. I'm thinking Zanzibar."

"Well then, get ready, dearie. When will you be back?"

"Tomorrow, around five."

◆◆◆

Charlie-2, the team shadowing Target-1 after relieving Charlie-1, had followed the Toyota Vanguard SUV without incident. Now, 30 kilometres from the house in Athi River, Target-1 came to a halt beside Nairobi's bustling City Market. The smell of crispy fried fish and grilled goat meat wafted through the air, making Charlie-2's mouth water, especially as they hadn't had time for breakfast.

Target-1 got out of his car and walked straight to one of the many flower vendors that dotted the street.

"Either he's a spontaneous guy, or the flowers were pre-ordered," Charlie-2's team leader concluded as Target-1 walked back to his car with a bouquet of roses.

"Funny, isn't it, coming all this way to buy flowers for your wife?"

"You know why, don't you?" said the team leader, his rumbling stomach almost drowning out his words.

"Why?"

"Nowadays, almost every man tries to win over his wife and children with flowers and sweets," the team leader speculated as he continued the tailing. "Their goal is to prove themselves as good husbands and fathers in order to avoid falling into the Duo's clutches."

"Holy moly!"

"I'm glad I don't have a wife and kids."

"Have you forgotten Constable Okocha? Married or single, with or without kids, none of us men are safe until we stop these terrorists."

"I guess you are right." The team leader's stomach rumbled even louder. "Damn, my sugar level is close to zero right now."

"Then we better call the backup team. We cannot afford a weakness that the Duo will exploit."

"Come on, dude! The Duo never strike in broad daylight. And if they do, they'll regret it. A hungry man is not to be trifled with."

Target-1 pulled into the car park of a gastropub, away from the hustle and bustle of downtown Nairobi. Clutching the bouquet of roses and a duffel bag, he got out, walked into the pub and headed straight for a corner booth occupied by two young women with curly Afros and a clean-shaven man in his late thirties. The table was laden with alcoholic and soft drinks.

The younger of the two women – his mistress– jumped to her feet. Her face lit up as she took the roses and inhaled their scent. She fell into Target-1's arms, hugging and kissing him passionately.

Target-1 greeted the others warmly. He shrugged off his jacket and draped it over the back of a chair.

"I'll be right back," he said. "I hope my room is still available."

"Haven't you paid for it, babe?" the mistress asked.

"I will now. I had made a reservation."

CHAPTER 38

Saturday, 31 March, 18:00

DS Bakari's eyelids fluttered and his nostrils flared as the smell, reminiscent of the foul stench in Dahdi Stoppa's backyard, shattered his peaceful slumber. He tossed and turned in his bed.

The stench intensified, suffocating.

"Scarface," he muttered. Driven by instinct, his hand darted to the Glock in the open drawer beside him. He leapt to his feet, whirled around and fired a shot. But Scarface remained unmoved, a fearless smile curling his lips. The magazine and clip rested casually in his hand.

Where is the assistant? Bakari wondered, looking around the room. He could feel a rush of adrenaline coursing through his body and his heartbeat quickening – not from fear, for he was the quintessential fearless police officer. It was the certainty that Scarface would not use the darkness as a shield.

Bakari flung himself onto the bed, rolled over to the side of the window and pulled back the curtains, letting the evening light creep into the room.

"No games in the dark," he purred, his voice barely above a whisper. But the most wanted criminal stood impassively, radiating an unsettling confidence that suggested he welcomed the daylight.

Scarface slammed the door with a resounding bang. The shrill vibration of Bakari's phone woke him up, shattering what was left of his dream.

"Hello," he answered the call, immediately checking the display as familiar voices chimed in with their respective "Hellos." The conference call consisted of Atieno-Masinde, Kebaso, and Mugo, the caller.

"Team Charlie-2 just woke me up from my office nap," Mugo said. "Looks like Target-1 won't be heading home tonight. He's with a mistress in a pub in town. I'm sending you ..."

He stopped mid-sentence. The faint but unmistakable sound of a yawn drifted through the phone.

"I'm sending you the coordinates of the gastropubs and a photo of his mistress," Mugo continued. "Killian, take command."

"What makes Charlie-2 think Target-1 will spend the night there?" asked Killian Bakari.

"Target-1 paid the bill for room sixty-four at reception and received a key card. Eric is on his way with a search warrant for room sixty-four. I need all three of you there before dark. Backup teams are already on their way."

◆◆◆

Charlie-2's team leader glanced over to Target-1's table, where a lively conversation was going on, punctuated by the occasional burst of laughter. The girls pushed the bottles aside to make room for the food a waiter had brought – a large tray of grilled leg of lamb, *kachumbari, managu* and steaming *ugali.*

The team leader stood up and walked towards the entrance. Halfway there, he stopped and checked the time on a double-sided wrought-iron clock, its vintage design reminiscent of those in New York's Grand Central Terminal. One face read 6:27 p.m., while the other showed 6:33 p.m.

Outside, he spotted DS Bakari in the car park. Backup-1, Backup-2 and Backup-3 arrived in unmarked police cars.

With a nod from Bakari, the Charlie-2 team leader slid into the back seat of an unmarked police car, a black Audi A6, and closed the door behind him. Atieno-

Masinde and Kebaso were in the car. Bakari climbed into the driver's seat and reached for a radio on the centre console.

"DS Bakari here," he said into the radio. "Backup teams, fan out. Cover the car park and access road. Anything suspicious moves, I want eyes on it before it takes its next breath."

A crackle of static followed before voices broke through.

"Backup-1 here. Copy that."

"Here is Backup-2. Copy."

"Backup-3. Copy that."

Bakari turned to Atieno-Masinde and Kebaso. "You two, go inside. Relieve Charlie-2. Charlie-2 will reposition to the pavilion and cover the back of the building."

Charlie-2's team leader sent a text message to his partner before slipping out of the car.

"We are lovers tonight, Henry," said Atieno-Masinde, her tone playful yet serious. She adjusted her shawl and jumped out of the car.

Henry Kebaso climbed out of the back seat and joked, "Let's get cuddly like lovers." He casually put his arm around Atieno-Masinde's waist as they strolled towards the pub entrance.

"Don't get used to it."

"Nothing to worry about, my darling. I am a well-behaved boy."

Inside, Atieno-Masinde and Kebaso slid into an empty table with a direct view of Target-1.

Bakari entered the building and made his way to the hotel lobby, scanning the area carefully.

A lone receptionist, seated on a stool behind her desk and absorbed in her smartphone, caught sight of the potential guest. She placed her device on the counter and stood up straight.

"Elizabeth," Bakari read out loud the name embroidered on the breast pocket of her vest. He flashed his service card and said, "I'm Detective Sergeant Killian Bakari. Where is the manager, Jacquey Kipsanai?"

"She stepped out for a moment."

"I am here to investigate a very important matter, and I think you can help me, Elizabeth." He held up his phone. It showed a photograph of Target-1 and his mistress. "What can you tell me about these guests?"

After a moment's hesitation, she replied, "The man is a regular. I've never seen the girl before."

"The man paid for a room today. I need the room number and the name he used."

Elizabeth's brown eyes darted to the screen and her index finger began to dance over the left mouse button and scroll wheel.

"He paid for room sixty-four on the sixth floor. It was booked in the name of Mr Olololo."

"When was the room booked?"

She checked the entry, looked up and said, "The twenty-fourth."

"A week ago."

"Yes."

"What time did you start work today?"

"At seven this morning."

"Have any other guests checked in today?"

She looked at the guest book.

"A couple in room forty-one. A woman in room fifty-five. Three men booked double rooms today but haven't checked in."

Bakari showed Elizabeth the warrant and said, "I need the spare key to room sixty-four."

The phone buzzed, pulsating in his palm. Almost in slow motion, Bakari tapped the green button, lifted the device to his ear and muttered, "Hello, boss."

"What is the situation like?" Mugo's voice came through from the other end.

Bakari nodded at the receptionist – a silent "thank you" – as she handed him the spare key. He stepped out of the lobby and replied, "We have our eyes in every nook and cranny."

"I have dispatched Alpha and Beta teams for reinforcements—"

"Boss, from what we know of the Duo, they don't carry anything fancy, just their regular torture gear," Bakari grumbled, feeling his competence underestimated. "Taking them down should be a piece of cake. We don't need an overpowering presence."

"It's the last day of March. My instincts are warning me of a possible showdown, like last year. If it comes to that, there will be chaos between the revellers and the workers. We cannot afford to make mistakes of any kind."

◆◆◆

Atieno-Masinde's eyes were fixed on Target-1 as he slipped a few notes into a waitress's hand and muttered something that brought a smile to her face.

The mistress picked up the roses from a chair and smelled the petals. Target-1 emptied his glass in one gulp, picked up his duffel bag from the floor and got to his feet. The companions followed in sync, and the foursome marched together to the lift.

Atieno-Masinde and Kebaso exchanged glances, their unspoken agreement evident – they needed to catch up with Target-1 without arousing suspicion.

Immediately, Kebaso stood up, swaying on unsteady feet, his lips curled into a lazy smile. He chuckled softly and leaned against Atieno-Masinde's side, who had come to his side.

"Time for bed, baby boy," Atieno-Masinde said as she took him by the arm.

Kebaso faked a hiccup, playing his part perfectly as Atieno-Masinde led him to the lift.

But then a waiter stood in their way and said, "You haven't paid your bill."

Atieno-Masinde cocked her head to the side and noticed that Target-1 was watching her. She fumbled for the money in her pocket and saw the lift door open.

"I'll get the change later," she spat, thrusting the money into the waiter's hand.

"Please wait for the change. I've finished my work and need to leave now."

The lift doors closed behind Target-1 and his companions.

Fuck! Atieno-Masinde cursed. "Get the damn change and give it to my husband."

Atieno-Masinde hurried to the next lift. But it was out of order. She took the stairs.

Kebaso sat down, took his phone out of his pocket and rang Team Beta-1.

"Hello," the team leader's voice came through.

"Target-1 is on the way up. Where are you?"

"We are in room sixty-seven, thanks to the guest's cooperation. Four listening devices in Target-1's room are ready to pick up any sounds of aggression should the Duo strike."

Bakari, watching the area from his car, reached for his buzzing phone.

"Shoot."

"Target-1 and his companions have taken the lift up," Kebaso's voice crackled over the line. "I'm waiting for the lift. Rahab took the stairs."

"I'll be with you in a minute."

Bakari ended the call and reached into his breast pocket. A hip flask of whisky appeared, followed by two pills – substances that generally put him in a psychedelic state of consciousness. He washed them down with the alcohol. Soon, he knew, his perception would change: The world would become sharper, the colours brighter, the sounds crystal clear.

"Beta-2, cover the lift and stairwell," Bakari radioed. "Beta-3, cover the emergency exits. Over."

"Copy that."

"Charlie-2, report your position," Bakari radioed.

"In the courtyard. Position in the gazebo."

"Do you have a clear line of sight to the rear of the hotel?"

"Affirmative."

"If you see flickering lights on the sixth floor, sound the alarm immediately. Over."

"Copy that."

Bakari got out of the car and entered the building, heading straight for the lift. He went up to the sixth floor and arrived just as Atieno-Masinde stood outside room 64 with a bottle of water.

She knocked on the door and called out, "Room service."

"Wrong room, we didn't order anything," came the reply – a woman's voice.

Bakari pressed the earpiece as the message from Team Beta-1 crackled through: "We have intercepted the response from Target-1's room."

"Any sound from Target-1?" Bakari asked.

"Negative. Shortly after arriving in the room, the man's voice said, 'Fancy coming?' and the girl's voice said, 'No, I'm exhausted'. The girl hasn't stopped talking since then, probably on the phone."

Bakari caught up with Atieno-Masinde and they retreated to the fire escape where Kebaso had taken up position.

"I spoke to the boss," Bakari said. "His gut instinct told him a showdown was coming."

"I have that feeling too," admitted Atieno-Masinde, "but I think it will happen somewhere else."

◆◆◆

Musamali Demba, sharp in a tailored brown suit, switched off the lights in his office on the tenth floor of a tower block in the heart of the city. His phone buzzed in his hand. He glanced at the screen – no caller ID. After a moment's hesitation, he pressed the green icon and put the phone to his ear.

"There's a police op about to go down. Big one," said the familiar voice on the other end.

Musamali Demba flipped the lights back on and strode to his desk. Sinking into his chair, he grabbed a pen and held it over his notepad.

"What kind of operation?" he asked.

"Can't say much yet. Be on standby. I'll call you with more details."

"Wait, wait. Where?"

"In Nairobi."

"The focus – what is it? Gangs? Corruption? Murder?"

"Just be ready. You'll want the story. Transfer the money."

The line went dead. Musamali Demba stared at the phone, then scribbled on his notepad: *Police op? Big one?*

CHAPTER 39

Saturday, 31 March, 23:05

Bakari checked the time again. Forty minutes had passed since Target-1 had left the bar.

"Charlie-2," Bakari radioed, "are the lights still on along the sixth floor?"

"They're still on. A woman has just closed the windows in one of the rooms."

Bakari felt his pulse racing. "What does she look like?"

"As far as I could see, she had no braids. She had a curly Afro."

"Next time, be direct, don't beat around the bush! Over and out."

Kebaso peered around the corner into the dimly lit corridor. He turned back to his colleagues with a frown and remarked, "Dalilah must be laughing at us for leading us on a wild goose chase this time."

"I don't think so. She has ..."

Atieno-Masinde paused as a bell-like chime echoed softly – the unmistakable signal of an arriving lift. The three of them turned and glanced inconspicuously around the corner towards the lift area at the end of the wing.

The lift doors slid open, revealing a figure draped in a white bathrobe, the hood pulled low over his head. The rhythmic slap of his sandals on the tiles echoed down the now-lit corridor as he walked. His face remained obscured, his downcast eyes fixed on the glow of the phone in his hand.

Pausing outside room 64, the man pulled a key card from the pocket of his robe.

Without a word, Bakari dashed off, with Atieno-Masinde hot on his heels. The man looked up, finally showing his face – it was Target-1's companion.

With urgency overriding his sense of professional decorum, Bakari forgot to introduce himself and demanded, "What are you doing here?"

"Excuse me?"

"This isn't your hotel room."

"It was the last time I checked. Who are you anyway?"

"CID, Detective Sergeant Killian Bakari." He flashed his service card. "Room sixty-four is booked in the name of Mr Olololo. Are you the one?"

"That's my mate. Is he in trouble?"

"You have no right to question an officer on duty," Bakari pointed out gruffly. "Where's your mate?"

"I'm an avid swimmer and didn't feel like taking the lift from the second floor to the rooftop in my bathrobe, so we swapped rooms."

"Which room is he in now?" The impatience in Bakari's voice was in every syllable.

"Room twenty-three, second floor."

Bakari sprinted away, Atieno-Masinde matching his pace step for step. He jabbed the lift button; the doors slid open, and they leapt inside. Without waiting for Kebaso, he hit button two. The lift descended.

On the second floor, they hurried to room 23.

"Open up, police!" Atieno-Masinde shouted in an authoritative voice as her knuckles rapped against the wood.

She let about a minute pass and watched as Team Beta-1 and Kebaso appeared and joined them.

She knocked again. "Police. Open up!"

"They were drunk; they could be fast asleep," Kebaso surmised.

Like a premonition, an oppressive feeling overcame Bakari, making him tilt his head sideways …

There she was, unmistakably in her school uniform, with a rucksack on her back.

"The assistant," Bakari shouted.

She disappeared behind the wall leading to the stairs.

"Where is she?" asked Atieno-Masinde.

"Accomplice sighted," Bakari reported over the radio, immediately taking up the chase. "I repeat: accomplice sighted on the second floor in her usual uniform."

"Beta-3, pick up a key to room twenty-three and gain entry," Atieno-Masinde radioed, following Bakari. "I repeat: obtain a key to room two-three and proceed inside. Over."

"Copy that."

Bakari paused at the top of the stairs. His eyes swept the unlit courtyard through the open window with almost military precision. Seeing no sign of the assistant, he turned, his hand moving, slicing the air with silent commands.

Team Beta-1 nodded. Armed with tasers, they crept up the stairs, barely making a sound with their boots. Kebaso broke away from the group and went down the stairs. Atieno-Masinde and Bakari slipped into the toilets on the same floor – she into the women's, he into the men's – hands on their gun holsters.

A deafening shot rang out from below. Bakari and Atieno-Masinde burst out of the toilets and hurried down the stairs. On the ground floor, they caught up with Kebaso, who was listening to a smartly dressed man.

"It's Scarface," said the man, pointing feverishly at the kitchen door. "He's gone in there."

Another shot rang out in the kitchen. Hysterical screams erupted, followed by stomping feet and objects crashing to the floor. Chefs and staff fled the kitchen in a panic.

The three officers moved forward. Atieno-Masinde and Kebaso flanked Bakari as he pushed open the kitchen door. Bakari stepped inside. Pots and broken china lay on the floor.

At the far end of the kitchen, Bakari spotted a hooded figure facing away from him. He aimed his Glock and shouted, "Police! Don't move!" At that very moment, a kitchen staff, who had been hiding in a cupboard jumped out and crashed into a large pot simmering on a gas burner. The pot crashed to the floor, splashing hot stew all over Bakari.

For the briefest of moments, Bakari's focus shifted. When he returned his attention to the task at hand, the hooded man was nowhere to be seen.

"Turn off the damn gas!" Bakari shouted, leaping over the spilt food. Dodging overturned pots and shards of broken china, he reached a kitchen counter in the middle of the room.

A shot rang out, the bullet narrowly missing Bakari's right ear.

Ducking, Bakari lunged forward and took cover behind a wall.

The double doors at the far end swung open to reveal a dark delivery entrance. Bakari stepped aside to give himself a clear shot and emptied his magazine.

The lights went out. Two shots rang out. Seemingly reflexively, Kebaso and Atieno-Masinde fired indiscriminately at the source of the fire.

"Beta-3 here. No sign of Target-1 in room twenty-three. His mistress is unconscious."

"DCI Mugo to all units: Take the Duo, dead or alive."

Bakari yanked off his covert earpiece, shoved it into his pocket, and slapped a magazine into his gun.

Kebaso and Atieno-Masinde switched on their torches. With synchronised movements honed by years of working together, they advanced towards the now-closed double doors.

Bakari paused at the door, his mind racing as he swiftly assessed the best strategy for the confrontation ahead. This wasn't just any criminal – it was most likely Scarface, the most wanted ruthless serial criminal known for his extraordinary night vision, near superhuman strength and intriguing ability to disappear like a magician.

Atieno-Masinde tapped Bakari on the shoulder, signalling him to move. She was ready to cover him.

Bakari flung open the door and burst out of the kitchen. He hit a slippery spot and lost his balance. His arms flailed clumsily. But in that fleeting moment of freefall, his gaze fell on a blue Mazda parked about 50 metres away with its interior lights on. Two hooded figures sat in the front seats, their faces reminiscent of Scarface. But Bakari noticed a subtle difference between the two figures – one that was impossible to miss.

No sooner had Bakari hit the ground with a heavy thud than the man in the passenger seat stretched out his arm, a gun glinting in his hand. Before Bakari could react, two deafening shots rang out.

Atieno-Masinde saw the greasy liquid that had knocked Bakari off balance. Without hesitation, she stepped back to get a running start. She sprinted off, leapt into the air, somersaulted over the slippery patch, and caught a glimpse of a man in a hoodie in a Mazda speeding away. Before landing, she fired four shots in quick succession at the car.

Guests and staff scattered in all directions. Some huddled between parked cars, others scrambled into vehicles, hands shaking as engines sputtered to life.

Amidst the pandemonium in the car park, Backup-3's radio crackled, and Atieno-Masinde's urgent voice cut through the din: "Suspect fleeing in a blue Mazda—"

The roar of an engine swallowed Atieno-Masinde's words. A blue Mazda sped through the car park, narrowly missing pedestrians and grazing parked cars.

"Suspect vehicle sighted," Backup-3 radioed. "Blue Mazda RX-8. Plates missing."

The two-person Backup 3 team sprinted to their car. About 150 metres ahead, they saw the Mazda hit a wooden sign and carelessly plough through a flower bed. It swerved back onto the road and turned right onto Lusaka Road.

"Backup-3 here," the team leader radioed as his partner sped out of the car park. "Suspect fleeing west on Lusaka Road. Repeat: westbound on Lusaka Road."

"This is DS Bakari. Two occupants in the getaway car. Both wearing dark hoodies. Similar appearance," he radioed. "Repeat: two occupants wearing dark hoodies. Similar appearance."

Bakari ran and jumped into their Audi, clutching the steering wheel like an anchor as he waited, almost impatiently, for Atieno-Masinde and Kebaso to take their places in the front and back seats, respectively.

Atieno-Masinde attached the magnetic police beacon to the roof of the car and plugged the power cord into the car's cigarette lighter. No sooner had she flicked the switch, bringing the blue light to life, than Bakari slammed his foot down on the accelerator, the tyres screeching against the tarmac and leaving a trail of scorched rubber in their wake.

Bakari's mind flashed back to the moment he had slipped and fallen – two shots had whizzed past him, one bullet on each side.

Was that bastard toying with me, or is he just a lousy shot? he wondered. And who is this other chap who looks like Scarface? Bakari was sure the driver was not Scarface. He had seen it in his frightened expression.

The radios crackled, Backup-3's voice cutting through the static: "Suspect on Mombasa Road C102. Repeat: Mombasa Road C102."

The dark motorway stretched like an endless belt, with only the occasional night bus and a few scattered commuters. The inconspicuous Backup-3 vehicle, with no lights or sirens, glided through the night like a predator on the prowl, silently stalking its prey. The speedometer needle teetered on the edge of recklessness, and with each passing second, the taillights of the getaway car became more pronounced.

"This is Backup-3. We're approximately three hundred metres behind the getaway car. Request permission to fire. Over."

Seemingly out of nowhere, a helicopter's searchlight pierced the darkness, flooding the motorway with blinding white light.

"DCI Mugo to all units: Hold your fire! Repeat: Do not fire. There's a camera crew in the helicopter."

The overzealous camera crew were at the top of their game. The thrilling chase, broadcast live on television, captivated viewers across the country. Emotions ran high, and the nation was divided as the rumoured motives of the Merciless Duo blurred the lines between heroes and villains. Some viewers – mostly women – rooted for the Duo, while others – a higher percentage of married men – cheered on the police, hoping that justice would finally catch up with the country's most wanted criminals.

The getaway Mazda hurtled down the motorway. The driver's heart pounded against his ribs. He tried to fight the rising tide of panic as his ears rang with the roar of an engine overhead.

"That's a police helicopter," he said, his voice quivering. "It's close, far too close. There's no escape."

The co-driver pressed the barrel of his Ceska pistol against the driver's temple and commanded, "Step on the gas and overtake the lorry."

"Don't you see? There's no way out! The police are everywhere."

"Step on it and overtake the lorry." The tone left no room for negotiation.

The driver swallowed hard, his foot hovering over the accelerator.

"We can't get away. If we don't stop, they will kill us. We should surrender, or else—"

The metallic click as the co-driver released the safety on the gun cut him off.

"Drive, or die right here and now. Me, I have nothing to lose."

Breathing heavily, the driver shifted into low gear, then quickly into high. He slammed on the accelerator, and the Mazda roared down the motorway at a blistering 210 kilometres per hour. In a desperate attempt to keep calm, he began to count under his breath. But the numbers slipped away as a gust of wind blasted through the passenger window, now suddenly open.

The forbidding presence of the weapon moved away from his temples. Then – BANG! BANG! Two loud shots rang out as he passed the lorry.

"Why did you shoot at the lorry?" he shouted, his voice cracking. In the rear-view, he saw the trailer swerve into the oncoming lane.

"Shit!" shouted Backup-3's team leader at the wheel.

Too late. The trailer came loose from the lorry and overturned on the road, forcing the team leader to jerk the wheel to the right to avoid a head-on collision. The vehicle veered off course, hit a pothole with a bone-crunching thud, and flipped over. Metal creaked, and glass exploded in all directions. With a final whine from the engine, the car came to rest upside down.

Bakari sped past the wreckage, his eyes fixed on the fleeing vehicle some 400 metres ahead. A quick glance in his rear-view mirror revealed two police cars stopped at the accident scene. The others sped past, their red and blue lights flashing and sirens wailing.

"Well done," Scarface drawled from the passenger seat of the getaway car. "Now, take your foot off the accelerator. But don't brake."

You have a screw loose somewhere, the pastor's son couldn't help but think.

The speedometer needle quivered at 130 kilometres per hour, and the steering wheel pulsed under his grip as the tyres skimmed the uneven road. Without warning, Scarface jerked the wheel to the left. The car crashed into a large boulder on the side of the road. Before the force of the impact hurled the unbelted pastor's son out of the car, he caught a glimpse of Scarface's face, contorted into a grin.

What kind of freak of nature is this ogre? was the last thought that crossed the pastor's son's mind.

An inferno erupted on a farm, just a few metres from where the getaway Mazda had finally come to a vertical stop after several rollovers.

The cameraman in the helicopter hovering above zoomed in on the scene below. Thick smoke billowed out, partially obscuring the view.

"Déjà vu? This is very reminiscent of the Duo's dramatic chase last year that ended in a fiery inferno," Musamali Demba continued his report, his voice barely audible over the roar of the rotor blades. Frantically, he scanned the ground beneath him with his binoculars. "The difference this time is that the getaway Mazda escaped the fire. The car, if you can still call it that, is a mangled heap of metal. It's hard to imagine anyone escaping without serious injury, if they survived at all."

A gust of wind whipped the smoke into a violent spiral, sending it towards the helicopter.

"Dear viewers, visibility is currently impaired by the smoke and ..."

The pilot banked sharply to avoid the danger, tilting the cabin dramatically and throwing Musamali Demba against the window.

CHAPTER 40

Sunday, 1 April, 00:17

Sirens blared in the distance as two ambulances and three fire engines hurtled through the darkness. Commuters whose journeys had been disrupted by the temporary closure of the motorway began to gather around the scene. Many had disembarked from an overnight bus, seemingly eager to see if the country's most sophisticated and elusive criminals would be whisked away in handcuffs or body bags.

From Musamali Demba's vantage point in the helicopter, the chaos below resembled a macabre disco – the crowd moving up and down, accompanied by a cacophony of sirens, roaring police cars and pulsing red and blue lights. Musamali Demba zoomed in on the suspect strapped to a stretcher. The man's features were unmistakable – Scarface. The protruding eye, the distinctive scars across his face and scalp, complemented by his signature outfit: a dark grey hooded sweatshirt, black tracksuit bottoms with two faded yellow stripes down the sides, and sturdy black boots.

The officers moved purposefully, their relief palpable despite the tension. Some formed a human barricade to prevent the increasingly restless crowd from approaching the suspect as they filmed with their mobile phone cameras.

"Prepare for landing," the pilot announced as she steered just above the road, skirting the charred remains of the farmhouse.

Dust and sand swirled through the crowd as the helicopter touched down on the uneven ground of an open field. The side door slid open, and Musamali Demba jumped out with a microphone. His cameraman and sound technician followed, and the three approached the spot where a group of officers surrounded the victim.

Musamali Demba tugged at his jacket and held up the microphone. The cameraman shouldered the bulky camera and focused on what was happening – paramedics lifting the stretcher carrying the victim into an ambulance. Two grim-faced officers rushed to a police car, one carrying a blue toolbox, the other a large evidence bag with a rucksack.

"We are back live at the accident scene," Musamali Demba reported, "where the feverish hunt for the Merciless Duo has reached its finale."

The ambulance drove off, flanked by a convoy of police cars.

"The scene behind me resembles an official security convoy," Musamali Demba continued. "That is the male suspect being transported from the scene in an ambulance." He stepped forward to the head of the task force and shouted, "DCI Mugo, can you confirm: was the man you just escorted away Scarface?"

Mugo stepped closer to Musamali Demba and, without warning, grabbed the hand holding the microphone and shoved it down.

"Who tipped you off?" Mugo demanded in a low voice.

"Part of our job is to keep our ears open. Let go of my hand. Don't embarrass yourself on camera."

Mugo looked into the curious eyes of the onlookers, their phones raised. He let go of the reporter's hand.

The tension dissipated. Musamali Demba held the microphone to his mouth and said, "DCI Mugo, can you please confirm that you have arrested Scarface and inform us of his condition and the fate of his accomplice?"

"It's too early to say anything about the suspect or his condition. We have secured two important items from the getaway car: a blue metal toolbox identical to the one seen with Scarface and a rucksack similar to the one carried by the accomplice. We also found a Ceska pistol, probably the weapon used in the gastropub shooting."

"Speaking of the gastropub, it's well known that the end justifies the means. This approach seems to have justified the illegal surveillance of citizens in order to apprehend the Duo. Did your team overstep boundaries and break the law to achieve their objective?"

"In view of the ongoing investigation, I must refrain from giving details that could compromise it. On the other hand, I would ask you not to quote sources that are professionally questionable. Such insinuations and publications hamper our progress and sometimes only contribute to unnecessary public anxiety. Please allow us to do our work without unwarranted interference."

Atieno-Masinde's voice rang out from the farm: "Guys, you have to see this."

Mugo hurried off, Bakari and Kebaso close behind. Once there, they found a gaping hole in the ground big enough to swallow a person. It had been exposed after the collapse of a burning barn.

"This is an opening to a tunnel," said Atieno-Masinde. "The farm owners are on their way here."

"The assistant couldn't have crawled out of the wreckage and disappeared down this tunnel, could she?" Kebaso asked.

"Something tells me the guy we got in custody isn't Scarface," Bakari said.

"Getaway car with two occupants, both wearing dark hoodies, similar appearance," Mugo began, "that's what you reported. Similar in what way?"

"They looked alike. Both with facial scars and an injured right eye. But the man in the passenger seat had a piercing, icy stare. He was the one who fired the shots in my direction. The driver looked scared."

Mugo turned to Atieno-Masinde. "Can you confirm that?"

"As I came out of the kitchen, the car drove off. I only saw the driver from the side."

"I didn't see the Duo either," said Kebaso. He turned to Bakari. "You'd spotted the assistant on the second floor when we were outside room twenty-three. She could not have gone downstairs; Beta-2 had covered the lift and stairs."

"Or maybe she took the risk and jumped out of the window on the second floor," Atieno-Masinde mused. "We found it open."

"Charlie-2 could have seen her from their position in the pavilion," Bakari countered, scratching the back of his head. "Backup-3 should be able to confirm that there were two similar-looking people in the car. The getaway car passed them in the car park."

"Both men were taken to hospital in critical condition," Mugo informed. His voice took on an imperious undertone as he asked, "How do you explain that only you and no one else saw the Duo?"

Bakari rubbed his chin sheepishly.

Mugo turned and stood a hair's breadth from Bakari. His voice heavy with disappointment, he whispered, "You've compromised this entire mission. Do you even realise that? Are you high or just reckless?"

"I am not high, boss."

"If I had you tested for drugs, would you pass?"

◆◆◆

The police had cordoned off the gastropub, transforming it from a bustling hotspot into something akin to a grim crime scene. The chaos inside seemed frozen in time, with puddles of blood here and there and broken glass glittering between overturned chairs. Both guests and staff were detained in the building and not allowed to leave until they had been interviewed and cleared. Downstairs in the hotel lobby, paramedics attended to the injured while police officers conducted initial interviews at various tables in the bar area.

The Beta-3 team leader opened the door to the conference room on the second floor. Her breath caught in her throat. A man lay on the floor, his naked, battered body motionless. His right hand was zip-tied to the leg of a table, and a business card lay beside him.

"Target-1," she whispered to her teammate. "No doubt, this is the Duo's handiwork."

Followed closely by her colleague, the team leader went over and knelt to check the victim's pulse. It was weak and irregular.

"Get the paramedics in here," she ordered, grabbing a tattered shirt from the floor and wrapping it around the man's groin. She pulled a pair of tweezers and a plastic evidence bag from her pocket and secured the business card.

A paramedic, who had just finished tending to Target-1's mistress, entered the room and got down on her knees to assess the victim's responsiveness. She felt for a pulse at the wrist and listened for breath sounds.

"Start CPR," she urged the male officer. "I'll get the doctor and a defibrillator." Turning to the female officer, she asked, "Is it true that Scarface has been caught?"

CHAPTER 41

Sunday, 1 April, 06:30

A massive search was launched for the assistant. A police helicopter circled the area and police patrols on foot and in vehicles combed the neighbourhood and surrounding area. Sniffer dogs with their noses to the ground followed the scent of the rucksack found in the getaway car.

The task force had conducted extensive interviews with the owners of the farm – a man in his 60s and his wife. They had also questioned their workers and neighbours, but they all denied any knowledge of the underground tunnel, which stretched almost 600 metres to a camouflaged exit.

The gates to the gastropub remained locked. The conference room where Target-1 had been found, along with the kitchen and adjacent delivery entrance, were cordoned off with yellow police tape. Forensic experts were busy collecting spent shell casings, documenting bloodstains, and securing biological samples. Many guests and staff had been interviewed, but some critical ones had fled before the lockdown – most notably the man who claimed to have seen Scarface enter the kitchen and the couple who had swapped rooms with Target-1.

Atieno-Masinde stifled a yawn as she entered room 23. Target-1's mistress lay curled up on the bed, her form under a white bedsheet, held tightly under her chin with both hands. Based on the slightly sweet, almost pleasant chemical odour detected by the paramedic during the examination, it was suspected that sevoflurane had been used as an anaesthetic to render the girl unconscious. Her blood sample was on its way to the laboratory.

"I'm Detective Sergeant Rahab Atieno-Masinde," she introduced herself as she sat down in a chair by the bed. "Your name is Anastacia Kemboi?"

"Yes."

"You're feeling better now, right?"

Anastacia nodded.

"I'm sorry your friend was attacked and is in hospital. We're doing everything we can."

She watched the sheet rise and fall over Anastacia's chest.

"You are safe, Anastacia." She paused, letting the reassurance sink in. "Now walk me through everything, from the moment you got on the lift."

"We went up to the second floor, and I came here with my boyfriend. I smelled something sweet." Her eyeballs twitched as if trying to reconstruct the sequence of events. "No. First I put my flowers on the table, then the lights went out. And then I smelled something sweet. The next thing I remember is waking up and seeing strangers around me."

"How many times have you been here?"

"It's my first time."

"How long have you been with your boyfriend?"

"Mmhh ... maybe three months."

"There were four of you yesterday. Who was the other man and the girl?"

"She is my friend. That man was her boyfriend. I don't know him. I didn't ask his name."

"I need your friend's name, phone number and the address where she lives."

Anastacia's hand slid under the sheet to retrieve her phone. With a swipe, she turned it on, opened the call log and pulled up the number.

"Her name is Trisha. I don't know her surname or where she lives," Anastacia said as she handed over the phone. "It was only recently that we got to know each other at her place of work."

Atieno-Masinde's eyes flickered to the phone before she asked, "Where does Trisha work?"

"Sakuti Food Court, in Parklands."

Atieno-Masinde dialled Trisha's number. After several rings, the call was disconnected.

She dialled again. This time, an automated message answered.

◆◆◆

The doors of the gastropub opened, releasing a stream of frightened patrons and distraught staff. Hours of questioning had yielded only vague answers. The kitchen staff had been particularly unhelpful: some had claimed to have crouched down, others to have taken cover or run out of the kitchen when the shots were fired. None had seen the shooter.

Seven members of the task force sat around a table in the gastropub.

Bakari's muscles flexed with every clench of his teeth. He was thinking: I had recklessly washed the pills down with whisky. Had they distorted my sense of reality?

Mugo's fingers drummed an irregular rhythm on the wooden table, a telltale sign of his burgeoning disappointment and frustration.

"This is unacceptable," he thundered, his eyes fixed on the pile of reports before him, each one a fruitless lead. "How is it possible that no guest, no worker, and not even the guards saw the Duo? The place was buzzing and packed to the rafters. Not to mention our presence."

"What's strange is the couple who swapped rooms with Target 1," said Beta-3 's team leader. "Their original room, number twenty-three, was booked for two days from Friday in the name of Joe Chituyi. But they only checked in yesterday and left in the middle of the night." She rested her elbows on the chair's armrest and interlaced her fingers. "Isn't that suspicious?"

"If Joe Chituyi was cheating on his wife – like Target-1," Bakari began thoughtfully, "and got wind of what happened to his friend, he could've had a reason to bolt just as fast."

"He could be a co-conspirator," Atieno-Masinde speculated. "Or a partner in crime."

"We'll take a two-hour break and reconvene at headquarters," Mugo declared. "In the meantime, go over everything again – every detail, every clue. I don't care how small or insignificant it seems. I need answers." He turned to Bakari and said curtly, "Blood test."

The task force rose from their chairs and walked to their cars parked outside the compound. A small crowd had gathered at the gate, their faces painted with anxiety and tense anticipation. Some were relatives and friends waiting to comfort their loved ones still trapped inside. Among them were two eager reporters with microphones, hungry to get a sensational first-hand account from the witnesses.

Mugo's eyes landed on a man standing slightly apart from the others, wearing a leather jacket that had seen better days and puffing on a cigar. The bold headline on the newspaper he was holding struck Mugo like a slap.

THE MERCILESS DUO ONCE AGAIN
ELUDES THE POLICE.

Mugo approached the man, his team close behind him.

"Excuse me," Mugo called out, "I need to take a quick look at your paper. Would you mind?"

"Go ahead, DCI Mugo," the man said, handing over the newspaper. "You can keep it; I'm done with it."

Disgusted by the smell of the cigar, Mugo turned to the feature page.

APRIL FOOL'S JOKE!

"Idiotic," Mugo grumbled, handing the newspaper back.

"Hardly idiotic," the man countered. "In fact, that's why I'm here. I was told I'd find you here."

"What do you want to talk about?"

"What the news won't talk about."

"Could you be more specific? What exactly are you getting at?"

"My office is on the sixth floor," he said, pointing to a towering building opposite the gastropub. "I was waiting for the lift when I heard gunshots. I ran back to my office and looked out the window. I saw a man in a hooded sweatshirt opening the boot of a car. Another man in a similar hooded sweatshirt got out of the boot. They drove off together in the same car. What is the news not telling us, DCI Mugo?"

"Did you get a good look at the two men?" asked Atieno-Masinde. "Can you describe them?"

The cigar dangled limply from the corner of his mouth and he looked indecisive. Suddenly, his expression changed, glowing with a hint of admiration.

"Aha, that was you," the man said, pointing his index finger in Atieno-Masinde's direction. "You did some impressive moves with the jumping and the shooting. That was sharp work."

"You can save the adulation for later," Bakari snapped. "Can you describe the men, other than they were wearing similar hooded sweatshirts?"

He drew the smoke into his lungs and curled his lips into a wry smile. Turning to Mugo, he said, "If one of your men hadn't fallen prematurely, you might have caught both culprits. Just saying."

Mugo kept his voice calm and steady. "Can you describe the two men? Anything that stood out – scars, wounds?"

"They looked like twins", the man said. "The gunman took the passenger seat."

CHAPTER 42

Wednesday 4 April, 15:10

The detectives' office at headquarters buzzed with urgency – the rustling of papers, the clatter of keyboards and the clipped, tense voices of officers at work. Analysts hunched over their desks, dissecting witness statements, while operators juggled a barrage of calls, each one a potential key to the mystery. Every scrap of information had to be catalogued, cross-referenced and, if warranted, followed up.

Senior Assistant Inspector Gitonga's eyes swept over the organised chaos as he strode through, heading straight for DCI Mugo's office.

No sooner had he closed the door behind him than he barked, "How long does it take to upload the bloody documents to the server?"

"We're working on it, sir."

"Key points," Gitonga snapped. The phrase, clipped and impatient, had become his mantra. He sank into a visitor's chair with cracked upholstery.

"Make and model of the weapon found in the Mazda: Ceska Zbrojovka CZ 75B, 9 mm calibre. Serial number obliterated, no registration, clearly obtained illegally. Gunpowder residue in the barrel confirms recent firing. Forensic analysis shows a perfect match between the markings on the bullets recovered from the gastropub and those fired during the testing of the Ceska."

"So, the Ceska is our smoking gun in the gastropub shooting?"

"Absolutely," Mugo confirmed. "But here's the rub: our man in custody didn't fire the Ceska. Hell, he didn't fire anything. Lab tests confirm that there are no traces of gunshot residue on his hands. He is clean."

"Someone else pulled the trigger?"

"According to Killian, he saw two perpetrators ... or rather, two men. The driver seemed ... timid. Hesitant, even. The man in the passenger seat looked menacing. He is the one who fired the shots before the car drove away."

"There were two men in the getaway car? And the man we have is probably the driver and not Scarface."

"That's the working theory. But something makes our suspect more than just suspicious." Mugo hesitated, leaning back in his thickly padded, dark brown executive chair.

His pause was a fraction too long, and Gitonga boiled over. "Out with it. I have a meeting to go to."

"The man is a ghost. We ran his fingerprints through every database. Nothing. Same with his dental records. Which is why we think he could be Scarface. He may have been wearing gloves, but we'll see if GSR can be detected on his clothing. We've tagged him John Doe."

"When will the gunshot residue test results be available?" Gitonga asked. "How soon will we know if he's Scarface?"

"As we speak, four witnesses are in the building to identify the man. They are cooperative and credible victims. Dalilah Beale is also a witness. We are waiting just for Oliver Morgan."

"Isn't Dalilah Beale's involvement a double-edged sword?"

"Why?"

"On the one hand, her clues have provided invaluable information. On the other hand, she is very close to her vainglorious lawyer Kizito and the unscrupulous reporter Musamali Demba. Her presence could mean that every detail of the investigation is splashed across tomorrow's front page."

Mugo smirked faintly. "We've come to an understanding."

The phone on the desk rang.

"Mugo," he answered.

"We'll have to start without Oliver Morgan," said DS Atieno-Masinde on the other end. "He has a health issue that needs to be resolved before he can join us."

"All right. I'll be there in a minute."

◆◆◆

The four cooperative and credible victims sat tense in the incident room, each absorbed in their mobile phones. They were volleyball coach Amos Mutisya, German model scout Moritz Rosenthal, Italian immigrant Francesco Lombardo and property mogul Francis Moshari. Dalilah sat in a corner, reading aloud from a picture book. Occasionally she looked up from the pages to check on Sammy, who sat quietly beside her, listening. She had brought Sammy with her to see if the boy could identify Oliver Morgan. DS Bakari and DS Kebaso sat at the head of the table, talking in whispers.

"I am Detective Chief Inspector Dennis Mugo," he announced, closing the door behind him. "Thank you for coming to identify the suspect."

Atieno-Masinde entered the room and walked over to Dalilah. Leaning forward slightly, she said in a low voice, "Oliver Morgan cannot make it today."

"Damn it!" Dalilah cursed.

Mugo walked to the front of the room and continued, "It's important to note that the head injuries the man sustained in the car accident may have slightly altered his face. He is in a coma."

"That will not prevent us from making an identification," Francesco Lombardo shouted. Every flicker of his eyes betrayed the raw pain seething beneath.

Mugo nodded. "As a precaution, you will be blindfolded before we set off for the identification. This is to ensure you don't reveal the suspect's location."

"Well, well! Look at that. Now he's being treated like a nobleman," Francesco sneered. "Of course, his whereabouts must remain top secret."

"The cost of his medical treatment and all these unnecessary precautions is draining the taxpayers' money," the volleyball coach grumbled. "Hasn't it already cost a fortune just to catch him?"

"That's why we need to temporarily confiscate all your electronic devices and blindfold you to prevent you from acting impulsively," Bakari reiterated.

"All right, let's get this over with," thundered the property mogul. He took off his dark glasses to clean them. An eye patch covered his left eye, which Scarface had permanently damaged.

◆◆◆

The room in which John Doe lay comatose was devoid of windows, its walls a dull, sterile white. Two fluorescent lights hung overhead, one flickering and emitting a low hum.

Atieno-Masinde and Bakari led the blindfolded Francesco Lombardo into the room.

When the blindfold was removed, Francesco found himself flanked by two tall, broad-shouldered guards, with DCI Mugo standing on the opposite side of the bed.

A surge of hatred, bitterness and rage consumed Francesco as his gaze fell on the unconscious man with tubes snaking out of his nose and mouth. He clenched his hands into fists and felt an insatiable urge to lunge at the man, to unleash a barrage of blows, to spit in his face and rip out the tubes. But the towering guards made it clear: any attempt to vent his rage would be futile.

"*Figlio di puttana*!" he cursed, resorting to the only weapon at his disposal.

"Excuse me?" Mugo responded.

"This is the *stronzo*!" His words crackled with the scalding fervour of his anger, his gestures dramatic and fierce. "This is the fucking *bastardo*."

"What makes you think this is the man who attacked you?"

For a moment, Francesco remembered what a urologist, who was also a sex therapist, had told him: *It's a psychological trauma. Time will ease the symptoms*. But time proved to be a fickle companion. The erectile dysfunction persisted, overshadowing his many ailments. Despite regular painkillers and a cocktail of medications, the after-effects of the attack remained uncontrollable.

Francesco spat out a stream of curses in Italian, each word dripping with menace.

"We are finished, Mr Lombardo," Mugo declared.

"What happens next? How will this *stronzo* be punished?"

The guards grabbed Francesco by the arms, blindfolded him and dragged him out of the room, his vile insults in his native tongue echoing behind him.

"Porca miseria! Vaffanculo"

Dalilah was led in. Her blindfold was removed.

Lips pressed together, she stared down at the man. A heavy, oppressive feeling settled over her, triggering a swirl of conflicting emotions.

Are you the man who made me name my foundation Daddy Stop?

She moved closer to the bed.

How I would have loved to meet you under different circumstances, if only to thank you for saving me.

"I'm afraid I can't help you," she whispered, her voice breaking.

Blindfolded, Dalilah was led out.

The volleyball coach was brought in. The blindfold was taken off.

When he saw the unconscious suspect, he felt dizzy and almost lost his balance. Breathing slowly and deeply, he shook off his fear and looked at the man with narrowed eyes.

"He smells like someone who hasn't had a shower in days," he whispered, sniffing around. "Scarface stinks horribly."

"What can you say about his face?" Mugo asked. "Is he the man who attacked you?"

"This is someone else. This is not Scarface; I'm one hundred per cent sure."

"What makes you so sure this is not the man?"

"Scarface's damaged eye never blinked ... somehow it couldn't. Here, it's half closed." He shook his head. "Unbelievable! You've got the wrong man."

Mugo walked over to the other side and whispered to a guard. Then he said, "Thank you for coming, Mr Mutisya,"

The guards blindfolded Mr Mutisya and led him away.

Next up was the property mogul. At the sight of the motionless man, his nose flared and he breathed heavily. He felt a lump in his throat, heavy and painful. His healthy eye wandered nervously around the room, half expecting the assistant to blow another chewing gum bubble and pop it with the same unnerving snap.

Suddenly, a doubt nagged at him: Is this really Scarface? There's something different about him.

"This is Scarface. This is the man who attacked me," he forced the words out. He wanted to find peace, to throw off the burden that had weighed on him for so long. "I'd recognise him from a mile away."

"I understand that you need closure, Mr Moshari," Mugo said. "But I sense that you are holding on to anything that looks like justice, even if it means accusing the wrong person."

Mr Moshari removed his glasses, his hand lingering mid-air before sliding them back on. Not a word left his lips.

"Is this the man who attacked you, Mr Moshari?" Mugo's voice was calm, but with the necessary assertiveness to break the man's silence.

"This is Scarface. He should be doused in paraffin and set on fire."

"Get this man out of here," Mugo ordered the guards.

The last witness of the day was the German model scout, whose near photographic memory had already proved invaluable during the interrogations.

"Ha," he chuckled as soon as the blindfold was removed, and he caught a glimpse of the suspect. "You've got the wrong guy. This isn't Scarface."

"What makes you say that?" Mugo asked.

"Scarface stinks unbearably. This man doesn't. And he's got stubble on his head and chin. Scarface does not have a single hair on his scalp or face."

"I'd say this man stinks," said Mugo. "As for the hair, maybe Scarface is such a freak that he shaved it all off before he went on his rampage. Now he's locked up, it's growing back."

"Scarface had three deep scars on the left side of his face, one on the right, one above his nose and one along his forehead."

"So does this man," Mugo countered.

"The right scar extended to his eye – more of a wound, really. It was the most prominent and still looked fresh and raw. That's not the case here."

"It's been almost a month since you were attacked. The wounds may have healed a bit in that time," Mugo argued.

"It's possible, but this man's scars are only on his face. Scarface had scars all over his scalp. Another thing is that Scarface had a prominent Adam's apple; this man has none."

◆◆◆

Dalilah Beale, Francesco Lombardo and Francis Moshari were blindfolded and led out of the building. At Mugo's behest, the German model scout and the volleyball coach were locked in a nearby windowless room, to be released only after the detective chief inspector had decided their fate.

Mugo scratched the back of his head, his eyes fixed on John Doe, his mind racing: *if this isn't Scarface, then who is he? A decoy? A victim of coercion?*

As he left the room, frustration and defeat hung over him like a leaden cloak. He couldn't shake the feeling that he had failed his team, his country, and himself.

"Hey, boss," Atieno-Masinde called as she caught up with Mugo in the empty corridor. Bakari was close behind.

Mugo turned to them. "What is it?"

"What should we do with the two men?"

Mugo ran a hand over his cheeks and sighed. For the first time in his career, he felt crushed by the weight of the decision, the pressure growing like weeds sprouting from the ground in spring, threatening to smother everything.

"First, we have to prove beyond a shadow of a doubt that John Doe is not Scarface," he said. "Until then, we can't afford any speculation, especially from these two men who say otherwise."

"We can't stop them from talking, boss." The tension in Atieno-Masinde's voice was unmistakable.

"The volleyball coach and the German model scout will be arrested immediately for child sexual abuse," Mugo said, his voice taut with tension. "Bail will be denied due to flight risk and potential witness tampering."

"Are you willing to risk a lawsuit for wrongful arrest, boss?" Bakari asked. "I wouldn't count on Dalilah Beale to produce evidence against these men."

"Scarface," Mugo breathed, brushing the question aside. "The Midnight Dancer of Dakacha, Dahdi Stoppa. What are we missing?"

"A suspect without a past is more troubling than one entangled in a web of aliases," Bakari said, half to himself.

Mugo's fingers lingered on his throbbing forehead. He massaged the spot in slow, deliberate circles, thinking of his impeccable track record. He had solved cases that had baffled others.

Then it hit him like a pang of malaria in the middle of the night – the retired OCPD's conclusion about the Midnight Dancer of Dakacha: *This? Looks like he left us some subtle telltale clues. I'll even bet he set up the board for a twisted game of chess.*

CHAPTER 43

Friday, 6 April, 10:20

File in hand, Mugo and the Digital Sleuth descended the stairs, heading for the Incident Room.

"Oh, I almost forgot," said the Digital Sleuth. "Musamali Demba has cancelled his appointment again. Says he's out of the country."

"Track down the traitor leaking our intel to that smug reporter."

"You still think one of us tipped him off?"

"Showing up in that chopper wasn't a fluke. And he knew about our gastropub op. Find that rat."

They entered the room, Mugo's eyes sweeping over Senior Assistant Inspector Gitonga and the eight task force members already assembled. Papers and files littered the table before them; some opened to reveal scribbled notes and highlighted passages.

Atieno-Masinde switched on the wall monitor. It showed a photograph of the hyena carcass found in the compound of the Midnight Dancer of Dakacha.

She opened the meeting: "We've received the initial analysis of the teeth found in the hyena carcass. The results confirm that they belong to the victims of the Duo."

"A glass jar inside an animal? Oh, how original," said Gitonga, his voice heavy with sarcasm and thinly veiled disappointment. "This is classic misdirection. Whoever staged this wants us to believe that Scarface is the Midnight Dancer of Dakacha."

"This is not a red herring, sir," Atieno-Masinde countered, brushing a fluff from her blazer to avoid Gitonga's piercing gaze. After years of working under the senior assistant inspector, she knew that Gitonga's instincts were rarely wrong. "We're working on the assumption that Scarface is the Midnight Dancer of the Dakacha."

"Working on assumptions is unacceptable," Gitonga thundered. "Why would a criminal leave his trophies unsecured in this way?"

"Criminals tend to get sloppy over time, especially if they've got away with several crimes," the Digital Sleuth argued.

"I'm sure I'm not the only one who thinks Scarface is flaunting his arrogance," Bakari said, gripping a cold cup of chai. "Maybe he left the evidence behind deliberately – a show of twisted superiority. Fact is, the whole thing was well-planned, and the timing was flawless. I'd even say Musamali Demba and his helicopter crew were a calculated distraction. The live footage tied our hands; shooting the car was off the table."

"Scarface and his assistant vanish without a trace. Is that what you call a well-planned, or was it a cock-up on your part?" Gitonga fumed.

Bakari rested his hands on the table, his posture stiff. "The Duo had it all figured out. The farmhouse, which went up in flames shortly after the accident, was probably their predetermined destination. The dogs picked up a scent in the tunnel. The Duo must have escaped through it, and the fire bought them time to slip away before it was extinguished."

Kebaso tugged at his tie, loosening it. "The man and his girlfriend, Trisha – the ones who swapped rooms with Target-1 – may have been involved. They've disappeared. I visited Target-1 this morning, but he still can't speak. He had a stroke after the attack, and his condition is getting worse by the day."

"Trisha works as a waitress at the Sakuti Food Court," said Atieno-Masinde. "She hasn't been to work for two weeks. None of her colleagues or employer knows where she lives, and her phone is switched off. Target-1's mistress, Anastacia, and Trisha met at the Sakuti Food Court four months ago and hit it off. A few weeks later, Trisha introduced her to Target-1."

"The coincidences are simply too numerous and too precise to be mere coincidence." Gitonga's stern face was a mask of disbelief. "It looks like we're dealing with a group of criminals, not just a lone duo."

Mugo nodded grimly. "We must be careful with that assumption. But we are digging deeper, following every lead, not overlooking the connections between seemingly unrelated events. There's a thread connecting them all, and we will find it."

"Why don't you think we're dealing with a gang?" Gitonga wanted to know.

"Given the reluctance of victims and witnesses to cooperate, it can be assumed that some of those involved acted under duress. We—"

The door opened, interrupting Mugo. His secretary poked her head in and announced, "Mama Daudi ... Mrs Saumu Ratego is in the house."

"Who the hell is Mama Daudi?" barked Gitonga.

"The mother of Dahdi Stoppa, the Midnight Dancer of Dakacha."

◆◆◆

Mugo's mind whirled as he and Bakari led the blindfolded Mrs Saumu Ratego down the corridor of the institute. Her multi-coloured, floral African dress matched the headscarf elegantly draped over her hair, which was grey at the sides. The ravages of time had scarred her face, the wrinkles reflecting a life of challenge and hard work.

They stopped in front of a heavy steel door. Bakari punched a code into the keypad, the lock clicked, and the door opened, releasing acrid air.

"We're here, Ma'am," Bakari announced.

"Just call me Mama Daudi."

Bakari led her into the room and removed the blindfold from her face.

Standing by the bed, Mama Daudi stared at the disfigured face of the comatose man.

"He looks like death has already claimed him," she whispered, clasping her hands tightly in front of her.

Despite her obvious efforts to maintain her composure, Mugo could see the cracks in her façade. Her trembling legs looked as if they could barely bear the weight of her trepidation. He instinctively reached out to steady her, but she pulled away, moving closer to the bed instead. With trembling hands, she reached out and grasped the edge of the sheet, pulling it down to reveal the man's torso. His unbuttoned shirt hung loosely on his frame, exposing a bare chest scarred with dark bruises.

Mugo watched the woman closely. He had almost resigned himself to the fact that the man wasn't Scarface, but part of him still clung to the hope that he was wrong.

Mama Daudi took a deep breath. Her eyes swept over the torso, searching for something. Then a smile lit up her face, and she looked relieved. She made the sign of the cross – touching her forehead, then her chest and finally her shoulder.

"This man is not my son."

Mugo stared at the woman, his mind racing but empty, searching for a follow-up question that wouldn't come. Years of experience had hardened him to the job's vagaries and inevitable vicissitudes, but this case felt like an affront to his intelligence, stretching the limits of plausibility. Although he would require DNA confirmation, his instincts told him that Mama Daudi was telling the truth.

"Why do you think this man isn't your son, Dahdi Stoppa?" Bakari asked. "Daudi Ratego – that's his real name, right?"

"Daudi has a large birthmark on his left side."

Bakari held up the blindfold. "I need to cover your eyes again before we leave the room."

"Is that really necessary?"

"Protocol." Bakari's tone was razor-sharp.

The three entered a windowless room, sparsely furnished with only the bare essentials: white plastic chairs and a wooden table with three bottles of water on it.

Bakari removed the woman's blindfold and led her to a chair.

"Time to answer a few questions," he snapped.

"May I?" she asked, her hand hovering over a bottle of water.

"Help yourself, of course," Bakari said, adjusting his chair to face her directly. "If you like, I can order you something to eat."

"I am not hungry, maybe later." She unscrewed the cap from the bottle.

"We're here to talk about your son – the Midnight Dancer of Dakacha," Mugo began, taking a seat opposite the woman. "Should I call him Dahdi Stoppa or Daudi Ratego?"

"Daudi will do." Her expression remained blank, giving nothing away.

"Or Scarface?" Bakari asked.

"Daudi," she said flatly.

"When was the last time you saw Daudi?" Mugo asked.

"It's been ages. But I don't blame him; he's been very busy."

"Busy doing what?"

A sardonic smile tugged at the corners of her mouth. She took a sip of water, her gaze fixed downward.

"Mama Daudi says Daudi has been very busy," Bakari said in a drawling tone as he scribbled in his notebook. "Busy with illegal attacks."

"Don't put words in my mouth. I never said anything about illegal attacks."

"Scarface – or Daudi, if you prefer – what he's doing is wrong by every standard of society and tradition." Bakari's gaze sharpened.

"Do you want to talk about Scarface or Daudi?" she asked, a cryptic grin spreading across her face.

"Let's start with Scarface. The name is now well known," Mugo said. "How did he get the scars and wounds on his face?"

"The last time I saw him ..." Suddenly, she stopped. She dabbed at her drooping, perpetually moist eyelids with the hem of her dress.

"Go on, Mama Daudi. The last time you saw him ..." Mugo urged.

She shook her head and said, "Nothing."

"The last time you saw Scarface, he didn't have any scars," Bakari said, scribbling in his notebook, trying to lure Mama Daudi out of her shell.

"Don't hesitate to correct my partner if he is wrong," Mugo invited her.

Mama Daudi said nothing. But sometimes silence says everything.

"Scarface ... excuse me, you call him Daudi," Bakari remarked. "Daudi breaks into people's homes and attacks them in a very inhuman way—"

"Scarface does what he does," Mama Daudi cut him off. "Not Daudi."

"What do you mean by that?" Bakari asked.

"You're so enthusiastic about Scarface, huh? You always have to mention him."

Bakari closed his notebook with a sharp snap. "Yes, Mama Scarface. This god complex that Daudi has adopted as Scarface is dangerous. It's self-destructive. Daudi needs help, and you can help us reach him before it's too late."

"God has different ways of making sinners pay for their sins. He made the Israelites conquer the Canaanites, didn't He?"

"God cannot be pleased with such disrespect and blasphemy as your son displays," Bakari admonished. "If I am not mistaken, you are a woman of God."

"Ever read the Bible, Mr Policeman? And if a man causes a blemish in his neighbour; as he hath done, so shall it be done to him: breach for breach, eye for eye, tooth for tooth. As he hath caused a blemish in a man, so shall it be done to him again."

"You must feel sorry for the comatose man," Mugo surmised. "We have a witness who saw Scarface drag him out of a car boot. He doesn't deserve to be in this state."

"I'm sure there are legitimate reasons why he ended up there."

"What would count as a justifiable reason?" Mugo asked, tilting his head, his expression open and impartial.

"Justifiable? Plenty – free will, moral stance, politics." She shifted in her seat and crossed her legs at the ankles. "But my bet is a guilt complex. He went along to avoid something worse. That's what people say, anyway."

"I haven't heard anyone say that. Who said that?" Mugo's tone hardened.

"Kavoi. Odhiambo. Njoroge. Kiplagat. Shall I go on?"

"Does Daudi have the right to punish people who have allegedly committed a crime?" Bakari leaned forward, his voice sharp. "What he is doing is against the law. It's illegal."

"Spare me the sermon, Mr Policeman." Her voice was suddenly defiant. "Preaching the law to me is like playing a guitar to a goat. It's pointless. Because we all know the truth. Those with power twist the law to suit themselves while the rest of us are left out in the cold."

"There's this young girl," Mugo drawled, "Scarface always drags her along. Doesn't she deserve better? Shouldn't she finish school?"

Mama Daudi wrapped her arms tightly around her belly, her hands disappearing into the folds of her dress. Mugo noted the gesture, a silent signal that she was erecting a barrier.

"Who is this girl?" Mugo asked emphatically.

With an inscrutable smile, she shrugged.

Bakari tapped his fingers on the armrest. "What is your relationship with Dalilah Beale, formerly Dalilah Majimbo?"

"Why are you derailing now? Mr Policeman, just because I'm a woman doesn't mean I'm a blabbermouth."

Mugo leaned in slightly. "We've confirmed that most of the men Scarface has attacked are guilty of child abuse."

Her face lit up. "Now you're talking, DCI Mugo."

"I promise you, Mama Daudi, they will be brought to justice."

"I believe you. I have heard that your track record speaks for itself."

"These child abusers are the worst criminals, Mama Daudi."

She clapped her hands once, raised them in the air and said, "Hallelujah! At last, you have recognised the selfless and noble cause."

"Your son Daudi Ratego, aka Scarface, aka the Midnight Dancer of Dakacha, aka Dahdi Stoppa, disappeared at the end of March last year, only to reappear in March of this year." Mugo leaned back, his posture relaxed, his tone warm and reassuring, but also probing.

Mama Daudi opened the bottle and took a drink.

"Dahdi Stoppa ... Scarface repeated the same pattern and stopped again at the end of last month. Can we expect him to come back in March and pick up where he left off with the child molesters?"

Mama Daudi smiled broadly and infectiously. But it was short-lived. A dark shadow fell over her eyes, and her frail hands gripped the bottle.

CHAPTER 44

Tuesday, 25 December, 16:30

The rented hall exuded a festive atmosphere, with Christmas decorations in every corner and twinkling lights bathing the room in a cosy glow. The tables were laden with delicious treats, sweets and biscuits. In one corner, members of the DS Savekids Foundation mingled with the press, including Musamali Demba, dressed to impress Dalilah. Across the room, sponsors who had contributed to the success of the event showed their continued commitment to the cause by their presence.

José Feliciano's "Feliz Navidad" blared from the surround speakers. High-pitched voices filled the room – some belting out the chorus with boisterous gusto, others stringing together playful gibberish in place of the actual lyrics. A few simply swayed, humming along, smiles flickering across their faces. These were children with a bleak existence, without a roof over their heads and, in many cases, without a family to love and protect them. Their beds were cold concrete, and the scraps of food they ate came from scavenging through dustbins – unless a passer-by dropped some change, which was rare. Many were victims of systematic sexual exploitation.

For the 129 children, the Christmas party was a rare treat, made possible by the main sponsor Oliver Morgan.

Oliver looked on with ambivalence as the DS Savekids carers and children enthusiastically held hands and began to dance. He and his wife Charlotte sat in an almost secluded part of the room usually reserved for the DJ. A babysitter was looking after their two children at their hotel.

Oliver's mind flashed back to the countless times he had reached out to Dalilah Beale, each call a desperate plea wrapped in half-truths in an attempt to win her heart. He had been determined to honour his deal with Scarface, and Dalilah had been unwilling to accept the million shillings. The stakes had been high, as the task force had finally confirmed that the comatose suspect was not Scarface.

"I am seeing a specialist to overcome my mental disorder," he had confessed. "I am a changed man now, Ms Beale. I have effective means at my disposal to curb immoral impulses before they lead to sexual assault."

"Omari Sekibo was your employee and also a pimp. The boy was only eleven. You should have realised immediately that he was far too young, probably forced or drugged."

Not one to be fooled by Dalilah's cunning and guile, Oliver had stood his ground: "I knew nothing of Omari Sekibo's shady dealings. All my affairs were consensual and with female prostitutes only. No male prostitutes."

"Where is Omari Sekibo?"

"*I haven't heard from him since his last visit to the hospital.*" Oliver hoped that Omari had invested his money wisely to start a new life in a distant land beyond the reach of the local police and their warrants. Omari had emptied the one million shillings from the safe in his hotel room.

"Are you sure you never set foot in that aparthotel in Nairobi and abused a boy?"

"*Please believe me, Ms Beale, I am not that kind of person.*" There had been no evidence linking him to the apartment hotel. With this happy turn of events, Oliver had agreed to come to Nairobi to identify the comatose John Doe. But things turned out differently. The sight of Dalilah Beale, hand in hand with the street kid – Sammy, if he remembered correctly – had struck him like a crushing blow to the chest.

Dalilah's relentless determination to find the truth had been evident in the way she had spoken to the boy, and Oliver had quickly seen through the intent behind her questioning. The boy's gaze had lingered on him – too long, too intensely. At that moment, Oliver had thought he was finished. But then he'd seen the flicker of pity in the boy's eyes – the hesitation, and finally, the inability to answer Dalilah's question.

Relief had washed over Oliver. "*Lucky I got bandaged up*," he had whispered, guessing that the searing pain carved into his face had masked any trace of guilt. Dalilah had not pressed further.

Finally, after countless phone calls, Dalilah had agreed to accept his donation to the DS Savekids Foundation.

The last notes of the Christmas carol faded into silence. A side door opened to reveal a white, pot-bellied Santa Claus with a long white beard and bushy white eyebrows. He wore a red pointed hat, a red coat lined with fluffy white fur, and a large brown burlap sack slung over his shoulder.

"Father Christmas, Father Christmas," cried a little girl, her face aglow with surprise.

"No, it's Santa Claus," squealed a boy who had seen a man like that in Christmas adverts.

The children ran up to the white-haired man and hugged him.

"Ho, ho, ho! Merry Christmas! Merry Christmas!" shouted Santa Claus.

"Who are you?" asked Sammy shyly.

"Where are you from?" asked another child.

"Ho, ho, ho! First of all, sit down and be quiet. Then I'll tell you who I am and where I come from."

Santa placed his sack on the floor and sat on a chair while two members of the DS Savekids Foundation brought more gift bags into the hall. Sharona Warinda, who was heavily pregnant, took a seat next to Father Christmas. No one had expected her pregnancy, as her on-again, off-again relationship with her boyfriend was thought to be over for good. The children sat down, some on the floor, to be as close as possible to the gift-giver.

With charismatic flair, Santa spun a humorous and quirky tale about his heritage. Sharona translated his story from English into Swahili for those who did not speak the language.

After finishing his story, Santa announced, "I have a present for each of you." He poured out the gifts from his sack. "When you hear your name, come and get your present."

"When you get your present, don't open it until I tell you to," Sharona added. "Is that clear?"

"Yeeees!" the children shouted in unison.

Charlotte Morgan watched as the children stood up one by one to receive their gifts. It reminded her of her husband's tremendous generosity to the Foundation and his commitment to social projects in Kenya. She wondered: *Oliver, the savvy shopper and thrifty man par excellence, who is constantly scouring the internet for Groupon deals and discounts*?

Santa picked up the penultimate present and called out, "Rosemary."

A girl of about thirteen rose to her feet with an exaggerated sigh. She approached Santa and said into his microphone, "I was beginning to think you'd forgotten me."

Laughter and applause filled the room.

"I rarely forget, Rosemary," Santa said.

Rosemary took her present, held the wrapped box to her ear and shook it.

"Thank you." She smiled mischievously and added, "Will you be back for Easter?"

Santa chuckled.

"You can make an exception for us, can't you?" called Mickey from the back of the room.

"This is the first time we have received a gift," said Rosemary. "Please come again at Easter."

"Pleeeease!" the other children shouted in unison.

Santa's mouth fell open, and his chubby cheeks turned a deep crimson.

"You can open your presents now," Sharona called out.

The rustling of wrapping paper filled the room, followed by excited and cheerful chatter.

Santa called out the last name: "Dalilah Beale."

Charlotte watched as Dalilah raised a single eyebrow, a wry smile tugging at her lips, before shaking her head as though she couldn't believe what she had just heard.

As Santa stood up and approached Dalilah with the gift box, Charlotte witnessed a bizarre exchange: Dalilah shot a questioning look at Oliver, who subtly shook his head in response.

What's going on between them? Charlotte wondered.

"Who smuggled a present in here?" Dalilah asked as Santa placed the wrapped box in her hands.

"Certainly not Father Christmas," said Santa. "It looks official."

Dalilah's heart skipped a beat as she saw the sender's typed name. She pulled herself together, prioritised the task at hand and took the microphone from Santa. First, she waited while the younger children were taken to an adjacent playroom.

"Um ..." Dalilah began. But no matter how hard she tried, the sender's name had her in its grip.

She handed the microphone to Sharona and whispered something to her.

With a healthy dose of jealousy, Charlotte watched Dalilah leave the room.

She turned to her husband and asked, "Why're you fibbing about not bringing Dalilah a present? She's touched. But she can't thank you in person, maybe 'coz I'm around, so she buggers off."

"Are you a comedian in the making? That's a bit of a giggle."

"You are—"

"Children, ladies and gentlemen, members of the press." Sharona's voice over the loudspeaker drowned out Charlotte's words. "First and foremost, I would like to extend my sincere thanks to all our donors and benefactors whose generosity has made this event such a success. I would also like to express my gratitude to everyone who continues to support our charitable projects. The list of names is too long to mention each one individually..."

Charlotte wondered: *Is there something going on between Dalilah and Oliver*? She had always relied on her husband's honesty, but everything changed when she met the members of the DS Savekids Foundation. The tension between Dalilah Beale and Oliver was palpable, but the looks they shared were devoid of affection or desire. Instead, there was an unmistakable distance between them, as if something once cherished had slipped through their fingers.

Charlotte listened with divided attention as Sharona continued.

"Our new project to help sexually exploited street children is a huge challenge. Many of these children are exposed to various forms of domestic and institutional violence and hostility. Some have fled violence and abuse at home only to face it again on the streets ..."

Charlotte's concentration slipped, and her mind drifted back to her sex life – or rather, the lack of one. She blamed Oliver's lack of sensual desire and emotional detachment on the lingering trauma of his attack. But one question kept nagging at her: *How could the thugs who attacked and robbed him cause such lasting damage to his libido*? The question had stirred up her insecurities – from the fear that Oliver no longer found her attractive to the suspicion that he was having an extramarital affair.

Charlotte watched as a pregnant girl walked up to the podium and took the microphone from Sharona.

"My name is Caroline Wambui," the pregnant girl's voice boomed. "I'm seventeen and this will be my second child. I dropped out of school to get away from the crap I was going through in my foster home and ended up living on the streets."

Charlotte perked up.

"Girls like me get pregnant because we get raped. We sniff glue or petrol to cope. It makes it easier to eat garbage, to kill the hunger, or to stay alert so we don't get jumped."

"That sounds like a drug advert," Sharona interjected, "but it's not."

"We are not drug addicts," Caroline went on, "it's naked survival. On behalf of my brothers and sisters on the streets, I want to thank you all for this wonderful day. I wish every day could be like this."

The crowd applauded.

"It would also be very, very helpful if the police would crack down on child abuse. I have a young daughter, and I don't want her to go through what I went through at the hands of paedophiles. Many of these paedophiles are much more brutal than the hard life on the streets."

The poignant words created a sombre and disheartening atmosphere. Tears welled up in the eyes of many, mostly women.

Surprised by the moist eyes of the usually insensitive Oliver, Charlotte teased him: "Are those tears of remorse?"

"Shut up," Oliver taunted her with his favourite phrase, just as a technical glitch silenced the speakers.

Nearby, Sammy was on his way to the toilet when he overheard the man.

Sammy stood paralysed, every muscle contracted in fear. The voice and the words were familiar, reopening an unhealed wound. He turned slowly towards the source, his breath catching in his throat as his eyes locked with the *mzungu's*.

Sammy felt the warm liquid trickle down his leg, powerless to stop it.

Charlotte noticed the boy staring at her husband, his face frozen in shock. Her sister's clichéd argument came to mind: *Men who work away from home for days on end are likely to succumb to the temptation of leading a double life.*

She turned to Oliver with a look that was nothing short of reproachful, and the words tumbled out of her mouth: "Do you have a child here?"

"For heaven's sake, I don't have an illegitimate child."

"Who is that boy?" Charlotte pointed to the boy who was hurrying away. "You got a thing going on with that … Dalilah Beale? She's been well dodgy, if you ask me."

"Please, stop! She's not even my sort … I mean …" His voice trailed off.

Charlotte's mind whirled like a storm as she weighed his every word.

"If Dalilah's not your sort, you into a particular type of chick, or you into blokes?"

"Come on, darling," Oliver said, taking Charlotte's hand, "let's talk outside."

◆◆◆

Dalilah opened the box, took out a white sheet of paper, unfolded it and stared at the typewritten signature. It was the same name as the sender: *L. Stoppa.*

L for Lillian, my missing mother, who supposedly ran off with her lover, Dahdi Stoppa?

Is she still alive?

Her fingers trembled as she removed the paper inserts from the box. Mouth agape, she stared at the pile of business cards, strikingly similar to her old ones, now depleted.

Her attention shifted to the accompanying letter.

> *Merry Christmas, dear Dalilah,*
>
> *I wish I could have personally presented you with this token of appreciation for your selfless support and dedication to the most vulnerable members of society. For the underprivileged, vulnerable, disadvantaged, and abused children, these business cards serve as vital protection. They are like a fire extinguisher – it is always better to have one and not need it than to need it and not have it. Should the souls, bodies and minds of these defenceless children go up in flames, these business cards will ensure that the arsonists responsible for inflicting such senseless physical and mental torment on them will have one implacable wish: that a millstone be hung around their necks and that they be cast into the depths of the sea.*

It goes without saying that it is more important to ensure that children grow up psychologically and socially healthy than to try to make up for the wrongs done to them when they are grown up and broken. No sane person should tolerate such cruelty against the weakest in society. Children are the future. No one should ever tamper with the future without facing dire consequences. Therefore …

The balcony door swung open. Dalilah caught a glimpse of Sammy in his damp trousers, his expression one of deep concern. He ran to her and grabbed her dress with both hands.

"What is it, Sammy?"

"I saw the *mzungu* that hurt me," he whispered in a frightened voice, glancing behind him.

"Are you serious … er … the *mzungu* is here? The one who said to you, 'Shut up!'"

"Yes."

"This sick son of a bi..." She bit back the rest and muttered under her breath, "How on earth did this bastard even dare to show up at my event? Has he come to choose his next toy?"

◆◆◆

"Let's go back to the hotel and have a chat," Oliver said, reaching for the car keys in his pocket. "I really messed things up. I'm dead sorry, love."

"Who is it?" Charlotte thundered, the immense weight of betrayal and breach of trust crushing her and leaving her unable to walk to the car. "It's Dalilah, isn't it?"

"No, not Dalilah. It's not a woman."

The words pierced her like a fisherman's knife, slicing through her mind and her sanity. Dazed, she leaned against the porch railing, struggling to process her husband's devastating revelation.

"That was a terrible mistake." Oliver's forehead was covered in sweat. "I'm seeing a therapist."

"What absolute madness are you talking about?" Charlotte shrieked. It took a great deal of self-control to keep her fingernails from digging into his lips, which dared to part and give free rein to the scathing words. "You are in therapy for homosexuality? What a load of codswallop! Are you in love with him?"

"No! I wasn't smitten. It was just … sexual. Nothing more."

"It was all about sex? What was it about him that turned you on, that I ain't got? His Adam's apple? His hairy, flat chest?"

"Let's chat somewhere else, shall we?"

"Answer me!" She lost control and punched him in the chest. "You had a fancy for a little bit of cock, huh?"

"No."

Tears welled up in her eyes. "So what the fuck is it?"

"It was a bit of a twisted kind of curiosity."

"Was it worth it? Is that why you can't …"

Charlotte fell silent as she saw the front door open.

Dalilah walked out of the building, hand in hand with Sammy. As soon as Oliver Morgan was clearly visible, she felt Sammy's grip tighten around her fingers.

She stopped in the car park and stared at the couple.

"Is that the mzungu, Sammy?'"

Sammy stepped sideways, almost disappearing behind her, and murmured, "Yes."

Dalilah felt her stomach churn, bile rising in her throat. Her breath came in ragged, shallow gasps as the words "betrayal" and "traitor" echoed through her mind. Every fibre of her being recoiled at the thought of being a traitor who had succumbed to Oliver Morgan's "blood money".

A man who can lie so brazenly is ... This is unforgivable!

Her disgust and contempt for Oliver Morgan built to a crescendo, consuming her beyond all self-control. As if in a trance, she pulled one of her new business cards out of the gift box and dangled it between her fingers.

Charlotte noticed the icy cold in Dalilah's eyes.

"What's going on here, Oliver?" she asked.

"Dalilah Beale has hatched a new plot against me. The Merciless Duo will execute it."

"A new plot against you? What on earth are you babbling about?"

"See the business card she is holding? The box she's clutching appears to be filled with more of the same. The Merciless Duo use them to track down their victims."

"Oliver, you're talking gibberish. Be clearer!"

"My health problems are the result of the Merciless Duo's attack. They properly messed me up."

Charlotte felt the colour drain from her face. "The Merciless Duo attacked you? You mean ... That's why ..." Her voice trailed off. She glanced at Dalilah and the boy, then back at her husband. "Is that why that boy over there wet himself when he saw you?"

"I paid for it ..." His voice cracked, the words barely coming out.

"Did you molest the child?"

"I paid dearly. You can't imagine what I'm going through. I feel like I'm hardly worth anything."

Charlotte suddenly felt an inexplicable twinge in her chest, a sharp point piercing her heart. She clutched at her left breast, but her legs swayed as the ground beneath her seemed to give way. Wobbling, she noticed that

Oliver's face had taken on an unfamiliar scowl, his features contorted into a predatory, menacing grimace.

"No way am I letting Dalilah Beale come after me again," he hissed, slipping the car keys into his pocket.

Charlotte shuddered; she had never seen this side of Oliver. His steps were heavy, his movements taut with an icy fury as he stalked towards Dalilah.

EPILOGUE

The new year began with a sense of foreboding. Ten months had passed since the infamous car chase on 31 March, and the Merciless Duo had faded into obscurity – no attacks, no sightings – but no one was fooled. Especially now that John Doe's identity had been established.

When John Doe awoke from his coma last August, doctors diagnosed him with retrograde amnesia, the result of brain trauma caused by the car accident. His mind seemed to have been wiped clean; he had no memory of his past, no idea who he once was.

The task force doctored photographs of his ravaged face and released them to the public, triggering a storm of desperate calls from people searching for missing loved ones. Among them was a delusional woman fixated on the belief that John Doe was her missing husband. Her claims meant that the search for possible relatives was put on hold while the task force delved deeper into the woman's story.

Gradually, John Doe's cognitive abilities began to recover, and he vaguely remembered that his wife had never greeted him with a kiss – unlike the woman who claimed to be his wife. The task force unravelled the woman's twisted story, cut off contact with her and reopened the door to others in October.

Blindfolded and flanked by two police officers, a pastor called Jacob Lamai was led down the corridor to John Doe's room.

The blindfold was removed, and the pastor saw the man, who had not yet been identified by the police. He was lying in bed with the headboard raised, his left hand

and legs cuffed to the bed rail. His face was recognisable, but strikingly different from his press photographs. On the other side of the bed were the two officers the pastor had met earlier – DCI Mugo and DS Atieno-Masinde.

Mugo noted the deep sigh and half-laugh that escaped the pastor's lips. The man looked relieved, as if a heavy burden had been lifted from his shoulders.

The pastor in liturgical garb closed his eyes and prayed: "Thank you, Almighty Heavenly Father. You have brought my son back to me. Thank You for Your mercy, for Your infinite grace. I praise Your name forever. In Jesus's name. Amen."

Mugo turned to John Doe. "Do you know this man?"

A spark of recognition flickered in John Doe's eyes, evidenced by the quick flutter of his eyelid.

"You are ... er ...my ... Pastor ..."

"Yes, I am your father, Pastor Jacob Lamai."

"Ah, that's why," John Doe exclaimed. He winced as he pressed down on his swollen eyelid. "The man ... he called me pastor's son. He said ... he told me the press christened him Scarface because of the scars on his face."

"Scarface, the Merciless Duo?" asked the pastor, his voice trembling with emotion.

"What's your son's name, Pastor Lamai?" Atieno-Masinde interjected.

"Noah Lamai. He went missing at the beginning of March. Oh, how many times have I appealed on various TV channels for anyone with information about my son's disappearance to contact me or the police?"

"That will be all for now, Pastor Lamai," Mugo said. "You will be escorted back to headquarters. My colleagues will take your full statement and conduct further investigations to verify your relationship with this man."

Alone in the room with John Doe, Atieno-Masinde and Mugo each pulled up a chair beside the bed.

"Tell us more about Scarface," Mugo pressed.

"Scarface," John Doe said, shaking his head, "he put a gun to my head and told me to drive faster."

"You drove away from a gastropub," Mugo said. "Do you remember the name of the gastropub?"

John Doe shook his head.

"Do you remember how you got there?"

John Doe shuddered, tears welling up. He tugged at the sheet with his free hand and wiped away the moisture.

"Scarface ... he swore he wouldn't kill me if I did what he said. Then he threw me in the boot of the car and ..." He paused, his eyes darting from side to side. "After a while, I heard shots. Then he opened the boot and told me to drive."

Mugo studied John Doe with a blend of sympathy and scepticism. For him, the distinction between victim and accomplice was blurred.

"Why did you lose control of the car?"

Signs of stress and trauma crept into John Doe's face. Whether it was fear, guilt or something much darker, Mugo couldn't tell.

"Scarface jerked the wheel," John Doe finally replied.

"Do you remember when you first met Scarface?" Atieno-Masinde asked.

"It was dark ... I think. Where did I come from?" His words came in halting bursts, as if he was struggling to put together a jigsaw puzzle with missing pieces. "He was in the car ... in the back. I didn't see him at first."

"Who was in the back of the car?" Atieno-Masinde inquired. "Scarface?"

"I think it was him – the voice and the smell. He had a knife to my cheek, his other hand around my throat.

He said I should take him to … er … Where did he want to go? Er … er …"

"You drove him," Mugo deduced impatiently. "What happened then?"

After a few minutes, he replied, "I don't know." The fluttering of his eyelids suggested the ebb and flow of his thoughts. I woke up in a dark room. It was so filthy and stinking. The schoolgirl …"

Suddenly, his handcuffed arm jerked. He seemed to be staring beyond the present. Mugo could see that the memory of the schoolgirl was deeply embedded in the man's nerves.

"What about the schoolgirl?" Mugo inquired.

"The girl is as beautiful as a painting …" He paused. As he continued, his voice dropped to a whisper. "How can such a young girl … she is the coldest creature I've ever met. She never said a word."

"When you left the gastropub, you were driving the car, and Scarface was in the passenger seat, correct?" asked Mugo.

"Yes, that's right."

"Was the schoolgirl in the car, too?"

"I don't know."

"How did you get the scars on your head and face?"

Suddenly, tears trickled down John Doe's cheeks in salty rivulets. He sucked in desperate gulps of air, and Mugo couldn't shake the feeling that misery clung to him like a shadow.

Between sobs, he murmured, "Scarface speaks so deceptively soft. But he is pure evil. He told me, 'Pastor's son, my assistant will make you look like me.' Then he sat next to me … That girl used hot iron rods from an oven to disfigure my face. She didn't show any emotion, not even when I screamed. She just did her thing, and blew out bubble after bubble of chewing gum. And she swayed gently to a rhythm that only she could hear. This girl ... she is a breed of her own."

Mugo and Atieno-Masinde exchanged glances. John Doe's memory fragments began to coalesce into a believable picture.

Unexpectedly, John Doe laughed and shook his head.

"What's funny?" Mugo asked.

"Scarface said, 'If everything goes according to plan, they will be amazed. And you, pastor's son, you will laugh'." He looked from Atieno-Masinde to Mugo. "Now I know what Scarface meant by that."

Mugo's stomach tightened. The words struck him like the sting of a scorpion.

◆◆◆

February began with the country on edge. This was heightened by the ubiquitous 'Most Wanted' posters and the incessant media barrage of sensational headlines about the expected return of the Merciless Duo. There were also wild theories about the Duo from street preachers and some clergymen, most notably Pastor Jacob Lamai. The pastor had become an overnight sensation and a familiar face on television screens after it emerged that he was the father of the suspect in last March's infamous car chase.

Musamali Demba's KNN television station capitalised on the frenzy by broadcasting Pastor Lamai's impassioned sermons live. It was the last Sunday of the month, six days before March. Among the countless television viewers who tuned in to watch the sermon were DCI Dennis Mugo and DS Killian Bakari. The latter had brought his family for a Sunday brunch hosted by Dennis and his wife, Virginia.

Dennis leaned forward, fingers digging into his chin.

Pastor Lamai was preaching:

"The Lord is gracious and compassionate, slow to anger and abounding in love. The Lord preserves all who love Him, but all the wicked He will destroy."

Dennis turned up the volume.

The pastor leaned forward, his tone sharp enough to cut through doubt:

"Verily I say unto you, this coming March will not pass lightly; it shall bring another month of brutal judgement. The vengeful archangel will dispense divine justice by punishing the wicked and bringing them to salvation through their suffering."

A man in the congregation shouted:

"Stop talking in parables. Call a spade a spade."

The voice of the pastor, who some believed to be clairvoyant, rose with fervour:

"Mark my words: this storm will not pass. It will consume all. There is no refuge. No protection."

His voice faded to a murmur, inaudible to Dennis and Killian. But they caught it – the silent movement of his lips forming the words: "Not from the Merciless Duo."

The camera swept across the congregation – hands clenched on pews, skin taut; eyes wide, frozen in terror; faces ashen, drawn tight with fear.

The anticipation of the inevitable – the Merciless Duo's vengeance – poisoned the air, choking the breath of the land.

ACKNOWLEDGEMENT

My deepest gratitude to Juliette, my beloved wife, and to my cherished daughter and son, whose discerning eyes meticulously reviewed the manuscript. Their invaluable suggestions and unwavering encouragement throughout this writing odyssey have enriched the creative process.

THANK YOU FOR READING!

Dear Reader,

I'm very grateful that you've taken the time to read this book – your time and support mean the world to me.

I hope you've enjoyed immersing yourself in the twists and turns of **The Merciless Duo Returns**.

If the story kept you on the edge of your seat, please consider leaving a review. Just a sentence or a brief paragraph on the platform where you bought the book can make a huge difference – it helps other readers discover the book and motivates me to write more compelling stories.

Thank you for your support!

ABOUT THE AUTHOR

George Milare is an author and poet who writes in both English and German. After publishing his first coming-of-age series in German, Ich glaub es hackt!, he spent nearly a decade honing his writing skills and pushing the boundaries of his imagination. When not weaving suspenseful stories, George Milare enjoys immersing himself in different cultures and exploring the intricacies of criminal investigation.

I'd love to hear from you – whether you want to share your thoughts, discuss the story or keep up to date with upcoming releases.

Send me a message on WhatsApp: Simply scan the QR code using your phone's camera.

SCAN ME

Follow Merciless Ink Publishing on social media:

Instagram: merciless_ink_publishing
Twitter: Merciless_Ink
Facebook: MercilessInkPublishing
TikTok: mercilessinkpublishing

www.merciless-ink.com
www.georgemilare.de

Subscribe to my newsletter.

If you liked this book and want to keep up to date with my next thrillers, join my mailing list! You'll get early release news, sneak peeks, exclusive content and special offers.

Subscribe to my newsletter:
https://merciless-ink.com/newsletter/

Or just scan the QR code!

MOST WANTED: BOOK 2

The hunt for justice continues in the Most Wanted series, and I can't wait to share more exciting tales with you. The Merciless Duo strike again in the explosive sequel: **THE MERCILESS DUO RESURFACES** (***Most Wanted – Dead or Alive: Book 2***)

Available for pre-order from **12.07.2025**

Released on **4.10.2025** – prepare for the next chapter of terror and pursuit.

Enjoyed the story?

Scan the QR code below to leave a review of **The Merciless Duo Returns** on Amazon.

Your feedback means the world!

Thank you for your support!

Printed in Great Britain
by Amazon

63175508R00188